Loving Number Seven

by

Rhoda C. Hill

book #1 in
The Love Shack series

Cover image: Rebekah Wetmore

Editor: Andrew Wetmore

ISBN: 978-1-7772937-2-7
First edition October, 2020

397 Parker Mountain Road
Granville Ferry NS
B0S 1A0

moosehousepress.com
info@moosehousepress.com

We live and work in Mi'kma'ki, the ancestral and unceded territory of the Mi'kmaq People. This territory is covered by the "Treaties of Peace and Friendship" which Mi'kmaq and Wolastoqiyik (Maliseet) People first signed with the British Crown in 1725. The treaties did not deal with surrender of lands and resources but in fact recognized Mi'kmaq and Wolastoqiyik (Maliseet) title and established the rules for what was to be an ongoing relationship between nations. We are all Treaty people.

You're my survival, you're my living proof.
My love is alive and not dead.

-Edwin McCain

This is a work of fiction. Any resemblance to actual people or places is entirely coincidental.

To Clifford for encouraging me to ignore housework.

Chapters

1

Penny Weis made a mental walk-through of her cottage, conducting a list of valuables and trying to place whether she'd remembered to store everything before the takeover began.

French chateau curtains from my bedroom?

Check.

Embroidered silk wall hanging from the loft?

Check.

She was down to mere hours now. After nine tonight anything left behind would have to be a sacrificial offering, given in the name of her father's one hundred twenty-five acre oasis.

Vintage hand knotted medallion rug from the living room?

Check.

The thought of work boots dirtying up her rug was almost too much to bear. She couldn't leave things the way they were and expect to return with everything the same. She was saving herself the headache and, if she were being honest, the heartache, especially since her father refused to make the workers sign a waiver of any sort.

"Faith, and good ol' camaraderie," is what he told her when she questioned his reasoning; blind trust was more like it, but Penny's trust was thin and she certainly didn't have the gumption for blind-anything.

"Things are replaceable," he told her, and although she knew he was right, the side of her that obsessed over vintage tapestry, fabric, and linen begged to differ. Did six rough-and-tumble construction workers really care if they had pretty bedspreads and fancy curtains? As long as they had a place to fall and food to eat they'd get on just fine, and she'd made certain to stock the fridge and the cupboards with every food she could think of. She'd even gone a little heavy on the carb-laden foods, and had stocked the fridge with beer.

She plucked an overlooked hand-laced doily from beneath a nearby lamp and folded it in a bit of the acid-free paper and added it to the cedar chest at the end of her bed.

French Normandy lace bedspread from my bedroom?

Check.

Vintage chenille bedspreads from the spare bedrooms?

Check.

Lamé piano shawl from the dining room wall?

She could definitely check that off the list. Her late husband had framed the ninety by sixty-five inch vintage shawl for her as a wedding present, and that monstrosity had been cumbersome to rearrange in her distillery. She'd enlisted the help of her father to remove it, along with an English regency stool and a three-piece French Victorian parlour suite from the sun room. Some things just couldn't be sacrificed in the name of any oasis, no matter how beguiling her father made it sound.

Turkish rug from the dining room?

Check.

With some reluctance she'd left a Grecian rocker, a pair of Queen Ann-style wing chairs, and a 1970s plycraft lounge chair and ottoman. She'd removed the Victorian frame that held her wedding photo, but had left the smaller frames peppering the walls. Although it would have been simple to remove the few textile samplers and ribbon dolls she owned, it left the walls too empty and a declaration of her intentions. The only framed tapestry sampler she'd removed was one from her bedroom, a needlework of graduated lines of alphabet. Below the alphabet panel were an embroidered mop and a pail overflowing with penny coins, and the words 'My little Penny Mop' stretched along the bottom panel.

She could picture each item neatly folded between papers and placed in the chest. The edges of a large white sheet spilled out over the sides of the chest onto the hardwood floor; they tickled the tips of her toes as she pivoted around looking for any missed treasures.

Grandma's Italian lace tablecloth?

Check.

The first Cantu bobbin lace doily my mom made?

Dropping to her knees in front of the chest she slipped her fingers inside and fingered the simple pattern on the doily.

Check.

If everything survived these next few weeks, she would find the perfect frame for the doily. If *she* survived the next few weeks.

Confident that she had safely stored everything in appropriate places, she pulled the edges of the white sheet around the trunk's contents, carefully tucked it all up nice and neat, and then closed the lid and turned the key.

Penny slipped the key into the pocket of her jeans and made her way to the window. From this side of the house she didn't have a view of her lavender gardens, but the aroma was thick in the air and wafted in through the open window, filling the cottage with its crisp sweetness.

Closing her eyes for a moment, she willed the tranquility the flowers evoked to enter her. As the gentle wind lifted the curtain of wheat-coloured hair from around her shoulders and bathed her in a cloud of sweet-smelling aroma, she allowed herself to be calmed.

"Penny-Laine?"

Her father's voice calling to her from downstairs pulled her from her reverie. She rushed to close the window quickly before answering, "I'm up here, Dad."

Squatting behind the cedar chest, she pushed it across the floor and toward the opening of her closet as her father stepped inside the bedroom. "Just tying up loose ends," she told him.

"Just squirrelling away your treasures, you mean."

Spencer McCalla wore an aura of greatness about him; it burst from him in leaps and bounds and was infectious to everyone around him. His smile was unforced, not something he just put on, but rather an effortless part of his being. People liked him, and what was there not to like? He was friendly and pleasant to be around, and even surrounded by the trappings of his wealth he stayed humble. He loved life and living, but above everything else Spencer loved his children.

But Spencer was no pushover, either; he stood for what he believed and could negotiate a hard bargain with an act of persuasion that left you reeling. His children were not impervious to his charm, which is why she found herself readying up her cottage and handing it over to six construction workers for the next few weeks.

"Can you blame me?" she asked, sitting back on her haunches to look up at him. "I can't go stay with you and leave these out to dirty, clumsy man paws."

"You'll be about a hundred feet away; you can peek in the window and insure their safety every hour on the hour if you want to."

She grimaced at that and continued to push the chest toward the opening of the closet. "I have no desire to peer through windows and spy on six grease monkeys."

He laughed. "Listen, Penny-Laine, if it'll settle your nerves at all, I came up here to tell you the six *grease monkeys*, as you put it, are going to be staying with me."

She rolled back on her haunches again and looked up at him, confused.

He held up a hand as if to ward her off. "No, no, we're still going to need your cottage. But instead of six grease monkeys you'll be contending with just one."

She dropped her hands from the chest and pushed herself up to standing position. "One whole three-bedroom cottage for *one* man?"

"Well, no, not exactly."

Crooking her head at him, she gestured for him to continue. "Enlighten me, please."

"He's bringing his family along."

"He's bringing his family with him?" She gawked, waiting for the punch line. When it didn't come she set her hands on her hips. "He's coming here to work, and he's bringing his *family* with him?"

He nodded, a smile still plastered to his face.

"Miles in the woods, away from life's little gadgets and gizmos? In the middle of no man's land? This man is bringing his *family*?" She squinted, and looked skeptically at her father. "What's the catch?"

She returned to the chest and dropped down in front of it again. Planting her hands on the sides, preparing to push again, she looked up at her father. "What are you not telling me?"

Crossing his large sun bronzed arms over his chest he leaned against the door frame and shrugged. "No catch. It was his only stipulation. If I wanted him, I had to take his family, too."

"And, of course, you wanted him?"

"Damn straight."

"And he's part of the construction crew?"

"Well, not the construction crew *per se*."

"So this is just a vacation for him?" She tilted her head and narrowed her eyes. "Am I just giving my cottage over to one of your vacationing friends?"

Spencer walked to the window to look out over the lake. "That's one hundred twenty-five acres of mostly woodland and wildlife." He spun around to look at her. "I just think it would be in our best interest to have someone on board who can insure we are upholding regulations."

"A police officer?"

"No, nothing like that. He's a game conservation officer, as well as a certified arborist and tree risk assessor."

"Why didn't you just say that from the get go, instead of tip-toeing around it like you have something to hide?"

He shrugged, "I'm not tip-toeing. I just wasn't sure how you'd react."

"I think it's a great idea." She reached out to squeeze his hand. "Mom would love you even more for it."

Pulling on his collar he cleared his throat, his smile a little more nervous than she was used to.

She watched his face for a long moment, and then turned back to the chest. "Well? Are you just going to watch me wrestle this into the closet or are you going to give me a hand?"

~

Penny slipped into the master bedroom of her father's home and closed the door against the laughter pouring in from the deck. She'd spent an adequate amount of time welcoming the six construction workers that she didn't feel inhospitable about retiring to her room. The men would no doubt be tipping back a few and getting caught up on the comings and goings of each other's lives until the wee hours of the night. Unlike her father, who was retired, she had business to tend to in the morning and couldn't while away the hours even if she wanted to. Weeding was best done in the mornings, when the sun was still on the horizon and the air was cool.

Her cottage was still unoccupied. Her father had told her that, although the arborist and his family had hoped to arrive tonight, things hadn't worked out and they would be arriving in the morning instead.

That was fine with her. Perhaps in the morning she would have enough time for one more walk-through. Although the thoughts of a woman living in the cottage with the man did calm her nerves to a certain extent, she still worried. Would she be the kind of woman who valued such things as vintage fabrics and tapestries? Was she the type who focused all her attention on making memories, and everything else be damned?

She stopped dead in her tracks at the next thought. Did they have children? Were they bringing along a little hellion with jittery legs and exploring fingers? She shuddered.

As laughter spilled into the house from the deck, Penny slipped from the front door and circled around the house. Although she had to pass in front of the deck where the men hung out, no one even noticed her slip down the path leading to her cottage.

The light from the waxing moon poured down through the treetops, casting shadows along the path. The sound of spring peepers filled the air, and the further she went along the path, the fainter the laughter from her father's deck became.

Under the blanket of night her lavender fields looked like a deep Tuscan red haze. Beguiling and mysterious, and misleading. In daylight the lavender was a sea of deep purple.

She closed the door of the cottage on the peepers and the sound of the laughter, still faint on the air. Leaning against the door she looked around at her home, everything cast in shadows. What would her home look like with a family? When she and David built the place, that had been their intention. That was the reason for three bedrooms. They were to be a perfect family of four, but things hadn't worked out, and instead she lived alone.

Her life would be so different now had David lived. From the small foyer she could see through the dining room and into the family room. The empty spot where she'd removed their wedding photo seemed forlorn and so final.

A small choke rose in her throat and she slid to the floor. He didn't deserve to be packed away. He had as much right here as any stray game conservation officer, complete with family. She'd already removed every trace of him, and now she'd taken down the one picture of him from the wall. Mr. and Mrs. Game Conservation Officer needed to see that any memories they made here were irrelevant. This home was a Weis home, already filled with Weis memories, and their memories were beside the point.

She pushed up from the floor and ran up the stairs to her bedroom, fishing the key from her pocket as she ran. In the closet the chest was pushed as far back as she had been able to push it, and she'd placed a couple empty laundry baskets in front of it, a miserable attempt at camouflage.

She tossed the baskets out and knelt in front of the chest, inserted the key into the lock, and found the picture wedged in the side of the chest.

She emerged from the closet with the securely wrapped frame, dropping the tissue paper and bubble wrap on the floor as she left the room.

Moonlight poured through the windows of the family room, and she used the light to guide her to the wall. Carefully she slid the picture back onto the hook, and then dropped back to look at it. That was better, it all felt right now. The room felt whole again, even with everything else still packed away.

She spun around in the dim-lit room. Now any family that came in would see this picture and know that memories had already been rendered here.

She gazed at the picture again, and sighed. She was tired. The storm of emotions had left her exhausted.

Running a finger down David's smiling face, she allowed a tear to roll down her cheek. She turned and headed up the stairs.

The bubble wrap popped beneath her feet as she made her way to the bed. The crisp sheets felt good on her bare legs as she slid beneath them, and as the familiar smells and feels wafted around her she allowed herself to drift off to sleep.

~

Reuben Lafford swung his jeep up past the big house and eased to a stop in front of the cottage beyond it. Solar lights lined the walk way, but the cottage was dark.

He had called ahead to let Spencer know they'd changed their mind and had opted for travelling at night rather than waiting for morning. It would be a much quieter ride with the girls sleeping. Spencer had explained where the cottage was, and what road to follow, and assured him the place was prepped and waiting for them. He explained that his daughter had retired for the night, but that the door was unlocked, and he would have her deliver the key in the morning.

He nudged his mother awake and stepped from the jeep. "I'll go open the door and take a quick look around inside. Then I'll come help with the girls."

With no key to fiddle with, he opened the door and found a light switch. Spencer had given him a brief layout of the cottage a few days before, and he knew the two smaller rooms were downstairs and the master bedroom above. His mother would take one of the rooms below and his daughters would share the other.

In what would be the girl's room, the lamp beside the double bed flickered a few times before it lit up the corner of the room. He turned down the covers and went back to the jeep.

His mother was hoisting Ember into her arms.

"The first bedroom to the right," he murmured, then circled the jeep to collect Terra. She whimpered as she snuggled into him, but didn't wake up.

He followed Gyla into the cottage and lay Terra beside Ember on the bed.

"You'd better bring Lacey, in case she wakes up and discovers her missing," Gyla said. She'd removed Ember's shoes and reached to remove Terra's, too.

Reuben stepped out on the deck and surveyed the surroundings. Spencer had told him he was building an oasis, but looking around now he had no idea what he meant by that. This place was already an oasis in his opinion. Just beyond his jeep he could see a tree-canopied path, with a string of solar lights lighting the way up to the big house.

The sweet smell in the air was almost overwhelming, but he suspected a few days here and he'd get use to it. It wasn't hard to find the source of the smell, though. To the left he could see acres of lavender.

At his jeep he turned the headlights on high beam and walked a few feet ahead to look out over the field. In the beam of the lights the purple was bright.

The cottage had a lower level, and the ground sloped down. The gardens almost came right up to the basement doors. He could recall Spencer telling him his daughter worked in the basement, a lavender business he presumed.

"It's just breathtaking and lavender is so therapeutic." His mother came up beside him and linked her arm with his. "And that smell is just heavenly."

They stood in silence for a moment before she reached up on her tiptoes and pulled his head down to hers. Planting a small kiss on his cheek, she caught his long braid in her hand as it fell over his shoulder. "You're a good man, Reuben. Your dad would be so proud of you."

He smiled back at her and wrapped an arm around her shoulder. "I needed to hear that, mom."

"Now come inside and get some sleep."

At the jeep she reached in to grab a bag. "Just take what you need for the night and we can bring in the rest in the morning."

He killed the lights and grabbed two bags from the back of the jeep. He was about to close the door when he spotted Lacey between the seats. The 1960's vogue doll had been his wife Eve's, and Ember had grown attached to it. Wedging it under his arm, he picked up the two bags, kicked the door shut, and returned to the cottage.

The master bedroom was at the top of the stairs. A dim light shone green from the face of an alarm clock next to the bed, enough to let him find his way about.

Just inside the bedroom was a door to a bathroom. He nearly kicked a laundry basket as he entered, and he bent down to place it out of the way against the wall.

As tired as he was, a shower was in order. He placed his bag on the floor, closed the door out of habit before turning on the light, and began to peel away his clothes. He'd just take a quick one, enough to cool down and help him settle for the night. Pulling the elastic from his braid he ran his fingers through his hair and stepped into the shower.

He'd brought his children and his mother with him after a lot of urging from Spencer. This was the first time he'd taken them to work with him. He'd accepted the offer because, truth be told, his daughters' lives had become monotonous. He wanted to break up the norm for them, and show them nature for a change. Eve had been a city girl, but he had grown up in the country, it's where his heart was. His family. His roots. Maybe it was time to be true to himself. Time to teach his girls about nature and their ancestors. Maybe it was time to set Terra, his wildling, loose. To let her explore the side of her that was begging for adventure. And maybe it was time to teach Ember that while pretty things were okay, being a child was okay, too.

If he got a moment he'd take his daughters out mushroom hunting, or berry picking. It had been ages since he'd roamed nature just for fun. With one hundred twenty-five acres at his fingertips for the next few weeks, surely he'd be able to find some free time on his hands to take the girls on a hike. He'd teach them the dos and don'ts and at the same time make a lot of memories.

Of course he was here to do a job and that took precedence, but he planned to spend every free moment with his girls. He wondered if lady slippers grew in the woods here in Ridgeville. He couldn't be sure, but he just bet they did. He made a mental note to watch for them. He knew Ember would enjoy seeing ballerina slippers in flower form.

Stepping from the shower, Reuben dried his hair as best as he could with a fluffy towel from the rack by the sink. He tied the towel in a clumsy knot around his waist and stepped into the bedroom.

After the glare of the bathroom light, the bedroom was deep in darkness. He found his way to the bed without stubbing any toes, sat down, and reached for the lamp.

As he did he felt a shift on the bed. Someone was in the bed, he was almost certain of it.

In the same motion Reuben turned the bedside lamp on and stood. And there lying in the bed was the most beautiful woman he'd ever laid eyes on.

For a moment he just studied her. This had to be Spencer McCalla's daughter, but Spencer had told him she was staying at the big house.

Long blond hair spilled out over the pillow in a golden border around her head. The sheet she lay beneath had fallen away, and her t-shirt lifted at the hem, exposing a flat stomach and a thin band of delicate beige panties.

He followed the outline of her body beneath the sheet to one foot peeking out over the edge of the bed. Then he looked at her face again, so peaceful in sleep. Her lashes were long and sat against her cheek, her tiny nose upturned slightly, and a light dusting of freckles peppered the bridge. She looked like sleeping beauty.

A better man then he would have looked away, but he couldn't. She was a rare sight. A raw beauty, with no augmentations, and it had been too long since he'd feasted his eyes on something so perfect. The t-shirt clung to the subtle curves of her breasts, and as he watched them rise and fall gently, his breath hitched in his throat, and an ache clinched within his chest.

Then she stirred ever so slightly, the sheet riding down to expose a hipbone. The band of her panties settled just under the hipbone and his teeth set on edge. He fought an overwhelming urge to catch the hipbone between his teeth and run his tongue over the flesh.

For a moment her gentle breathing stopped. He stood stock still, willing the stirring in his groin to abate, willing her to continue sleeping.

When the rhythmic breathing returned he slowly stepped back to leave. But, as he did so, his heel came down on something squishy and a popping sound filled the room. Her eyes flew open and locked onto his.

He knew she was going to scream. He could see it on her lips and in her cornflower-blue eyes. In one swift motion he was on the bed beside her, a hand clamped over her mouth.

He leaned in closer; the smell of lavender clung to her hair and rose to circle around him. His eyes locked onto hers, her lips inches from his own.

He lay a finger to his lips in a hushing motion and slowly moved his hand from around her mouth, then pressed the finger to her lips.

"Shhh," he said. "You'll wake my daughters."

2

Penny was almost certain this was a dream, mostly because of the man leaning over her. He could not be real. Men like this did not exist in the real world, did they? But the finger pressed onto her lips felt real.

"If I move my hand are you going to scream?" he asked.

She shook her head and his finger left her mouth. She immediately regretted her decision.

With his hands off her, he moved from the bed, his long fingers rechecking the knot at his hips.

"Number seven," she said, more to herself than to him. She scooted up in bed, her eyes roaming over him. His shoulders were broad and the muscles in his arms well defined. His hair dropped down past his shoulders and dripped water down his torso, a light dusting of dark hair splayed across his chest and tapered down beneath the towel. His copper skin glistened in the dim light of the bedside lamp. It had been years since a man stood before her naked, or stood inside her bedroom even.

His fingers fiddled with the fabric at his hip. "Seven?" He asked, pulling at the knot unfolding in his hand. "If I drop the towel, do you think that will raise my score seven notches?"

His long fingers circled the loosened fabric, and he thrust his hips forward in an insinuating gesture.

What had she been thinking? What kind of a person just gawked at a stranger like this? And naked, no less? Grabbing the sheet up around her she sprang from the bed, a string of apologies on her lips.

"Oh God, Oh God!" She repeated over and over as she squatted to retrieve her shorts. "I wasn't expecting you until morning, I'm so sorry, this is all my fault." She bunched the shorts beneath her elbow and squatted again, the corners of the sheet in one fist against her breast. Grabbing the tissue papers and bubble wrap from the floor she stepped into the closet and fell to her knees in front of the still-open chest.

Shoving the paper and bubble wrap inside she closed the chest and turned the key in the lock. Standing again, she made to come out, but then changed her mind. "Just give me one second," she said and closed the door in his face.

She emerged from the closet fully dressed. He hadn't moved, nor had he retied the knot.

"I'm sorry," she said again.

"You said that a few times already." His smile widened; a dazzling contrast against the deep bronze of his skin. "Please stay."

She shifted uncomfortably unsure what he was suggesting, but not liking where her thoughts were leading her.

"This is your home, and we've inconvenienced you." He took the bunched sheet from her arms and tossed it to the bed. "It's after 2 am, and there's no reason for you to go."

Penny pulled a fresh sheet set from a shelf above the closet and set them on the bed. "I'll just remake your bed and leave." She plucked the fitted sheet from one corner of the mattress and started for the opposite side, but he reached forward to splay his fingers on the sheets edge, preventing her from removing it.

"I'd feel better if you stayed," he said.

The crazy notions rolling around inside her head were flashing every shade of red on the colour wheel, Her cheeks, she was certain, were their form of medium. The jellied knees and fluttering hearts such invitations must have evoked on the ladies in his life must be too numerous to count. She wondered if he left a pile of victims in his wake everywhere he went. She would not be one of those blathering fools who would fall prey to his charm. It may not be easy but she would do it. He seemed to have an overly huge dose of magnetism though. Clearly whoever had been in charge of doling out charm had accidentally tipped the bottle in his favour. Well she liked to think she'd been given more self-control than others, and she planned to kick that into overdrive in memory of all the innocent women who had fallen prey to his charms in the past.

Although his invitation may have been purely innocent, her overactive brain kept sinning it up. Well that would stop right now. She would be the voice of reason-starting now. "I'd rather not," she said pulling on the corner of the sheet again. It stretched beneath his hand, but did not give way. Her insides were shaky; a muscle the size of a fist had tightened in her chest and dispersed tiny rubber bands to the ends of her toes and the tips of her fingers. She tried to ignore the zinging, the shake of her fingers, and the wobble in her knees.

Even as her concentration focused hard on righting the chaos in her body his hand closed over hers and everything she'd managed to place right fell away to shambles within her again. With no control over her own body, she allowed him to turn her away from the bed.

"If daily routine followed me from the city, my girls are going to have me up in less than five hours. If you'd be so kind as to step out for a moment, I'll make myself decent and see you to the big house."

Her breathing grew shallow at his nearness, and she couldn't speak.

"Unless of course, you've changed your mind," his voice was deep, and his words spilled out like honey, their warmth washing over her. She felt like a mindless fly going crazy at the first inclination of sweetness. "My bed is your bed," he said a slow smile tugging at the corners of his perfectly etched lips.

She didn't trust herself to speak; instead she dropped the sheet and walked from the room.

Penny didn't stop there. She needed out of this cottage and away from the copper god with hypnotic powers over her. She needed space and time between them. A good night's sleep might screw her head on right.

At the front door she bent to slip on her sandals, and stopped short. There, on the mat, was a pair of size eight lady's shoes. The guilt that washed over her was palpable. She had been lusting over another woman's husband. What kind of a person had she become?

As she pulled the door closed behind her, she peered inside looking for any clue that he'd followed. It would help her to know at what pace she needed to get away. No one was visible, but just as she turned something caught her attention. She could only see it faintly, but the brownish-orange was unmistakable.

The mantel was a good thirty-five feet away and the house was dimly lit, but she could plainly see her mother's velvet wheat embroidered mantel scarf. She'd forgotten to pack it away and the door had locked behind her.

She wanted to scream and lash out, but a shadow moving in the stairwell kept all that at bay. The mantel scarf would have to wait. She would devise a plan to get it out of the house in the morning. Preferably without ever having to encounter number seven, his children, or the woman who'd snagged him.

Glancing at the stairs again, she watched as the stairwell gave birth to the sexy Mi'kmaw who would sleep in her bed—without her.

The sounds of his footsteps on the path behind her added the extra pep to her step that she needed to reach the front door of her father's cottage before he caught up with her.

From the open doorway she could see him emerge from the canopy of trees. For a moment their eyes met along a molten pathway of lust and bad intentions. His silhouette a promise of many hours and days of trip-ups and bad decisions; a test of her willpower and dignity.

"Have a good night Miss McCalla," he called just before she closed the door behind her.

Shivers cascaded down her spine and she leaned against the door to wait for them to pass. It had been a long time since anyone had called her Miss McCalla. Even after three years of being without him she wore David's name proudly, and just like the band on her finger she had no intention of getting rid of either.

She was the only one sleeping on the main floor of her father's cottage. Spencer had given up the master bedroom downstairs for her and he slept on a pull-out in the den upstairs. He'd purchased three additional cots to add to the three bedrooms, so that each room had a bed and a cot. The six workers had taken those rooms.

The place was quiet, but Penny's body was screaming. Everything rolled into one, making a jumbled mess of her thoughts. She lay in bed trying to bring order to the chaotic mess.

Number Seven was sexy as hell; her reaction to him was so full of sin that the devil himself would have trembled. She couldn't allow herself to be alone with him again, and yet her mind kept playing the images of him and begging for a rerun. Then there was the matter of the mantel scarf, it's sentimental worth far outweighed its monetary value, and she had left it behind. He had children; what did that mean for the scarf? Were they good children? Surely their mother would confine all food and beverages to the table. But what if she didn't? Maybe they only drank water, but that was a preposterous thought, what child didn't love juice? And Penny had bought five litres of Welch's, the purple kind too. She wanted to kick herself for being so stupid.

She would say a simple prayer for the mantel scarf, she decided, and there lying in bed she closed her eyes.

"Oh God, please watch over my mothers velvet mantel scarf."

Would that do? She wasn't a praying woman, had never felt the need to ask God for anything. It was all new to her really. What was the protocol for such a request? Did God sit up there taking in the thousands of prayers he got in the run of a day and divvying them up into piles? That would be how she would do it. It would help add some order to it all. What would the piles be labelled? Maybe four piles labelled urgent, soon, later, and never. Did God have a slush pile? Of course he did. If he didn't we'd all be rich and beautiful and happy. So what was his system then? Did he judge each one by their urgency? How does one prayer grab his attention over another? Does he require a more in-depth lament? Probably, or probably not, she couldn't be sure, but on the off chance that he did, she wanted to cover all her bases just-in-case. So she tried to lie still and drum up all the emotions she could muster.

"Dear God, it's been a few years since we've touched base and I apologize for that, I really do. But, you see, I've just been down here happily making do with what you've already given me. I rarely ask for anything, because I know how busy you must be, and my mother taught me to not be too greedy. So I've prettied up my life with little things from the past, trying to upcycle rather than waste. My mother's velvet mantel scarf is an heirloom passed down from the last three generations. I am from a long line of earth conscientious people. Our motto, you could say, is waste not, want not. If the mantel scarf gets destroyed I will need another, and I'd much rather keep this one. I don't want to be greedy, so I don't expect to make your urgent file, but if you could add me to the *soons* I would be so grateful. Thank you for listening to me God. Amen."

Would that do? She'd been considerate of others with more pressing problems; maybe that act of empathy would tug at God's heart and he'd stick her in the urgent list to show his appreciation for her compassion. She reevaluated her request. Here on earth you give something to get something. Was that God's form of bargaining too? Down here if you grease the right palms you could make anything happen, but what did one grease God's palms with? And did that stuff even work on him?

He created the earth, so he probably adhered to the same set of rules. But she'd already sent her prayer off. She'd even added the 'amen' which meant that all lines of communication had been cut. Maybe if she just sent a quick sidebar it would automatically accompany her request. But what would she promise in return? She didn't have much to offer, but she had to think of something quick before her request got too far down the line.

"Dear God, just a quick little note to help you in your decision making. If you do this for me I will… I will…"

She would what? Her mind was drawing a blank. She had to hurry; it would be too disjointed if her sidebar lagged too far behind her initial request.

"I will purge my mind of all sexual thoughts of Seven."

There. That ought to do it. Hadn't it been God who said that lusting after someone was committing adultery in your heart already? Yes it was, and if she remembered correctly he'd even gotten melodramatic about it too. According to his records there was a domino effect that followed lustful thinking: a person lusts, gets dragged away by the temptation, commits the act, gives birth to sin, sin grows, and then everyone dies.

If he were that fastidious about the issue then her promise was a good one, it halted the whole assemblage in its tracks. Didn't he also say that lust was a poor, weak, whimpering, whispering thing? Wait, no, that was C.S. Lewis, wasn't it? Yes, it was, but she just bet God approved of it and that was almost the same as if he'd said it himself.

Now what was she expected to do? Wait? Did her promise kick in now or only once the request was fulfilled? Probably once the request was filled, but all the same she intended to push the sexy man out of her mind, for practice's sake.

How did one remove grape juice stains from velvet anyway? Maybe a dry cleaning solvent would do the trick. There was that one time she'd stained the edge of a tablecloth and easily removed it with a mixture of lemon juice, baking soda, and water. Cleaning velvet was tricky though, and by all rights she should probably take it to a professional dry cleaner. But truth be told she didn't trust anyone with her vintage fabrics.

Would it hurt to use a scrubbing brush on velvet? How long could it be left soaking in a solution? She wouldn't dare to machine-dry it, so it would definitely need to be hung on the line. Would that be safe? Maybe a hair dryer would be the better solution. Or Maybe God was at work on her application right now and if so the mantel scarf was in good hands? Right?

Somehow she managed to fall asleep, but sleep was fitful. She dreamed of a little girl carrying a sand pail full of grape juice. She was walking towards Penny. The child stopped in front of her, dropped the pail, and pulled out the velvet wheat-embroidered mantel scarf from the juice. It was dyed a splotchy purple. She held the scarf out to Penny and said "there you go Miss McCalla. See, I fixed it for you."

But it was another dream just before morning that sat her bolt upright in bed.

3

The decoy laundry baskets were stacked neatly against the wall. The closet doors were closed and there was no sign of the bubble wrap. The top sheet from the bed was still wrapped around her, its edges clinched in her hand against her breast, her shorts tucked up under her elbow.

Penny tried to take a step toward the closet, but couldn't. A gentle tug on the sheet made her realize she couldn't move because someone was holding on to the other end.

"My bed is your bed." A deep voice spoke from behind her.

She spun around, the sheet twisting around her ankles. Number Seven lay stretched over her bed, looking sexier than any man had the right to. His hands propped behind his head and his tantalizing smile tempted her forward. His eyes, like swirling wells of molten copper, begged her to join him.

She moved her gaze down the length of him, expecting to see the towel around his hips; instead her mother's velvet, wheat-embroidered mantel scarf lay across his groin.

"If I drop this, do you think I could raise my score seven notches?"

Penny sat bolt upright in bed, her heart racing a mile a minute and her head swirling. She promptly fell back again, forced down by the dizziness that overtook her.

How many weeks of this did she have to endure? According to her father the project was open-ended; it would be over when it was over. She'd simply referred to the time as a few weeks and had been happy with that, up until now. Now she wanted an honest-to-God number. She wanted something to circle on the calendar, so she could cross off the days with big red X's.

She'd beat the alarm by eighteen minutes, but rather than hit snooze, she got up and began her early morning routines.

These routines didn't include breakfast, so fifteen minutes later she had freshened up, dressed, perked a pot of coffee to refill her travel mug, and was out the door. Breakfast would come later.

Although she'd put down weed cloth between the garden beds, green invaders still managed to sprout up around the cloth. She liked to keep everything clean; it made for a better crop.

The small garden cart was laden with all the essential equipment needed; she wedged her travel mug in to the allotted spot and adjusted her knee-pads.

If Seven's routine had followed him from the city, he'd be waking up right about now. She pushed the cart to the bed nearest her cottage and squatted at the end. She wanted the best view she could possibly get in the hopes of spotting his children. She didn't want to see him, or that was the lie she told herself. She just wanted to see his children so she could get some idea as to what future her mantel scarf had to look forward to should God Slush-pile her request. Trying to think happy thoughts she took the messy little girl she imagined earlier and tried to pretty her up into a white-gloved little princess whose hands were as foreign to dirt as day is to night.

Shamefully, she wanted a glimpse of the woman who had managed to tie down the ridiculously handsome man who slept in her bed. Of course, thoughts of the woman ruined that image, which was a good thing in light of her recent promise. They were a couple, though, so naturally she couldn't expect one to be sleeping in her bed and not the other.

A pang of jealousy lurched in her chest. She must be a pretty amazing woman to have him wrapped so tightly around her little finger that he can't even go a few weeks on a work assignment without taking her with him. What kind of a woman was she anyway? Classy, vivid, dull, or sassy? Or maybe she was all those things rolled into one. Penny would guess that she was the hair in a chignon at the nape of her neck type, who wore straight pinstriped skirts and heels and carried an Armani bag. Or per-haps the bold kind with four inch heels, patent leather pants, and big hair. Well she'd be a little over dressed here in the woods if she were.

But then she could be the mousy kind of woman with a girl-next-door kind of beauty. That was just as much a possibility as any other. Mrs. Game Conservation Officer probably had a tiny upturned face, brown eyes and mousy brown hair. She would have that kind of beauty that isn't right in your face but rather sneaks up on you and, bam, before you know it you're snagged good and hard. Or perhaps she was the kind of self-pro-claimed independent woman who wants him, but swears she doesn't need him, but yet as soon as he's gone she's all over him like a bad rash.

It could be any type of woman really, but one thing was for certain: she would be beautiful and irresistible.

And here Penny was looking as ordinary and inadequate as it was possible to look. She plunged her nails, bitten to the quick, into the dirt at her knees, but then she remembered her upturned nose and unearthed one hand in order to push down on the tip and swipe the back of her hand over the spray of freckles on its bridge. All her efforts at concealing them were futile, because at the end of the day she would still have the freckles, the upturned nose, and the nails bitten to the quick.

She rummaged in the garden cart for a pair of garden gloves and put them on. It didn't matter what she looked like anyway; he already had a wife and, besides, she wasn't looking. She was getting her life on track, and this life wasn't for the faint of heart. This life was an acquired taste. A taste she had grown to savour insatiably, and was not willing to give up for any man, no matter how sexy he was.

Why had he flirted with her? He'd thrown insinuating remarks at her, too, and led her to believe that he meant them. What kind of a man did that when he already had a wife? Not a faithful one, that was for sure.

He'd had her imagining all kinds of horrible things, and he'd done so intentionally. She could tell by the tone of his voice and the twinkle in his eyes.

She circled her hand around the fresh buds of a new lavender shoot, holding its bulk in her palm, with the stem between her fingers as though she meant to lift it for a toast before she drank the sweet bud.

Before she saw anything she heard the door close. The deck of her cottage was elevated above the basement. From where she sat, squatted in her garden, she couldn't see over the railing of the deck. She waited with bated breath, willing whoever had stepped out onto the deck to come into view.

As if on cue, the devil himself stepped into view. He held a mug, and…

Did he even own a shirt? So far she hadn't seen any trace of one. His hair caught in the wind and whipped out behind him as he looked out over the lavender field.

Their eyes met and held for a brief moment before he lifted his mug toward her in a good morning bid. Completely distracted her hand closed around the lavender plant and before she realized it, the plant lay limp in her hand.

"Damn, damn, damn," she said plunging her fingers into the empty hole in the earth. Without properly eyeing the plant's descent into the earth again she kept a not-too-obvious eye on the man on her deck.

He leaned forward, his elbows propped on the railing. He looked like he belonged there, like the deck had been made with him specifically in mind.

But that was absurd. She and David had made this home, and here she was cheapening that memory with imaginings of a tenure that would never be.

Forcing her attention to the plant again she packed the earth around its roots, and then scooted to the left to focus on some debris that had managed to weave itself into the leaves of the next plant.

Her hand stilled on the plant when she heard the door open a second time and the sound of hurried feet racing across the deck. Seconds later a small head popped up to the left of Seven.

It wasn't her intention to rise, but she did. Her mantel scarf's future was riding on this little girl.

She was so short that she had to step on the bottom guard to see over the railing. How old would that make her? Three? Four? From this distance Penny couldn't tell if she were a safe candidate to live in the same house as an important heirloom.

Penny waited with anticipation for something to happen that would either make or break the whole thing, and as she watched an identical head popped up to the right.

The voices from the deck were low, and although they carried on the wind, she couldn't make out the words.

Completely undone, Penny dropped to the ground again. With two children not even as tall as the deck railing, the mantel scarf didn't stand a chance. Penny wrote off the scarf, her heart pounding wildly at the memory of it.

She didn't want to intrude on their little party, but she couldn't keep herself from glancing up at the trio. So she was watching as Seven shifted slightly and hoisted Lefty up.

Gravity pulled on the contents of Penny's stomach while at the same time bile rose in her throat. The dishevelment of Lefty's hair and the holes in the knees of her jeans killed any niggling of hope that she would be a tidy child.

But hope was hard to kill, especially when it was all a person had left. And so everything was riding on the mother now. Perhaps she was trying to tame the unruly children. What could Penny do to help speed up the process? She began mentally combing through the books on the shelves in her father's den, trying like hell to remember a book on parenting, although the likelihood of her father having such a book was low.

"Good morning, Miss McCalla."

It took a second to realize they were calling to her. The two little girls were waving and her heart leapt for a moment.

"Good morning," she called back. That's when Seven lifted Miss Right up into his arms.

Her hair was in pristine condition, a little pink-bowed headband sat on the top of her dark head. She wore a pretty pink dress and flat shiny black shoes. Penny's breath caught as she suddenly saw a little ray of hope.

It all became obvious to her now. Mrs Seven has been working on Miss Right and, by the look, she has succeeded. Now all her attention could be devoted to Lefty.

Even as she thought this Lefty dropped back down onto the deck again and Penny watched all she could see of her, the very top of her messy hair, as she walked to the railing in front of the sunroom. The ground to railing ratio was greatly reduced here and Lefty realized that. With one swift movement she climbed up over the railing and leapt off, rolling on the grass on her landing. The little girl righted herself and made a mad dash for Penny.

Penny closed her eyes and prayed for a small favour.

~

Reuben watched as Terra, his little whirlwind, raged into Miss Mc-Calla's life. Like any good windstorm victim, the beautiful woman looked flustered as Terra bounded upon her and wrapped her arms around her legs. Her spirit was what he loved about her, just as he loved Ember for her reserve. The two were as opposite as day and night, and while it was good to be as they were to a certain extent, it would be better if each could be a pleasing mix of both. While he didn't want the girls too trusting, he did want them to trust; and he didn't want them cloistered, but he wanted them to cope well with solitude.

"Do you want to go meet Miss McCalla?" he asked Ember.

"You take me," she said clinging to his neck.

"Well, I do need to properly introduce myself," he said, setting her back down on the deck. "Just let me grab a shirt."

Seconds later he and Ember where walking down the steps to the lower level of the cottage and moving toward the lavender garden, Ember's little hand clinched tightly in his own.

Terra was squatting beside Miss McCalla, and when she rose she held a weed in her hand.

"Look, Daddy! Mrs. Wise let me pull a weed," she called, then turned to toss the weed into basket in the garden cart. "Mrs. Wise says these are good plants when they're growing somewhere else, but here they're bad and we have to throw them away."

"Mrs. Wise?" He asked, looking at Penny.

She stood when she saw him approaching. He couldn't help but notice the skin at her midriff, visible from the sides of her coveralls. She wore a heather grey crop top beneath, and the coveralls hung loose over them on her small frame. There was a smear of dirt across her nose.

"Weis," she corrected, removing one of her gloves. She ran her palm down her pant leg before extending it to him. "Penny Weis."

He let go of Ember's hand to reach for hers. "Reuben Lafford, and this is my daughter Ember, and I guess you've already met my other daughter, Terra."

"Oh Terra," she said surprised. "No, but I did meet Rah."

Terra tugged on his hand, "Daddy, remember? I want to be Rah now."

"Oh, right, I forgot."

"But you can't forget, Daddy. It's important."

"I've been calling you Terra for four years; it's hard to change now."

"Oh yeah, I forgot you have an old memory."

"Hey, don't embarrass me in front of Mrs. Wise now."

"Weis, Daddy, remember?"

It was Ember who spoke, her voice so low they almost missed it.

Penny laughed. "That's okay, I understand. It's your Daddy's old memory. Why, I'm surprised he remembered to wear a shirt today." She reached out to touch Ember's cheek. "Next time maybe he'll actually re-member to button it."

The two little girls giggled at that.

Reuben met Penny's eyes. "You don't like how I dress?" he asked pulling the edges of his shirt together. He began to button it from the bot-tom to the top.

"That's just it. You don't dress, not totally."

"Is that a crop top under those overalls?"

She ignored him and turned back to the garden. "Ember, would you like to pull a weed?"

"No, thanks," Ember answered timidly.

"Ember doesn't like dirt," Terra said.

Penny plucked the gloves from her hands and held them out to Ember. "You could borrow these."

"No, thanks."

"Okay, maybe another day when you're dressed for it."

"But Ember doesn't like dirt." Terra said again, "and she doesn't like getting her clothes dirty either."

"Well in that case, maybe one day *you*," she said, tapping a finger on the end of Terra's nose, "can loan her a set of *your* clothes, and she can pretend for one day that she *does* like dirt." She turned to Ember again. "How does that sound?"

"No, thanks."

Penny smiled, defeated. "Well that's okay, too," she said, dropping to her knees again. "I just thought weeding would go faster if I could drum up some help, but that's okay, I totally understand."

"Are you being a lazy bone?" Ember asked from behind Reuben's legs.

Reuben loved how Penny's eyes widened in surprise before they lit up with amusement at his brassy child, and he knew he should correct Ember, but he was enjoying the scene playing out before him a little too much. He wanted to see how Penny handled this.

"Oh you think I'm a lazy bone do you?" She reached forward her hands poised to tickle Ember but the state of her fingers made her stop. "I wouldn't say I'm lazy," she said sticking her upturned nose into the air and peering down at Ember. "I just saw two awesome-looking helpers and thought I'd try to lighten my load.

"I'll help," Terra said plucking another weed from the ground

"Maybe another time, Terra. I'm sure Mrs. Weis has a lot of work to do and will no doubt need to schedule time for your training before she just let's you delve in and start pulling things."

When Terra began to protest, he interrupted her. "Besides, Nana's making blueberry pancakes, and I'm sure you don't want to miss out on those."

Terra's face lit up at the reminder and she bounded out of the garden and up the path chanting "blueberry pancakes" as she ran.

"I want pancakes, too," Ember said.

He sniffed in the air, "Well if my nose is right, and it always is, they are just about ready to eat."

"I'm gonna go eat some," she said and started up the path behind her sister.

"Save some for me," he called after her.

"They *are* twins, aren't they?" Penny asked.

"Biologically? Yes, but in every other sense of the word? No."

Penny laughed again. Her laugh was different. A cross between a giggle and a chuckle, and seemed to end on a hiccup. He liked it. It was cute, and it made him smile. It matched her small face, upturned nose and the playful spray of freckles littering the bridge.

"They're great," she said staring after his daughters.

"Yeah, they're okay," he dragged it out in an exaggerated tone.

"Yeah, right," she laughed again. Her hickle making his insides quiver.

A hickle? She had him coining words now? Well it was the only way to explain her laughter. It was unique and ought to have its own word.

"Those girls have their Daddy wrapped around their finger," she added.

"You got me."

"How's the cottage? Are you finding everything you need?"

"You mean after I scared Goldilocks away?"

He saw the blush spring into her cheeks and watched as she nervously fiddled with the contents of the garden cart, righting tools that were already righted, and shifting the weeds in the basket so that they spread out along the bottom evenly. Her long braid fell forward and knocked against the cart. When she rose again she held a travel mug.

"I apologized for that. But in my defence I was told you wouldn't be arriving until morning."

"That was the plan, but we changed our mind at the last minute. I called ahead and Spencer gave me the go ahead. I assume he had no idea you'd gone back to your cabin?"

"No, I kind of snuck out," she curled her nose mischievously.

God, she was cute. Who knew coveralls, dirty purple garden gloves, and a smear of dirt across her nose would make him want to devour her even more. He remembered the tiny hipbone and the beige band of her panties and wondered if beige was a recurring colour with her? Did she wear a matching bra?

"Like I said last night, I truly am sorry to have inconvenienced you. If you'd like to stay in your own home, I'll gladly take the sofa."

"Not at all," the travel mug hovered near her lips. "I tried to stock the cupboards with essentials to last at least three weeks, and I also bought some non-essential snack foods. I realize some parents don't allow their children to have juices, so please just move those or anything you don't want to use to the back of the lower cupboards. And if I missed anything, just make a list, and the next trip into town I'll pick it up for you."

"We'll be fine. We packed a few things of our own as well. I doubt we'll need anything more."

"Okay, then. Just let me know if I can do anything for you." She took another sip from the mug, and smiled. "I'm trying to beat the sun," she said looking up into the sky, "but I don't think I'm doing a great job of it."

He knew she was dismissing him, but his mind was still reeling from her former statement, and he was finding it hard to walk away.

Let me know if I can do anything for you?

That was a loaded offer. Right now he could easily tick off at least five things she could do for him, but he was a gentleman with two small daughters and it would do him well to remember that.

Returning the cup to the cart, she bent down, exposing a side view of the bare skin beneath her overalls. The hem of her crop top stretched and hitched further up as she reached forward to remove some debris from a plant. As her blonde braid fell forward and hitched in the side gap of the overalls, there was a stirring in his groin. He'd learned self-control at a young age, but keeping himself in check around Penny Weis was becoming more difficult by the minute. She looked as sweet as the air smelled, and he wanted so badly to taste her. To nip her cute little nose, nibble her scrumptious hipbones, strum his tongue up and down her delicate rib cage, and scrape his teeth across the small knobs of her ankles.

He wanted to hook his hands in the straps at the back of her overalls, and pull her up from her kneeling position. He wanted to pull her back against him, turn her towards him and taste the coffee that clung to her perfect pink lips.

He shook his head, trying to clear away the images and thoughts. All they did was scatter, and when he looked up at her again he could sense all the pieces converging again. He had to leave before the images completed themselves and he gave into the temptations each image depicted.

"I'll leave you to it, then," he croaked, and stepped backwards away from her. She had him inventing words, breathing from a much shallower place than usual and thinking thoughts he could usually coax to a halt.

He stopped short at the next thought and nearly keeled over at the sickening feeling that overtook him.

She made him forget Eve.

4

Four of the six men staying with her dad were out on the deck having morning coffee. The other two were hovered over the stove when she came in from the garden.

"Having trouble there, boys?" She asked.

"I think Tim here's having troubles."

"No trouble at all," Tim said, dishing white particles from a pan with a slotted spoon and adding them to a pile of glop on a nearby plate. "You just watch this, Kyle, third times a charm, I promise you."

Penny reached the stove just as the third egg plummeted into the rapidly boiling water. The egg instantly pulverized into pieces and foam rose to the surface. Kyle fell back against the kitchen island in stitches.

"Poaching eggs, I assume?" she asked.

"Wasting eggs is more like it," Kyle said. "But get this, he poaches his own eggs every morning," he erupted into squeals of laughter again.

Tim looked affronted, "Well I do, and I use one of those microwave egg poacher things. I've never actually had to just wing it before."

"Let's start over, shall we?" Penny said.

"If we intend to eat today, someone's going to have to start over, and I'd much rather it not be Tim," Kyle said.

Penny poured out the hot gooey water and added fresh to the pot. While she waited for the water to come to a slow simmer, she discarded the pulverized eggs and laid out paper towels. Once the water began a steady gentle simmer she poured a small amount of vinegar into it. With the slotted spoon she stirred the water in a clockwise direction until a gentle whirlwind formed in the pot. Then she cracked an egg into a ladle and tipped it gently into the water. The white wrapped up around the egg in a perfect poach.

Tim gasped beside her. "Hot damn, how'd you do that?" He watched the egg for a second. "Pretty, and she can cook."

She dropped three more eggs into the water and set the timer for three minutes. Then she thrust the slotted spoon into Tim's hand. "It's just eggs," she said. "Let's not break out in song and dance just yet."

Kyle grabbed her overall straps from behind and twirled her around. Catching her around the waist with one arm, he laced his fingers into hers and started a slow tango around the island. "I think successfully poaching eggs is worthy of at least a dance." He paused, holding their arms poised out to the side. "And I am happy to oblige."

With that they were off again, and she was letting him lead her around the island, into the dining area, and around the table. At the table he dipped her backward, her back flat on the table. "And, if you were my girl, here is where I'd kiss you."

"Kyle, you perpetual flirt, come make the toast, like you promised."

With that Kyle flipped her upright again and with fluent expertise spun her down the length of his arm and released her. She twirled in front of the French doors for a second before she stopped herself. A bit dizzy from the excursion, she reached for the door jamb to steady herself, laughter bubbling up in her chest.

"I came for coffee, but I think someone may have already drained the pot?"

The voice stopped the bubble of laughter before it spilled from her lips, and she turned. Reuben stood in the doorway, mere inches from her.

"Nah, we were just celebrating our successfully poached eggs. There's still plenty of coffee," Kyle said. "Me and the boss man's daughter don't need caffeine to get our hype-on."

Reuben had braided his hair and wore a cap. He still wore jeans but had added a t-shirt beneath the khaki shirt. A pair of sunglasses jutted out from the shirt pocket. His eyes swept over her from head to toe and then the hiking boots he wore scuffed on the floor as he sauntered across to the coffee pot.

He pulled a mug from the mug tree. He turned, and with the pot poised over the mug to pour, took in the three of them. "If she'll dance for poached eggs, what would she do for an omelette?" His voice dragged, and his head dipped to watch the liquid slosh into the mug. As the coffee neared the brim he looked up from under hooded eyes and smiled rakishly at her.

The proverbial marbles within her scattered, and as they rolled around inside trying to find purchase, everything quivered. As her breathing became restricted she parted her lips and allowed a shaky breath to escape.

She heard the toast pop, and was grateful for something to do, but when she stepped around the island and reached for it, Kyle beat her to it and she was left empty handed. And as if him looking at her wasn't enough, she was now shoulder to shoulder to him, facing opposite directions, and when she stepped back he reached out to take her forearm.

"Coffee?" he said, offering her the cup he'd just poured for himself.

Because she needed something to do and an excuse to get away from him, she accepted it, making sure to avoid his fingers. She didn't meet his eyes, but she could feel the molten swirls of chocolate reeling her in just the same. She didn't dare chance it, one more look and the ugly hand of addiction would wrap its fingers around her and pull her in. The distance and time of one night had not been enough. She would have to find another way to cope, another way to survive Reuben Lafford.

The coffee, too much for the mug, slopped against the walls of the cup and dripped down the sides. In the privacy of her own home she would have caught the drops with her tongue, but here she let them drip to the floor instead.

"I guess omelettes will have to wait for another morning," Tim said, taking his plated up toast and eggs and hooking his fingers into his own coffee mug. "Thanks for rescuing me, Penny-Laine."

"Penny," she corrected. "That's just a silly name my Dad pinned on me. I've long given up hope that he'll drop it. Please just call me Penny."

All three men raised their mugs in toast-fashion and she heard both Kyle and Tim murmur "Penny" in agreement. Although he'd raised his mug with the others, Reuben stayed quiet.

For some reason it irked her and when she looked in his direction his half smile made her heart momentarily stop beating. He lowered his cup from his mouth and let a drop of coffee plop to the floor, his eyes following hers from his drop to hers. Invisible fingers squeezed her lungs.

In one quick motion she swept her foot across the floor letting the drops of coffee soak into her white ankle socks.

She couldn't breathe.

With number seven standing so close to her, she forgot how to do it naturally and found herself mentally prompting her lungs to inflate and deflate. In and out. In and out.

She needed fresh air.

"Thanks," she said, and took her coffee to the deck.

Her dad had pulled a table closer to the cluster of deck chairs and had spread out papers in which he'd jotted notes and doodled pictures of his vision for the woods.

Jeff, the man sitting next to him, was a long-time friend of her father's. He'd lent a hand in many of Spencer's visions before they'd both retired. Now Jeff had pulled himself away from his own seaside oasis to lend Spencer a hand with his own. He had his landscape planning program of choice up on his heavy-duty laptop and the two were adjusting their plans to accommodate the new notes and drawings. The three other men were crowded around as well, each leaning forward occasionally to volunteer a suggestion.

"It's probably best if we take a look around first, walk or ride the land and get a feel for things before we start tweaking anything."

"Royce just wants to get rolling," Kyle piped up from behind them. He and Tim grabbed chairs and scooted closer to the group.

"Best time of day to work, and that sun's gonna be a scorcher later, by the look of things."

Penny sat a fair distance from the men, and it was only when she lifted the cup to her mouth and sipped that she realized she had straight up black coffee. The bitter liquid spread over her tongue and she nearly gagged and spit it back into the cup. She'd been so distracted she'd forgotten to add sugar and cream.

Making a move to get up, she saw Reuben in the French doors leading inside. He leaned against the door jamb with his own coffee. Not wanting another battle of wills with him, she settled back down and balanced her coffee on the arm of her Adirondack chair. She wouldn't drink it, but it made for a good distraction should she feel the need for one.

Reuben didn't join the other men. He just stood there being intimidating and setting her nerves on edge, and she was sure he intended to stay there too had her father not looked up and caught sight of him.

Spencer pushed up from the papers instantly. "Reuben," he said, approaching him with outstretched hand. "How was the drive? And Gyla, did she come with you?" He grasped Reuben's hand and clapped him on the shoulder with the other hand.

"She did. She's at the cabin with the girls, they're going to unpack and take a little walk along the brook later. The drive was fine too." Reuben's smile was big and genuine.

"I'm so glad you could make it. So you think Gyla will be okay with me popping in later to formally welcome her?"

This was a side of her father that Penny had never seen before. While he was typically polite and friendly, he seemed a little more so than usual.

"Mom would love that," Reuben said.

Spencer released Reuben's hand but turned him towards Penny.

Penny stiffened and instinctively gulped a swig of the bitter coffee. Her face curled up and her eyes began to water and although she tried to work her taste buds around the bitter liquid she couldn't, and instead she spat it forward.

Although her dad was as much in front of her as Reuben was, the majority of the coffee spray landed smack dab on the front of Reuben's jeans.

She wasn't able to react to the horror that filled her as she erupted into a coughing fit. With the mug extended in front of her, she made a mad dash for the kitchen. Pouring the offending brew down the drain, she quickly filled the mug, still tinged with coffee, with water and gulped it down.

As the nagging cough ebbed away the horror took over, and she spun around, the third mug of water raised to her lips. And her eyes widened.

"Are you okay?" Her dad asked, reaching out to her.

Reuben was smiling from beside him, paying no mind to the stain on his jeans.

"I'm so sorry," she croaked, her voice raspy. "There was no milk or sugar in my coffee and the bitterness was just too much to handle."

Reuben chuckled.

"I'm sorry about that," she said indicating the stain.

"No worries, Penny-Laine," he said, his voice a deliberate drawl as he spoke her name, adding emphasis to the hyphen.

Spencer dabbed at her chin with a kitchen towel, but the towel stopped short and he turned to look at Reuben. "Oh, you two have already met?"

"I've met Penny-Laine..." his words trailed off in thoughtful trepidation.

"Early this morning," she finished for him.

"Yes, very early this morning," he conceded.

"I think I'll just refill my travel mug and head to the distillery," she said, stopping her dad's hand as it rose once again to her.

She stepped away from her dad and around Reuben. This time she remembered to add milk and sugar to her coffee. Then she grabbed an apple, bade her onlookers good day and left the house.

~

Reuben had no intentions of changing his pants until Penny walked from the house. Then he gave a feeble excuse about dealing with the stains and rushed out after her.

Telling himself he shouldn't, he couldn't deny the reaction she caused in him. He would be here for less than a month, and then he would return to Halifax and she would stay here in Digby County. Three hours was too far a distance between them, but he could deal with it if he let her alone now. If he refrained from interpersonal relations with her, if he refrained from touching her or even looking at her for too long...but for whatever reason, a reason he was having problems laying his finger on, he was having a hell of a dandy time trying to do that.

She was a Weis. Where was her husband? Away on business? Had they separated? Had he passed away? He'd seen no trace in the cottage that he lived there, so he assumed that in some way he was no longer a factor. She obviously still loved him since a wedding picture still hung on the wall and he'd seen her ring.

He was as guilty of hanging on as she was, though. Although he'd removed his wedding ring, he still carried it in the folds of his wallet.

Even though every indication was pointing to the permanent absence of a husband, if there were one it would make his situation less difficult. He would not disrupt marital happiness at any cost. Hell, he wouldn't disrupt marital *anything* at any cost. Marriage had room for only two people, whether the situation was pleasant or not.

"Penny-Laine," he called down the path, but she continued to walk, her step only faltering slightly. He watched her rounded bottom sway from side to side, her loose overalls a light whisper against her skin and panties.

She was being stubborn, he could tell. It turned him on. "Penny," he tried.

She stopped in her tracks, turning. Her arms crossed against her breast as he neared her, a green apple jutted out to the right and a white travel mug to the left of her.

"I already said I was sorry," she said. "Do you want me to launder them for you as well?"

"I'm not worried about my jeans," he said. "I'm worried about my thoughts."

"Your thoughts? I'm pretty sure I can't control those."

"You have more control over them than you think.'

"What does that mean?"

He sidestepped that one. "I have a question. The answer will help how I deal with my thoughts."

She inclined her head at him, her corn-flower blue eyes confused.

"Your Dad's the great founder of McCalla Potatoes, and you are his daughter, yet you are a Weis." He looked down at her upturned face, shaded by the umbrella of trees. "I see a wedding picture, and you wear a ring, but I see no husband."

"Why does it matter?"

He tapped his temple and smiled at her. "My thoughts, remember?"

"Yes, we all think, but what does my marital status have to do with your thoughts, Mr. Lafford?"

He wanted to cup her face in his hand, to circle his fingers around the back of her slender neck, and trace the delicate line of her jaw. If only he could deal with the aftermath, and if she were unattached and in agreement, he'd make these next few weeks something they'd both remember.

"My thoughts are impure," he confessed.

"And my marital status will change that?"

"Knowing your marital status would help me know if I need to rein them in or if I can continue to let them run rampant."

"Oh, please," she said and turned to head up the path again.

He caught her elbow. "You just spat coffee all over me, and all I can think about is how much I liked it."

She stepped out of his hold and held up the travel mug. "If you get that excited over a spray of coffee, how would you feel about a whole mug of it?"

Her face still looked cute curled up in a sneer. In fact it made him want to knock the coffee from her hand and back her up against a tree and wipe the sneer off her face. He wanted to take her around the waist and pull her feisty little body to his. Take her cute little plump bottom lip between his teeth and suck it until it swelled against his tongue.

He laughed at her retaliation, and instinctively moved closer to her. She lifted the apple-laden hand and pressed it into his chest in an attempt to keep him at bay.

"Married? Divorced? Separated? Widowed?" he asked circling the apple hand with one of his own. "I just want to know if you're single."

"I wear a ring," she said. Lifting the other hand she wiggled her ringed finger as best as she could.

"But where's your husband?" He still held her hand, his fingers splayed along hers and extended out to grasp the apple too.

"If you really must know, he passed away," she said, her eyelids fluttering down.

He knew he ought to apologize for her loss, as was custom, but he also knew how tedious hearing such statements became, and he didn't want to be just another well-wisher.

"I guess my next question would be, how long ago?"

"Does that even matter?"

"I guess the answer defines the asker's next move. How I proceed certainly depends on the time frame of your widowhood."

"Did you really just say widowhood?"

"If it'll make you feel better, I can tell you that I have been fourteen months living in widowerhood."

"You're a widower?" she asked, relief flooding her face.

He tried to smile. "Did that just make you happy? I lost my wife, and you're happy about it."

She tried to twist her hand free from his, but he held tighter. "Don't be such a pig." She tried to splay her hands open beneath his.

"Okay, okay, I'm sorry," he said snaking a hand around her waist. "I didn't mean you were happy someone died. If I had meant that then you could call me a pig, but I could see the relief on your face."

She twisted in his arms, and it took no struggle at all to contain her.

"Why did that ease you, Penny-Laine?"

"I still love my husband," she spat.

"And that's as should be."

His body reacted to her closeness. He wondered if she could tell.

"I still love Eve, too, but loving someone who's gone doesn't stop the wants and the needs, does it? A gone person can't fill either of those." He breathed deep, his restraint stretching thin. "How long has it been, Penny-Laine?"

"My fucking name is Penny," she said. "And if it's so damn important for you to know, it's been two years, seven months, sixteen days, and," she twisted her hand and peered at the watch on his wrist, "three hours, and about forty-two minutes."

"Then it's been too damn long for both of us," he growled

With a flick of his wrist the apple rolled down the pathway. The travel mug fell at their feet. He swiftly readjusted his arm to circle her waist beneath her coveralls and crushed his lips to hers.

For a second he felt no resistance as she breathed deep. He could feel her breast push against him as her lungs filled with air, and her lips move on his. But as soon as their tongues collided he felt her draw back.

He let her. He'd felt enough to know that she wanted him as much as he wanted her.

She stared at him wild-eyed, her lips parted and moist from his kiss. Then she looked at the mug at her feet and its spilled contents that had splashed up onto their pant legs.

"You're a manipulative pig," she spat and ran up the pathway towards her cottage.

He watched her disappear out of sight before he picked up the mug and the apple. He wiped the apple on the leg of his pants and bit into it as he started back up the path toward the big house, a smile as big as all outdoors on his face. Penny-Laine was as sweet as she looked. He wanted her now more than ever. And better yet, she wanted him, too.

5

It was the threat of rain that broke the dry spell. Penny hadn't seen hide nor hair of Reuben in more than twenty-four hours. Not since she'd called out his piggery, and wobbled away on jellied knees. She'd heard the eight men board their ATVs shortly after and head into the woods to make notes and get a feel for the area, and then again this morning they'd geared up machinery and she could hear all sorts of commotion going on within the wooded area around her.

In light of the impending rain they'd gotten an early start today. Their schedule had almost clashed with her own, but she had expected it and managed to sneak from the house as soon as she heard the first creak on the stairs. She knew she couldn't avoid them forever.

As soon as the rain started, they would all be forced together. With any luck at all Reuben would head to her cottage to be with his family, and she would be left with just her father and six rowdy men to contend with. She could handle that.

Reuben, on the other hand…

She wouldn't dwell on that, she told herself. He'd kissed her once, and even though it was an earth-shattering, curl her toes kind of kiss, she was going to make damn sure it never happened again. She liked her world right side up, and her toes were fine just as they were.

However cooping herself up in a bid to avoid him was not going to happen either, especially here in her own home. If he attempted to even touch her again she would set him straight.

A whole day after and she could still feel his hands on the small of her back, and the trace of his thumbs grazing along the hem of her crop top. It still left her breathless.

She caught her bottom lip between her teeth and ran her tongue across it, tasting the coffee that hung there. She wondered if coffee would ever taste the same again. This morning's coffee seemed to be lacking something, and all she'd had was one small taste of him.

Well she was just going to have to retrain her taste buds. They'd become like an addict, one small taste of him had them craving more. Her traditional morning coffee contained two creams and one sugar, and there was no room for a dash of Reuben.

She sat at the desk in the distillery, reading emails from customers and printing out order forms. *Land of Lavandula*, her small online business, had become more popular in the last year, and so last fall she had expanded from three acres to five. Good reviews were pouring in from free samples she'd offered, and although initially she had worried that free sampling would hurt her financially, she was pleased to see that a lot of the people she'd sent the samples to were returning to purchase. It was looking like a good return on her investment.

Just as she was about to reply to a comment on social media a knock sounded on the door.

"Mrs. Weis? It's Gyla Lafford, may I come in?"

Penny's fingers froze on the keyboard. Although she couldn't explain why, the need to straighten herself and appear as presentable as possible was great.

She ran her hands down her loosened hair and tucked the front strands behind her ears. Today she'd chosen a pair of black leggings and an asymmetrical lace tunic. Although she'd been sure to wear a tank-top beneath the barely see-through tunic, she still wondered about it. She'd removed her white canvas shoes, but she slipped them on again in an attempt to feel more pulled-together. It didn't work, but she couldn't ignore the woman forever.

"Come in," Penny called, standing as the door opened.

"Hello, dear," the woman said as she slipped through the door. "We haven't had the chance to meet yet."

Then she stopped short. "Oh, dear, you're just beautiful."

Gyla circled the desk and, although Penny extended her hand for a shake, wrapped her in a hug. She squeezed Penny gently. "I've heard so much about you, I feel like I know you already."

Penny froze. Had Reuben told his mother that he'd met her? But that couldn't be it. This woman made it sound as though she could pass a trivia test on the subject of Penny Weis, and a couple of short conversations and a kiss from Reuben wouldn't yield a loaded statement like that.

"You've heard so much about me?" Penny asked. "From whom?"

"From your dad, of course." Gyla pulled away, but kept Penny at arm's length. "He's so proud of you, and of your brother, too, of course, but you're right here close to him and he really appreciates that."

Her smile was toothy. "And you gave up your home for us. That was so kind of you."

Penny instantly thought of her mother's velvet mantel scarf.

"Don't worry, I am being extra careful, and making sure you get your home back in as pristine a condition as when you gave it." She stopped short. "Oh listen to me, babbling like a brook." She raised a finger and thumb to her mouth and mockingly closed the proverbial zipper.

Penny couldn't help but laugh. The woman had spirit that spilled over onto Penny. "I hope you're finding everything you need. I tried to stock the place with all the essentials, although truth be told I was expecting seven rowdy men, so I went a little heavy on beer and snacks."

"Don't worry about a thing," Gyla said, laying a hand on her arm.

"I wasn't expecting children, or I would have chosen healthier snacks, and by the time Dad broke the news to me it was too late to run into town."

"We are making do," Gyla smiled. "Speaking of the children, they are the reason I came down here."

Where were the children, anyway? Had she left them alone in the cottage? Alone with her mother's mantel scarf?

"They're sleeping now," she said, as though she could read Penny's mind. "But I promised the girls I would invite you to dinner with us."

Dinner? She hadn't expected that. She tried to recall if Reuben had eaten dinner at the big house yesterday, but she wasn't entirely certain.

"It'll just be something light since I'm spending the afternoon up at Spencer's preparing a big supper for everyone, but you made a good impression on the girls and they really want you to come for dinner." She grabbed Penny's hands and the endearing look was almost more than Penny could bear.

Gyla winked and leaned in to whisper, "Its how I got them down for a nap, with the promise that I would extend the invitation, so you can't refuse." She laughed again, a good-hearted laugh that made Penny's heart happy. "We'd love to have you," she said straightening again. "They even chose the meal. So, I have a macaroni salad chilling in the fridge. I've got some cold chicken for biscuit sandwiches, and I made fresh iced tea."

"You had me at 'I promised the girls'," Penny laughed. "Can anyone really refuse them anything? But I have to admit the promise of macaroni salad and biscuit chicken sandwiches sealed the deal."

Gyla patted her hand before she let go and started for the door again.

At the door she turned. "Oh, good: the rain is starting early, by the looks, so Reuben will no doubt be joining us."

Penny deadpanned.

"We'll see you at noon, dear," Gyla called as she closed the door behind her.

~

Rainwater pooled around Reuben's feet and soaked into the doormat. The rain had started out lightly and, although they'd packed up and headed in at the first hint of a sprinkle, they hadn't made it before it was coming down in sheets. It was invigorating. It seemed to seep into his soul and rejuvenate him. Of course now he was drenched to the core and he would need to change his clothes, but it was a small price to pay for the deluge.

As soon as the door shut behind him, Terra leapt into his arms. "Daddy, Mrs. Wise is eating with us." Ember jutted a tiny finger in Penny's direction and Reuben's eyes met hers.

Reuben noticed that Ember had moved her chair to the right, closer to Penny. It was just a subtle bit, and he doubted Penny even noticed, but he did. Ember liked everything balanced, and when she deviated from her norm, he noticed. To be honest he relished it.

"I see that," he said, planting a kiss squarely on Terra's lips. "Did you have to bribe her?"

"No, silly, she wanted to come, right, Mrs. Wise?"

Penny moved her eyes from Reuben's and smiled at Terra, "Absolutely," she said.

Ember jittered and beamed to one side, her shoulders hunched up level with her chin. Reuben could see her feet kick happily under the table. She was trying really hard to contain her excitement and remain a lady-like girl, but her excitement was slowly spilling over the top. He admired her self-restraint. She liked Mrs. Wise more than she cared to show.

It kind of worried him. Although he wanted her to let down her guard, he also didn't want to give her false hope.

"I'll change into something dry," he said, walking across the floor to set Terra down at the table.

On his way up from the stoop his eyes locked with Penny's and he smiled, "Glad you could join us, Mrs. Wise."

Penny shifted uneasily, and mumbled a feeble "thanks."

"Terra, go change your wet t-shirt, please," Gyla said.

Reuben took the stairs two at a time. In the bathroom he pulled off his wet clothes and towelled himself dry. His braid was soaked, so he removed the elastic and pulled the braid apart and towel-dried it as best he could before flipping it up into a bun at the back of his head.

He had to be careful. He had to go downstairs and treat Penny-Laine like any other person he knew. He had to pretend he didn't want to kiss her again. Pretend that he didn't want to continue the exploration of her mouth with his tongue, and pretend that at the first sign of her willingness to comply he wouldn't ravish her into oblivion.

Terra's unadulterated happiness at just having Penny-Laine for dinner, and Ember's coy acceptance, were warning flags for him. He had to be extra careful for their sake. He couldn't harbour any false hope for them. He had to keep Penny-Laine in the friend zone, no matter how badly he wanted her in his arms and in his bed.

He looked at the bed. The sheets she'd slept beneath were still there.

In a quick motion he ripped them from the bed and let them hit against the wall before they fell to the floor. That was the first step. Sleeping beneath sheets that smelled like her was a sure way for him to trip up. One slip and he could shatter the perfect world he'd been trying to create for his babies for the last fourteen months, six days, ten hours, and seventeen minutes.

He would go down to dinner and focus on being kind, no insinuating remarks or looks. He would talk about his morning and make polite conversation, and then he'd excuse himself and head to Spencer's for a beer with the boys.

He entered the kitchen a few minutes later and took his place at the head of the table. Penny sat directly across from him. His stomach muscles clenched as his eyes met hers.

The tray in the middle of the table was laden with a heaping pile of freshly cooked chicken and more biscuits than they would ever eat, but it was his mother's habit to overdo meal times, especially if there was a guest. She'd also prepared macaroni salad and iced tea, and had set out a pitcher of grape juice for the girls.

He had been taught that meals didn't start until the man of the house took the first serving, but that didn't apply when they had company. He leaned forward and lifted the bowl of macaroni. Reaching over the biscuits, he passed it to Penny.

She looked taken aback, but quickly caught on to what was expected of her. To Reuben's surprise she took a healthy portion and turned to Ember.

"Should I help you?" she asked her. Tongue in cheek, Ember gave a tiny nod.

"You tell me when," she said and began spooning macaroni onto Ember's plate.

After a couple of small scoops Ember said. "When," and giggled when Penny mistakenly dropped another unwanted spoonful onto her plate.

"Oops," Penny said and tried to pick the macaroni back up with the spoon. Ember's laughs grew hysterical when most of the macaroni fell off the spoon back onto her plate.

"Oh, don't you laugh at me," Penny teased, reaching over to tickle Ember on the tummy. Ember's head lolled back in the chair and her laughter rollicked from her as Reuben had never heard before. On the other side of Penny, Terra was laughing, too.

"You're just being a silly goose," Penny said to Ember and turned to Terra. "How many scoops would you like?"

Terra had covered both her hands over her mouth trying to hold in her laughter, but she dropped them and extended her hands. She held down her thumb in order to hold up two fingers, "This many," she announced.

Penny leaned forward and counted each individual finger.

"One, Two. So you want two scoops like your silly goose sister over here, huh?" And she proceeded to scoop the salad onto the plate, incident-free.

Then it was like she remembered the others were there. She looked up apologetically and passing the bowl to Gyla. Her eyes shifted from Gyla to him nervously. "I'm so sorry. Was it okay that I did that?"

God, she was making this hard for him. "It was fine," he said.

"Just perfect," Gyla beamed, taking the bowl from her. "However, if you help them with their biscuits, I made little bitty ones for them. They're on the side and don't use too much chicken on them. Their eyes are always bigger than their stomachs."

Reuben watched as Penny helped prepare each of his daughter's biscuit sandwiches, spreading each child's preferred condiment on the appropriate biscuit, mayonnaise for Ember and barbecue sauce for Terra. Then he watched as she squirted mustard on her own sandwich, and pouted at the girls when they poked fun at her choice of condiment.

Why hadn't she had children of her own? If her interactions with his girls were any indication, she seemed to enjoy them. She would make a perfect mother. He wondered if one day she would get the chance. Was she dating anyone?

He hadn't seen a man around, unless he counted Kyle. He had seemed comfortable enough around her, but still it wasn't the kind of cozy comfortable one was with a person they knew intimately. Still he wondered about it.

He studied her over his glass of grape juice. He had only been here a couple of days. Maybe her beau only got round to see her on weekends. If that were the case he was a different kind of man than Reuben was. There was no way in hell he'd wait even twenty-four hours to see her. She was not the kind of woman you tucked away until time was convenient. She was more along the lines of 'let's get this work day done, so I can devour her' kind of woman. A seven days a week, fifty-two weeks a year, always and forever kind of girl.

Hell she wasn't even his and he missed her. It had been too long since he'd tasted her. Too long since he'd felt her flesh beneath his fingers.

"Shit," he said, and sat his glass down on the table, a little harder than he intended. Some of the juice splashed out onto the table. It was only then that he realized he'd cursed aloud.

"Sorry," he said as he scurried to sop up the juice with his napkin. But as he did the glass wobbled and more spilled out.

"Fuck," he proclaimed, rushing from the table to grab a wad of paper towels and catch the juice before it travelled too far down the table.

"Daddy dropped the f-bomb," Terra said, her mouth a complete *0*.

"He needs to put a quarter in the swear jar, Nanna," Ember said.

"I think he needs to put *two* quarters in the swear jar."

Reuben could hear the anger in his mother's voice.

Shit, if they only knew his thoughts he'd have to take out a small loan and the swear jar would need to be bigger.

"I'll pay my dues, I promise."

The whole point of the swear jar was to clean up his potty mouth around the girls. Although Ember was too lady-like to cuss, Terra had started to repeat some of his words. "Did we even bring the swear jars?"

His mother was the only person who had the ability to reprim-
and him with a mere look, and the look she gave him now could
have pinned him to the wall. He knew that her anger wasn't because he'd cursed in front of the children, although he was sure she
was plenty mad about that, but rather because he'd done so in
front of a guest.

"We brought the swear jars, daddy," Terra piped up. Dropping
her fork she slipped from the table to run to the family room. She
stopped at the mantel and pointed up at the four jars in a line on
the mantel scarf. "See, Daddy."

"Okay, Terra, come back and finish your dinner now," Reuben
said.

"But, Daddy, you owe the swear jar," she whined. She pulled an
ottoman over to the mantel. Balancing precariously she grabbed
the jar labelled 'daddy', and flipped the clamp lid open.

The spring of the clamp lid was just enough to unbalance her,
and she teetered on the ottoman. Reaching a hand up to catch herself, she grabbed the edge of the scarf and the three remaining jars
fell to the floor with a crash.

~

Penny's heart was already wedged in her throat, blocking off a
scream that tried to surface. Terra still stood on the ottoman, un-
harmed, the daddy jar wedged up under her arm. She stared down
at the broken glass on the floor.

Penny hated to look at her mother's velvet mantel scarf, convinced God had deemed it too trivial to warrant his attention, so
she rushed over and took Terra from the ottoman instead.

Reuben was there as well. Seeing that Terra was okay, he bent to
deal with the shattered jars.

"You're so hard headed," he said at Terra, and Penny tightened
her arms around the little girl protectively. "Now look what you've
done."

The three remaining jars had broken in such a fashion that it was still pretty easy to tell what coins went in what jar. The mantel scarf had acted as a cushion.

Some glass fragments had scattered over the cloth and onto the floor. If Penny hadn't stored away the medallion rug, the glass shards would be embedded in it now, and if it weren't for the mantel scarf the hardwood floor would no doubt be gouged.

Gyla dropped to her knees with three ziplock bags and a waste basket. "I'm very sorry," she said to Penny.

Terra curled into Penny, the daddy jar wedged between them.

"It's okay. Don't worry about it. It was just a little mistake."

She squeezed Terra tightly. She wanted to stay upbeat for the little girl's sake, and she found it easier than she would have thought it would be given the fact that she didn't yet know the status of the precious mantel scarf.

"You all go ahead and eat your dinner," Gyla said, waving them all back to the table. "It'll just take me a minute to clean this up."

"I've got it, Mom," Reuben said laying a hand on Gyla's wrist. He took one bag from her and began to fill it with the coins from one of the jars. "Do you have a marker around here somewhere?" He asked Penny.

"I do, upstairs in the loft," she said. "Would you like to help me get it?" She asked Terra and the little girl beamed.

She took the daddy jar from her and placed it on the dining table in front of Ember. "Ember, would you mind getting two coins from your daddy for the two swear words he did today and then a third one for the swear word he threw at *me* yesterday?"

Penny heard Gyla's surprised gasp from behind her, and turned to walk up the stairs with Terra still on her hip. Although she didn't turn to look, she could feel the heat of Reuben's glare burn into her back. As she neared the landing she heard Gyla reprimand her son and couldn't fight the smile that broke out across her face.

In the loft she sat Terra down and pulled open a drawer. She had a small array of coloured markers and she let Terra choose a dark purple that Penny already knew dried to a near black.

The little girl bounded down the stairs with the marker held tightly in her fist, anxious to do something right and maybe win her father's praise.

Penny lingered at the top of the stairs for a moment, watching Terra's descent. There were children living in her home, and, although temporarily, it still felt right. The house had originally been designed with children in mind, but since then it had taken on an almost eggshell demeanour. The dream of children had been so long in the grave that she had allowed everything around her to become brittle, and as a result she lived a careful existence.

But she had been happy. Her life may not be for everyone but it had served her well until now.

Had been? Until now? What was she doing? She was happy before The Laffords showed up, and she would be happy long after they were gone. There was no *until now*, there was only *always*. Her life would always serve her well, and Reuben would not change that, even if he had been right. It *had* been too damn long for her, but there were plenty of men who could hold her as efficiently as Reuben had, and could kiss her just as thoroughly.

She crossed to the loft again and looked over the banister down onto the scene at the fireplace.

Terra was squatted slightly to look into her daddy's eyes, and her small voice carried up to the loft.

"Daddy, are you mad at me?" she asked trying to level her eyes with Reuben's.

Penny knew by the way Reuben squared his shoulders that he was going to play the tough love card with her, but as soon as her tiny hands reached out to clasp his face she saw his shoulders loosen and he turned to her, allowing her to hold his face in her tiny hands while she talked.

"But daddy, you sworeded, and you told me when I sworeded that the fastest I paid for my swores the fastest I'd get forgiven." She said it so matter-of-fact and so straight-faced and sincere that a smile stretched across Reuben's face.

"You're right, the faster I pay my swear debts the quicker I'll be forgiven," he said, repeating what she'd said but in proper English.

He took her small face in his own hands. "Thanks for worrying about me, Terra," he said and kissed the tip of her nose.

Finished with the cleaning he stood with the mantel scarf in his hand. "I do forgive you for not listening, especially knowing now that you were doing it for my own good, but now you're going to have to seek forgiveness from Mrs. Weis."

He opened the scarf and held it up. A horizontal slash, about two inches wide, leered out at them from across an embroidered bundle of wheat.

6

Penny spent part of the morning poring over invoices and packaging up orders. The packages were ready to go, thanks to online shipping tools, and so it would be a quick drop-off in the morning and then she had plans to meet Claire, her best friend, for lunch in the village.

With the rain coming down there wasn't much to do outside, so she had gone down to the big house to lend Gyla a hand. The girls had grown tired of *helping* and had rolled a small trunk of toys out to the deck. They brought innocence to the group of rowdy men and it made Penny's heart happy to see burly men go from tough to tender in the presence of children.

On the few occasions she'd peeked out she'd been pleased to see the men comply with stethoscopes, reflex tests, and tongue compressions, and on one occasion she'd even seen bandages on some of their faces and arms. The girls were enjoying their willing patients, and it didn't take them long to clue in to the wealth of fun they could be having; their patients were versatile and could be anything their minds could imagine.

Before long they had begged for tea in their tiny tea pots and a small tray of crackers and cookies, and the next time Penny looked out four of the men, Reuben included, were sipping tea from tiny pink princess mugs.

Penny had envisioned that Gyla would prepare a rack of lamb or a roast with all the fixings, but instead she and Penny sat down to pick chicken and before long a couple pans of rapure pie were in the oven while freshly-baked rolls cooled on the sideboard.

The place smelled divine, and Gyla's company was equally as pleasant. Her nurturing ways didn't stop at Reuben and the twins; she made everyone feel cared for.

Penny was used to herself and Spencer making up their family for the most part. But on some weekends and on special occasions her brother, Warren, would come and then they were a family of three. Although Penny loved their family time she hadn't realized until now how much she'd longed for this feeling. She missed her mother. No matter how much family togetherness the three of them had, something was always missing; the loving touch of a mother's hand. That hand had the ability to turn a simple existence of a house into a home, and although Penny believed one could still thrive without a mother, she also knew from experience that nothing compared to the completeness a mother *and* father provided.

As the supper hour drew near, the rain eased and the smell of rapure pie baking poured from the open windows, drawing the men in from the deck.

The long dinner table was fashioned to seat eight comfortably, but Gyla had wedged in three extra chairs at the corners. Penny had a twin on each side, and was thankful that Reuben was at the opposite end of the table. Gyla had seated herself next to Penny's dad and the two seemed eager to pull their chairs close together to make room for the additional chairs.

"How long have you known Mrs Lafford, Dad?" Penny asked.

The two looked at each other before saying in unison, "Since November eleventh." Then they fell into laughter at their in-time answer.

"Of last year?" Penny asked.

"Yes," Spencer said.

"Although we didn't officially meet until January," Gyla said. "Your crazy father drove through a blizzard to come to the city that day."

Spencer rested his hand on Gyla's. "Well, I waited two whole weeks, I wasn't going to let a blizzard keep me away."

"I remember that," Penny said. "I thought you went to the city that day because you had some meeting that couldn't be postponed."

"Well, I did," Spencer laughed.

"I thought you were old friends?"

"It feels like we're old friends," Gyla said, splitting a roll in half and spreading a pat of butter on each half. She placed one half on her plate and the other on Spencer's before turning to Penny with concern. "Does our friendship bother you?"

It did, a bit, but Penny couldn't say that. Mostly she was bothered that her dad hadn't told her about it, and that she hadn't realized it until now. "No, no, not at all." She split her own roll in half and buttered it. "I have no issues with anyone being friends."

"Good, then," Gyla said, reaching out to take the salt shaker from Spencer before he could sprinkle some on his food. She said nothing as she reached past Kyle, sitting beside her, and placed the salt shaker well out of Spencer's reach.

Penny watched the quiet show of concern for her father's health with confusion. They obviously knew enough about one another to have discussed something as personal as medical problems and already felt comfortable reprimanding each other for not taking care of themselves.

She looked at Reuben for a sign that this was news to him as well, but he didn't pay it any mind.

"Mrs. Wise," A small voice from the right drew Penny's attention away from her father and she turned to look at Ember. "I spilled juice on my dress." The front of her lacy dress was blotched cherry red.

"Oh no," she said wiping at the lace with a napkin. "I bet your granny knows a trick or two to get stains like that out easily, though, and if she doesn't I have a few tricks of my own. Is this dress a favourite?"

She shook her head solemnly.

"We better not get any more stains on it, just in case." She tucked the napkin in the collar of Ember's dress and smoothed it over the front as best as she could.

"What about here?" she asked showing her exposed lap.

Penny reached for Roger's unused napkin and, getting his nod of approval, draped it over Ember's lap. But as soon as Ember adjusted in the chair the napkin slid down her legs to the floor and she looked up at Penny with a look of dire distress in her eyes.

Penny clamped a hand over her mouth and stooped to get the napkin, and that's when she noticed her father's hand splayed on Gyla's knee beneath the table. She hit her head on the table edge on her way up, but she ignored the stab of pain as she looked down the table at her father. There was no denying the look that passed between Spencer and Gyla.

It was right there, not only the fact that there was an obvious attraction between the two but that they had either already acted upon the attraction or were right at the threshold.

Unsure what to do. She moved from the table and pulled a dishcloth from the counter. At the table she busied herself securing both the napkin and the dishcloth on Ember's lap, tucking the edges in under her legs. "There that ought to work," she said as her eyes flitted back to Reuben.

She was looking for signs of his unease, but he showed no hint of a care, and when her eyes locked on his she tried to will a response from him. Tried to summon up a telepathic pathway between them in which he would confirm what all the signs were pointing to.

When his stare became too much, she focused her attention on the rapure pie on her plate, but suddenly the delicious south-western dish no longer looked appealing to her.

Why did this bother her so much? While she pushed the chicken and potato concoction around on her plate she tried to work out the reason. Hadn't she just minutes before been enjoying Gyla's company and compassion so much that she had even likened her to her own mother?

Hadn't her presence here made Penny wish for a mother figure in her life? It was true, Gyla had such a welcoming way about her that in the short moments of knowing her Penny could easily picture her in her life permanently. But where did that leave Reuben?

He was Gyla's son. They were a package deal. And herself? She was Spencer's daughter. They were a package deal. Combining the two packages didn't work for her. What would that make Reuben? Her step-brother?

She looked at him across the table. His liquid chocolate eyes swirled as they looked around the table and came to a stop on her, and even the few seconds she afforded to look at him, she could feel herself getting lost in their pools.

Her step-brother? The thoughts he evoked in her were anything but brotherly.

"That was a meal fit for a king, Mrs. Lafford," Jeff said, and an echo of agreement circled the table.

"There's plenty more left in the oven," Gyla said. "But save room for dessert. I thought we'd have strawberry shortcake, but I prepared the strawberries earlier in the day and left them in the fridge at the small cottage." She turned to Reuben. "Since you've finished eating, would you mind taking a run down and bringing up the dish of strawberries from the refrigerator, and the dish of whipped topping in the container beside it?"

"I'll help," Penny said, springing up from the table just as Reuben stood to leave.

All eyes turned to her she fumbled for an excuse. "I, I," her eyes flitted down to Ember. "I want to get Ember a change of clothing."

"But you haven't finished," Gyla said. "I'm sure Reuben can manage a change of clothes as well."

"Well, I– I," she fumbled over her words again, her eyes flitting around in search of some excuse, the smirk on Reuben's face hard to ignore. "I need to close down the computer in my distillery, too, and shoot an email off to Claire to confirm our dinner date tomorrow."

"Oh, okay, then," Gyla said.

Penny moved around the table towards Reuben and the doorway. She slipped on her shoes and stepped through the door as Reuben held it open for her.

Out on the deck she walked around the corner toward the stairs. She heard the door close behind them, and waited until she heard his footsteps close before she rounded on him.

In a swift movement she had him against the side of the house, and a hand pressed into his chest. "What do you know of this relationship between my dad and your mother?"

"What?" he asked, taken aback.

"You're too comfortable around them. I can tell. You knew." She slammed her palm into his chest. "Is that why you came?"

"What? No." He said catching her hand just as she was about to deliver another blow. "Yes, I knew about their friendship, but his request for me to work for him was legit. It was me or someone else, and of course he chose me because of Mom."

She stepped away from him and started pacing the front of the steps. "Well, what are we going to do?"

"What are we going to do? It seems to me you're the only one with the problem. Spencer is good for Mom, he makes her happy. Who am I to get involved?"

"Then you're okay with this?" She threw her hand back to indicate the door of the cottage, and ultimately their parents inside.

He laughed. "Sure, why not? The question is, why aren't you okay with it?"

"Have you thought about what will happen if this lasts between them?"

"Of course it will last between them."

"Okay, okay, sure, so let's say it does go okay between them, and they decide to make it official. Have you given any thoughts as to what will happen should they decide to make this relationship a permanent thing?"

"Like what?"

"Like say come Christmas time. Gyla's going to want to spend time with her grandchildren and her son."

"I certainly hope so."

"And I live down a pathway two minutes away. I spend every Christmas in that big house with my dad and my brother."

"Good. I hope that doesn't change. Family is important, you of all people should know that."

"Don't patronize me, Reuben."

"What are you so worried about? I'm sure Spencer has enough room in his heart to love my mom and still love you and your brother. He's not going to forget about you just because he loves my mother, and me and the girls by association."

She squeezed her clenched fist tight in front of her. "Don't pretend you have no idea what I'm talking about."

He moved from the house toward her, a wicked smile playing at the corners of his mouth. "Are you talking about us, Penny-Laine?"

"There is no us," she spat.

"Then what are you talking about?"

"I'm talking about me and you." She stepped closer to jab a finger in his chest. "You will never be my brother in any way, shape, or form."

Then she took off down the steps. The rain instantly soaked her hair and seeped through the lace tunic she wore, soaking the black tank top beneath.

"I have no intentions of being your brother," he said, coming down the steps behind her. Catching up to her he reached for her hand and spun her around, but she guessed what his intentions were and pushed away just before his arm encircled her waist.

Her canvas shoes slapped on the ground as she ran up the pathway to her cottage, but just as she reached the front door he closed in on her and flipped her up into his arms.

With a swift movement he opened the cottage door and walked inside, with her still struggling in his arms. He didn't bother to remove his shoes, and still holding her up in his arms he braced her against the wall of the entryway and claimed her lips with his own.

Unable to resist him she opened her mouth on his and moaned when his tongue slipped inside, their tongues colliding, and her cries the only indication of the silent battle going on inside their mouths.

Then he released her and she spun away. She yanked open the fridge and removed the strawberries just as he came up behind her, his hand coming around to turn her face back up to his. She allowed him to press her back against him, his erect manhood pressing into her behind.

The container of strawberries was forgotten as his hand pulled the wet fabric of her top away from her body and reached beneath to cup her breast. And as his fingers found her taut nipple her insides shattered, and the strawberries fell to the floor.

He released her mouth and dropped his head to her neck. "I want to make love to you, Penny-Laine." His lips trailed hot kisses down her neck.

He slipped a hand beneath the band of her leggings and ran his palm over her flat stomach, the tips of his fingers tracing the delicate outline of her panties. "I want to feel you beneath me more than I've ever wanted anything in my life."

He slipped his fingers beneath her panties, and dipped into her warmth. "I want to feel myself inside you," he groaned in her ear as he slipped his fingers within her. "I want to watch you moving on top of me, to see your perfect breasts dance, and feel you quiver in my arms."

His other hand cupped her breast gently and tweaked her nipple. "I don't want to be your brother anymore than you want me to be." Deftly he slipped his fingers out of her and manoeuvred her around so they were facing one another.

She flopped against him, weakened by his touch, and working her fingers at the band of his pants she released the shirt and slipped her hands beneath. Her fingers flitted around his torso and circled him, pulling him closer. Her face turned up to his, she sought his mouth with hers and moaned deeply when he closed the distance between them.

"Please,' she said against his mouth.

"Please what, Penny-Laine?"

"Yes," she groaned when his hand reached to cup her bottom.

"Yes," he agreed, as he hiked her up the length of him and she wrapped her legs around his torso.

It took two strides to reach the table. He lowered her atop it.

~

Reuben watched the smouldering hot Penny arch and purr on the table beneath him. It wasn't how he pictured their first time. He'd pictured candles and soft music and, at the very least, a warm bed, but she pulsed beneath him. Her everything screaming out for him as loudly as he was screaming out for her.

Just this once, he told himself. He would take her quickly, and that was it. Maybe this would quell the craving he had for her, and if not, then the next time he would love her the way he longed to. To explore every inch of her body, trace all her contours and memorize her the way a man losing his sight drinks in his surroundings– with utmost attention and care.

"Please," she said again and then he felt her fingers working with the clasp of his jeans and he was suddenly free, pulsating within her hand. He needed to have her and all else be damned.

Pushing her back on the table, he caught the band of her leggings and yanked them down around her ankles, and then stepped within the circle of her legs. For just a moment he let himself admire her. Her thin beige panties created a bridge from hipbone to hipbone.

Cupping her tiny hips in his hands he slid his fingers beneath the elastic and slid the slight fabric down. The panties came to a halt against his groin, and he reached behind to yank a sopping shoe from her left foot. The leggings slipped off the freed ankle and dangled from the opposite one.

Grabbing the sides of her panties, stretched taut from the spread of her legs, he deliberately pulled them down. Bending her right leg he slipped her foot out of the leg hole and watched the panties spring free across his stomach to dangle from the opposite leg. Unable to wait another second he pushed forward and entered her.

Penny's cries of pleasure echoed all through the cabin as he bucked and pushed within her. She met him thrust for thrust, her fingers eagerly exploring his chest and clawing at his back in an effort to get closer still.

And when he felt her spasm beneath him, her inner muscles clenching and unclenching around him, he released himself within her. Their cries mingled together and they clung to one another, their bodies melded into one continuous whole. *He* and *she* an *us*, despite the promise of *never*.

Reuben held her to him, afraid to release her. Afraid to see the regret he knew would be in her eyes. Her head fell forward on his chest as she tried to control her breathing. He was still within her, still semi-hard but deflating slowly. Her legs still wrapped securely around his waist and her arms bunched up between them, her hands cradling her own face as her head lulled to and fro, her lips quivering against his skin, her body slowly coming to grips with reality.

He felt the small space between them almost instantly as she lifted her head, and heard her small cry before he dragged her face to his and grabbed her swollen bottom lip between his teeth. He kissed her as though it would be the last time, trying to make it slow and purposeful. The purpose of harvesting the memory of her taste for future reference. When her ankles unclasped behind him, he groaned regretfully and tried to hold her tighter, but she pulled away.

Separated from her now, he felt cold and empty despite the warmth within him. He watched her scrambling to dress. When she dropped to the floor, he did all he could think of to do.

He lied.

"I'm sorry," he said stooping to her, his own jeans still wrapped around his ankles.

But she reached up, without looking, to dig her fingers into his lips, and then she looked up at him. Her eyes filled with tears as she said in an angry whisper, "Don't speak."

'But," he started, but she twisted her fingers again and scratched at his mouth.

"But nothing," she said.

He refastened his jeans as she retied her canvas shoes and rose to her feet, readjusting her tank and tunic, both still soaked from the downpour, and then she looked around frantically. The horrified look that crossed over her face made him look in the same direction.

The strawberry container was on its side, a puddle of red juice, laced with clots of strawberries, pooled out around the container.

She rushed to retrieve it, moving to the sink to wash away the spillage from the sides, and held it up to look at the contents. At least half had spilled out on the floor.

She thrust the container in a bag and retrieved the whipped topping from the fridge.

"Ember's clothing?" she asked, not meeting his eyes.

He pointed to the bedroom further down the hall and she took off towards it.

"Let me," he caught her hands as she fumbled through the closet. "You catch your breath." He moved her to the bed. She didn't resist as he set her down on the edge. He moved to a set of drawers to retrieve a pair of pjs. It was closer to bedtime, and made more sense.

As he chose between the sets of pjs he watched Penny give herself some time to calm down.

"I'm sorry," he said. "I didn't want our first time to be like that."

"There was never suppose to be a first time," she croaked.

"Penny, don't kid yourself," he said from the other side of the room, still not sure it was safe to approach. "We are both adults. Single adults at that. We don't have to answer for what we've done to anyone."

He chanced a step toward her, and she raised a hand to ward him off.

"It happened, just as we both knew it would, but it doesn't ever have to happen again." He ignored her hand and stepped even closer. "I'm not going to lie, I want it to happen again, but it takes two to make that decision, so ultimately whatever you decide I will abide by."

He reached out to close his hand over her raised one. "If Spencer and Mom stay together for the long haul, it will be hard, but not impossible." He placed her hand to his mouth and kissed her palm. "I have spent days burning inside for you. Naturally I want to do wickedly sinful things to you, but I can be a gentleman if need be."

She didn't speak and not knowing was killing him.

"But you need to tell me, Penny, so I can know what my limits are."

She rose from the bed and grabbed the pjs from his hand.

"It was slippery and you fell. You dropped the strawberries, and although we managed to save some, you hit your head pretty hard. You decided to retire for the night to nurse a headache."

"What?"

"You hit your head and retired for the night." Her voice was low, but hard.

"But I want dessert too," he said.

"Your share is on the floor. Clean it up, and don't show your face back at the big house until tomorrow."

She turned to leave the room. He followed her, but she didn't stop.

"And what about us?" He asked as she opened the door and made to leave.

"I told you already," she said, turning to look at him. "There is no us."

~

For the rest of the night Reuben pined like a jilted lover. Which was, in his opinion, exactly what he was. He'd gone rooting through the laundry basket in his room and came up with the sheets he'd torn from his bed earlier, but his wet clothing had soaked down onto the sheets and they now smelled mostly of earth. The lavender from her hair still clung to the pillowcase but the organic earthy smell overpowered it.

Strictly prohibited to join them in the big house and having to make the lie of a headache believable, he stretched out on the bed, resigned to his predetermined evening agenda.

What if his Mom and Spencer did marry? As things stood now, he had expected to never see Penny again once he left for the city. But if there was a wedding between their parents he would be seeing a lot more of her.

A smile tugged at the corners of his mouth at the thought of all that entailed. All the things that had turned Penny off from the idea were more like icing on the cake to him. Christmas with Penny would be a gift in itself, but if a repeat performance of their escapades just now was a possibility then he'd be sure to spend every holiday with his mom in hopes of a retake. Thanksgiving, Labour Day, Easter, New Year's. Why, he'd probably wear out his welcome. He'd even forgo the costume party his daughters attended every year, and make up some new traditions, in order to spend Halloween with Penny, minus the trick and heavy on the treat.

How long could their affair last? A woman like Penny couldn't stay single forever. That would be an outright sin, and not something he wanted to see happen. She deserved to find love, and to start a family of her own.

And if that happened? Then what? Would he still want to spend holidays here? Would he be okay seeing her with someone else? Seeing her happily married to someone who wasn't him? She had every right to move on with her life, and while an occasional lover would be okay for short-term, she'd need more eventually.

And he would never commit. He'd already loved and lost, and he had no strength left to do it all over again. He had Ember and Terra to think about now, and so he would get by on occasional lovers and save the bigger part of himself for his girls. He would put his all into raising strong independent women. Women very much like Penny herself.

In fact, now that he thought about it, having her as honorary auntie could only be a good thing. She was good for his girls. Having her in their life would take away some of the burden. Maybe when the time came she could be the one to talk to them about menstruation, and boys, and respecting themselves.

Had he respected her? Would he be considered a good example? Or would she use him in her illustrations of how not to use a woman.

But just now, downstairs on the table, it had been consensual. She had wanted him as much as he wanted her. Her 'yes' had answered all the nagging questions he wanted to ask. Can I kiss you? Can I touch you? Can we make love?

But had they made love? As much as he enjoyed it, it had not been what he'd longed to do. True, it still had the same outcome, but he preferred time to explore and bear witness to the glories of her body.

And oh God, what a body.

A groan escaped his lips and his thoughts zeroed right back to square one. Penny-Laine Weis was a delicacy he was going to have a hard job shaking. His fantasies would never be the same again. Beige panties dominated his colour wheel now. It was her signature colour. Or at least that's what his mind appended to her.

That first night in the bed she'd worn beige panties and just now, downstairs on the table, he had pulled beige panties down around her ankles. In most of his fantasies the lady of choice wore black or red, but now, thanks to Penny and the two times he'd been exposed to her undergarments, beige was his favourite.

Reuben groaned again as his little friend prodded at his underwear, wanting out. He needed Penny.

He shook his head at that bold thought. His needs and wants were all over the place. What he really needed was a cold shower. Without the intent of offering her a future, Penny was just a want, and one he had no right craving and ought to keep his hands off of.

He pulled the pillow out from under his head and placed it over his face, clamping it down on either side with an arm, trying to close his mind off from his overactive imagination.

7

By the next morning the rain had stopped, but the ground was still soggy. Penny knew the dirt road leading out of Ridgeville would be a nightmare to drive through, so she loaded up David's power wagon for the trip into town. Putting the last of the packages into the crew cab, she closed the door, and went back inside the distillery for the more sensitive items that would travel up front with her.

Returning to the truck minutes later, she saw her dad walking up the garden pathway. His step turned into a jog when he saw her and as he approached he reached to take a box she was balancing.

"Thanks," she said, and offered her cheek to him for a kiss. He obliged and opened the crew cab door.

"I'm going to put those up front with me," she said, and so he circled around the truck instead. "Did you need anything in town?"

He set the box on the floor and reached to take the basket and gift bag she held. Placing them on the passenger seat he shut the door and turned to her. "No, I'm good for now."

"Okay," she said, confused. "Coming to visit Mrs. Lafford then?"

"I am," he said, a big smile spreading across his face. "The boys are working without me today. I thought it would do them good to not have me hovering over them for a change, and Gyla and I are going to take the girls to that big maple tree down along the brook and set up a picnic for dinner."

"You're a little early," she said. "I checked a few minutes ago and it was barely eight thirty."

"That it is," he said awkwardly. "I thought I'd, I'd...I'd come down and confirm the time she wants me at the cottage."

Penny laughed and reached forward to cradle her Dad's face with both hands. "Daddy, you know you don't have to lie to me, right?"

"Lie to you?"

"I'm not completely blind. I saw the two of you last night."

"Saw what?"

She pinched his cheeks before releasing him. "You and Mrs. Lafford were all over one another like a bad rash." She laughed when he turned bright red.

He lowered his head bashfully. It looked awkward on such a burly man. The gentle giant never cowered for anyone.

"How do you feel about it?" he asked, reaching to take one of her hands in his own.

Her mind flickered to her conversation with Reuben the night before, when he assured her that he thought a relationship between his mother and her father would most definitely work out. If that was the case, and he'd seemed adamant about it, then it was just silly of her to be upset and therefore add hostility to the situation. Her father and Gyla were both adults.

We don't have to answer for what we've done to anyone.

Who was she to tell her father what he could or couldn't do, when the skeletons in her own closet were stacking up?

"You're both single adults," she said, mimicking Reuben. "You don't have any strings attached to anyone, so what you do is up to you."

"That's where you're wrong," he said, squeezing her hand. "My string's attached to you and Warren, and I don't ever want to break that string. Not for the world."

"Daddy," she moved to cup her free hand around his. "My string is stuck far too deep for you to ever lose me. Besides, I love seeing you happy, and if Mrs. Lafford does that for you, then who am I to interfere?"

He smiled and raised her hands to his lips. "Good," he said, his laugh a little giddy. "She doesn't know this yet, but I'm going to ask her to marry me."

"What?" Penny hadn't meant to sound so shocked, and she tried to tone her voice down as best she could when a look of alarm flashed across Spencer's face. "I mean, right now? Is that why you're coming here so early in the morning?"

"Well, no, not right now. But soon."

"Good."

"Penny-Laine are you sure you're okay with this?"

Yes, I'm sure I'm sure." she said, pulling her hands from his and wiping them down her pant leg. "It's just, a marriage proposal shouldn't just be blurted out on a surprise visit early in the morning, when I doubt Mrs. Lafford is even out of her night clothes yet, and the twins are probably awake, too."

She laughed and reached out to wrap her arms around him. "You scared me." She said pulling back to look at her dad. "She deserves a pretty proposal, with all the bells and whistles. A proper proposal isn't just blurted out, and I thought that was what you were up to, you big goof."

"I hadn't thought about that," he said running a hand across his face. "It's been almost forty years since I've done this, so I'm a little out of touch."

"You'll be fine." She poked him in the chest. "That ole big heart of yours will kick in when the time is right, and you'll know just what to do. You always do."

Penny reached on her tiptoes to kiss his sweaty cheek. "Now I have to get going."

She circled the truck and pulled open the door.

"Wait, wait," her father said, rushing around the side to catch up to her. She slipped inside the truck and rolled down the window to him. "Can you help me?"

"No, Dad, I won't help you," she laughed. "This has to be special from you."

'Okay, okay." He fidgeted in front of her awkwardly.

"Trust me, Dad, whatever you come up with, she'll love. Now I really have to go."

She started to roll up the window, but he rapped on it and she lowered it again. "Okay, I guess I will be needing something from town then."

"Okay, sure." It was the first time she'd seen her father so nervous and it amused her. Her powerful, supportive father who always knew what to do and say was fumbling with his words and actions and it was so endearing to her. "What do you need?"

'Hold on." He fumbled in the chest pocket of his shirt, produced a small coil notebook and a pen, and began jotting down a list. After several minutes he ripped the page out and passed it to her.

She tucked the list up under the visor and rolled up the window. She couldn't fight the smile that stretched across her face as she drove away.

Although she was confident that supporting her fathers decision was the right thing to do, she worried about what it would entail for her own future. It would definitely mean more time with Ember and Terra, which was a huge plus. She'd fallen head over heels in love with the two polar opposites, and would miss them when they left.

It was their father she worried about. With Gyla in the family, she'd have to attach new strings to her life, and already the idea of their family growing made her heart swell with excitement. But that didn't remove the issue of Reuben. She just couldn't trust herself around him. He tested everything she thought she was. He made her turn herself inside out and study the person she'd become. He made her long for more.

The power wagon bounced over ruts in the gravel drive. Penny drove slowly so as not to bounce the parcels around too much. When she reached the edge of the woods, where the ground was worn and the trees and brambles parted for entry, she stopped, put the truck in park, rolled the passenger window down, and listened to the work being done beyond the trees.

She hadn't seen Reuben since the night before, but that didn't stop her from wanting to catch a glimpse of him. Her actions confused her. Not only her cravings to see him now, but also her reaction to him last night.

When she'd offered to accompany him to her cottage it had been with the sole intention of berating him for not warning her about the relationship between her father and Gyla, since he had so obviously been aware of it. But then he'd scooped her up in his arms and kissed her, and all her wits flew out the window. All she could focus on was how much she liked it, how right it felt, and how she never wanted it to stop.

She had tried to stay on task with what they were sent to do, but then he'd started listing all the things he wanted to do to her, all the while touching her with the expertise of a man fluent in exactly what it took to arouse her, and her guard hadn't just fallen, it totally abandoned her altogether.

She hid a smile behind her hand and bit the inside of her thumb to suppress a giggle. There was no denying the spontaneity of it all. Although she could certainly feel the attraction between them, this had still come out of left field.

But on the table? They'd acted like barbarians. Completely uncivil. She hadn't had even an ounce of care for any kind of acceptable order. She'd had no self-control at all, and couldn't remember ever being that impulsive in her life. The moment had definitely been earth-shattering.

And after? The body-wracking orgasm had swallowed her whole. It had felt like a million tiny elastics pinging off beneath her skin and the affect left her zinging from head to toe. If he'd slid her to her feet right then she wasn't entirely sure her knees wouldn't have buckled beneath her. She was aware of him holding her, and her hands between them cradling her own face, and dwelling a little bit longer than she probably should have in the Utopia they'd created together.

When she'd finally floated back to earth she'd had an onslaught of emotions that she hadn't been able to file away in their proper places fast enough, and so she'd resorted to anger, and then reasoned with herself while she sat on the edge of the bed. Distance between them seemed like the best thing in that moment. She'd been too afraid of what she might say or do, and she didn't want to have any regrets come the light of day.

And now here it was the light of day and she still felt torn. She wanted to run away, which was sort of what she was doing, but at the same time she longed for just a glimpse of him. Just one small peek to tide her through. A *coup d'oeil.*

She threw the truck into gear and continued down the long driveway, resigned to the idea of a Reuben-less day. She told herself that all she'd really wanted, in seeing him, was to gauge from his mannerisms if any-thing had changed.

Of course nothing had changed. It's not like they'd made love. It was just straight-up sex with no romantic overtures. No hidden meanings. No fine undertones. Just two people getting their rocks off. Two *single* people letting off some steam.

But she'd just wanted to see if he seemed more at ease, or different somehow. In truth, she had no idea what she wanted to see. She just wanted to see him, but not for the simple joy of looking at him. She wasn't *that* shallow. Was she?

She turned the radio up. A subdued rendition of Depeche Mode's Per-sonal Jesus filled the cab as she rolled down the dirt road to Ridgeville, which was more dirt road but at least recently graded by the department of transportation.

~

Penny walked into *Six Owls* at 11:45 and took the table closest to the window. Calleigh, the owner, threw her a smile and rushed over to greet her.

"Claire told me you two were coming for dinner today. I had strict in-structions to purchase freshly shucked clams and whip up a batch of broccoli salad." She straightened a placemat and fussed with the condi-ment tray. "Which I did."

"You're the best," Penny said, and Calleigh beamed.

"Do you want to look at the menu while you wait?"

Penny held a hand up, "No menu needed, but I'll wait for Claire before I officially order. Besides I'm still debating on coin fries or sweet potato fries."

"I made béarnaise sauce this morning, if that helps with your de-cision." Calleigh smiled slyly at Penny.

"Oh you know me so well," Penny laughed. "Coin fries it is, then."

Calleigh leaned forward, an excited gleam in her eyes. "I heard Spencer has a crew of men working for him."

"That he does. They've been at it for about a week now, when it isn't raining."

"That must be intimidating."

"How so?"

"Well, you being the only woman amongst all those men. I know in here sometimes, especially the breakfast crew, it gets pretty rowdy. All that testosterone is overwhelming."

"Everything's been fine so far," Penny said, not feeling like it was necessary to tell her that not only wasn't she the only female, but that there were two small children to soften up the atmosphere.

"I just can't imagine anything making that spot any more lovely."

"I'm guilty of not even peeking at what they've done so far, but I know my dad had a few ideas that seemed appealing. Pathways, look-outs, gazebos. It should be nice when it's finished, and if nothing else it gives my dad something to focus his energy on, and will give him someplace to hike safely."

"Sounds lovely."

"Drive out when it's finished and we can take a walk-around. You can stay for supper after, or the night even. I'm up for anything."

"I just may take you up on that offer," Calleigh beamed, genuinely delighted with the invitation.

The door chimed. "Can I get you anything while you wait?" Calleigh asked before turning to greet another customer.

"A tea would be nice, but only when you have a minute. No rush."

Penny was leafing through *The Village Way* and sipping her tea when Claire arrived.

"Have you been waiting long?" she asked, folding Penny in a friendly hug. The black asymmetrical bob of her hair shimmered in a stream of sunlight pouring through the window.

"Just outside of fifteen minutes is all."

"Did you order yet?"

As if on cue, Calleigh was at their table. "Doctor Larkin," she squealed, and slid into a seat. "I have to know if the rumours this morning are true. Did your meeting with the Village Committee go as well as the gossips say it did?"

Penny flicked the paper closed and folded it out of the way. "Claire?"

"It's not official yet, so this is strictly off the record, but it's looking like a go."

"Oh that's wonderful," Penny said reaching over to clasp Claire's hand.

"It's about time," Calleigh said, standing again. "You'll do wonderful things there, and Lord knows the demand is high enough."

"Actually that's a lot of the issue right now. The demand is *too* high," Claire said.

"There's not enough of you to go around," Penny conceded.

"Exactly," Claire said. "I can only comfortably take on half of Dr. Wells' patients. And although I will be added to the on-call circuit, so anyone can walk in, I'm not sure it's good enough."

"Well, it's a start," Calleigh said. "You're only one person. You can only do so much."

"And still have time for yourself, and your mom," Penny finished.

Calleigh's expression softened at the mention of Claire's mother, and she reached out to touch Claire's hand. A tattoo of a small olive-coloured bow circled the distal crease of Claire's ring finger. "And how is Pidge?"

Pidge Larkin was the reason Claire had returned home. Extreme bouts of loneliness originally brought her back from Toronto, and although no one else had noticed, Claire saw the telltale signs of early dementia and knew Toronto would have to go on without her. Claire's father had already passed, and there was no one to care for her mother.

Penny knew the decision to stay had not been as difficult as Claire had thought it would be. Claire would not be happy anywhere else, knowing her mother needed her. She was too kind-hearted a person to just walk away, and so here she was.

Although Penny wished it had been under better circumstances she was happy to have Claire back. She'd missed Claire. And it hadn't been until she returned that Claire realized the dire straits of her hometown. The village needed her, too.

"She's doing okay," Claire said. "She's taking an inhibitor and memantine, although we're still tweaking the dosage. Of course there's no cure, but we're trying to slow the process as much as we can."

"That's good to hear," Calleigh said. She glanced to the door and said, "I'll be right with you," to the couple who entered. Turning back, she flipped open her order pad. "Clams for both of you?"

Fifteen minutes later Calleigh set a plate of clams, coin fries with béarnaise dipping sauce, and a small broccoli salad in front of each of them. "Enjoy," she said and sped away to tend to other customers.

"So tell me about the oasis," Claire said, slipping a gloriously golden clam into her mouth.

"There's not much to tell, really. I haven't actually walked through to look at anything yet."

"And your cottage?"

"My cottage?" Penny dipped a coin fry into the sauce. "It's fine."

"Are the *rowdy* men destroying it like you anticipated? Or have you even gotten a chance to look yet?"

"Oh yes, I've been inside it since the workers came." Her mind instantly turned to the memory of strawberries pooling on the floor while she and Reuben romped on the table a few feet away. "Everything's fine."

"So the men aren't as rambunctious and disorderly as you thought," Claire asked piercing another clam onto the prongs of her fork.

"Mm hm. Everything's fine."

Claire lowered her head and squinted suspiciously at Penny. "Why do I get the feeling that everything is far from fine?"

Who was she kidding? Claire was her best friend and could see right through any lie Penny tried. She always did. If not right away, then eventually. Penny doubted she'd make it out of *Six Owls* without spilling all the sordid Reuben details.

And why not? One of the great purposes of a best friend was for such an event as this. It would be nice to hang everything out in the air and hear the perspective of another person. Especially if she admired and valued the opinion of the person mulling over her dirty laundry.

"There's seven men," she started. "Jeff, my father's long-time friend. Then Jeff's brothers Roger and Blaine, and his friend Royce. Then there's Kyle and Tim, a couple of men around my age, whom I get along with great. They seem to have taken me under their wing, like a little sister of sorts." She drew another long pull on the straw and let the cold pop's burn fizzle before she continued. "They all stay at the big house with me and Dad."

"Okay, and the seventh?"

"Reuben," she said, her answer a long drawn out sigh. "He stays in my cottage."

Claire dropped her palms to the table, wide-eyed with shock. "Spencer swindled your cottage out of you for one man?"

"Well, not exactly. Reuben brought his mother and two children with him."

When Claire started to protest, Penny reached out her hand and stopped her. "Long story short. Reuben's a conservation officer, and that's part of the reason dad hired him. He could have hired any game conservation officer, but he didn't, he hired him because he met Reuben's mother online and they became *friendly*."

"Oh Pen, I'm so sorry. It has to be tough seeing your dad with another woman," Claire said.

"Oh no, not at all, Gyla's great."

Genuinely confused now, Claire furrowed her brow. "That's good, then."

"No, it's not," Penny was unable to stop the tears from springing to her eyes.

"It's not?"

Penny shook her head. "It's Reuben." Her heart clenched in her chest. "I'm not sure I can keep my hands off him."

Claire set back in her seat, relief flooding her face. Then a smile spread slowly across her lips and she studied her friend skeptically. "You're serious?"

Penny blinked rapidly, trying to suppress the tears. She couldn't explain why she was crying. Perhaps it was just being able to talk to someone about it. "Unfortunately, yes," she said and then she too was laughing amid the tears that finally won over and rolled down her cheeks. She caught them with the napkin. "Everywhere I turn he's there, he's like the temptation that won't go away."

"Is he married?"

"According to him he's been a little over a year in the *widowhood*."

"Does he have a girlfriend?"

"No, not that I'm aware of." She blanched at that thought. Was there a girlfriend waiting for him in the city? She hadn't thought to ask.

Who was she kidding? It wasn't as though she would have stopped him before he placed her on the table and asked, "By the way is there a potential someone pining away in the city for you?" or maybe just before he stepped between her legs to enter her she should have cock-blocked him with, 'Is there someone in the city who's going to be upset if you put that in there?" She choked on a laugh at that thought. No, she wouldn't have thought to ask, because in all honesty she wasn't doing a whole lot of thinking just then.

"What's the problem, then? Are his children little terrors?"

Her face softened at the mention of the twins. "Ember and Terra are perfect."

"Then what is it? You're obviously attracted to him. Are the feelings not mutual?"

She remembered his confession under the trees. *My thoughts are impure.* And then her thoughts flashed to their first kiss. He wanted her, that much was obvious.

And then last night. She could almost hear the creak of the table as it rocked beneath them and she had a quick flash of a police officer interrogating a witness who can only remember the blaring obviousness of the crime and so he passes her a card and says, "Here's my card in case you remember anything else." She understood now why they did that, the small bits that she hadn't remembered directly in the aftermath were slowly coming to the surface as the moment settled within her.

It was the pulse of Reuben's cock in her hand that floated to memory when she looked up at Claire, a little breathless from the unexpected stroll down memory lane, and so it was with bated breath that she answered, "The feeling's definitely mutual."

The flush on Penny's face and the fluttering of her eyes must have been a dead giveaway for Claire. "You slept with him, didn't you?"

Penny turned three shades of red. "What? No."

"Have you kissed him?"

She bit the inside of her mouth, and looked side-long at Claire. "We never actually made it to a bed."

Claire laughed and then her mouth formed a complete O as she stared at her friend. "You hussy,' she chided, slapping Penny's arm playfully. "This is more serious than I thought." Then she became serious. "So, is this going somewhere?"

"It's going nowhere. I don't intend to ever let it happen again."

"That bad, huh?"

"It was most definitely not bad," Penny said dunking a fork full of coin fries and a clam into the béarnaise sauce and shoving it into her mouth. "It was," she said through chews, rolling her eyes up to the ceiling, "better than clams and coin fries dipped in béarnaise sauce."

~

It was nearing the supper hour when Penny and Claire parted ways. Penny was returning home with a few items she'd found at the thrift store, and four swing-latch jars from the hardware store. They were a little smaller than the original swear jars that had broken so she'd picked up four in case the twins wanted symmetrical bottles. There might be one left over for herself.

At the used-clothes section of the thrift store she'd picked out two pairs of denim overalls for Ember and Terra and two tank tops, using a guesstimate on the size. At the hardware store she'd found kid-size garden gloves. She picked up two extra pairs of kneepads and sunhats and two additional travel mugs. If she had willing help, it was her intention to at least make sure they were outfitted properly.

Ember would be a tough one to break, but she had to at least try. But because she didn't know these children as well as she hoped to eventually, she needed to cover all her bases, so she'd bought them each a bug explorer set, a small backpack, a colouring book, and crayons.

She'd also picked up the items from her fathers list, which required stops in several different stores. The items were odd, but she'd complied and so she was returning home with a medium-sized terra-cotta plant pot, potting soil, a simple, white-faced, battery-operated wall clock, floral tape and wire, four different colours of tissue paper (she'd made sure one was green as per instructions), a black permanent marker, a small bottle of white acrylic paint and a set of artist's paint brushes, a bag each of white and chocolate chips, and a bag of balloons.

She placed the bags in the crew cab and turned to Claire. "Promise me you'll come out to Ridgeville soon?"

"First chance I get, maybe a day next week. I have mom's respite in place now, so I won't have to worry about leaving her alone."

"Come early," Penny said.

"I will. I want to check on Dad's cabin anyway," Claire said. "I've been so busy this summer I haven't had a chance to."

Claire dug in the pocket of her jeans for her keys and prised one off the ring. She held it out to Penny. "Take this."

"What's that for?" Penny asked, taking the key.

"It's the cabin key, in case you need it."

"Did you want me to look in on it for you?"

"Just take it," she said reaching forward to close Penny's fingers over the key. "In case you need somewhere to go."

"You're encouraging bad behaviour."

"If that's what you want to call it, then yes, I'm encouraging bad behaviour," Claire said triumphantly. "It's been over three years since I've seen that glow on your face, and if a little time-out with Reuben is what's causing it then I most definitely approve and encourage it."

She encased Penny in a hug and dropped a kiss on her cheek. "I'll see you soon."

"Very soon," Penny called. She stuffed the key into her pocket and slid behind the wheel of her truck. A smile spread across her face at the thought of Claire's words. Maybe she did need a time-out with Reuben. After all, it was just what the doctor ordered.

8

A belt of fog hung over the lavender garden the next morning, the smoky grey making the purple more prominent. With the moisture, the aroma was thick and mingled with the organic smell of dew, and as the sun slowly warmed the air and lapped up the dewdrops, the smell spread and was twice as potent as ever.

From where Penny stood at the door to the distillery, the lavender field looked like a huge purple blanket one need only lift the edge of to slip beneath. On days like this she took her morning coffee to the deck and lingered a little longer than she should, basking in the splendour of it all.

Today she would settle for the lower level and hope that the occupants of her home took a moment to enjoy the view from above.

Inside the distillery she sat the bags she'd brought with her on a nearby table and removed a small container from one. Lifting the cover she looked at the strawberry shortcake, and wondered about what she was doing. She wasn't going to go out of her way to find him and give it to him, but even if she did it was just an apologetic gesture. A way to make amends for how she'd acted. A simple act of kindness in which she silently admitted that she was wrong. What they'd done was no more his fault than it was hers.

Last night, lying in bed, she'd made up her mind. She would broach the subject of a no-strings attached affair. A private affair that ended when he left and was never talked about between anyone but themselves.

It was all she knew to do. Otherwise sleepless nights were going to become chronic insomnia. She had to indulge in the craving or she might never sleep again.

If he agreed to the proposition then she would be well-on her way to a cure. Eventually she'd have her fill and be finished with it, and with him. Too much of a good thing was bound to get tiresome.

She put the shortcake in the small fridge and laid out the items she'd purchased for Ember and Terra. She placed the items in little purple baskets she already had in the distillery for display at trade shows and fairs. She set up a table and covered it with an old plastic tablecloth, and dug out stencils, stickers, acrylic paints, and brushes from the storage room in the lower level.

She placed the four swing latch bottles in the centre of the table, and with thirty minutes left before it would be time to tuck her tail between her legs and face Reuben among his family, she slipped behind her desk and booted up the computer.

She wanted to log into email and social media to check for messages that might need addressing, but before the computer had even purred to life a tap sounded at the door. Before she could answer it the door opened and Reuben stepped inside.

Her heart leapt into her throat. She'd been mentally preparing herself to do this in thirty minutes, not now. She wasn't ready.

"Is it okay if I come in?"

"It looks like you're already in," she answered, willing her heart to calm down. He was just a man, but the way her heart was beating out of control you'd have thought God himself had stepped through the door.

"Okay, then," he said smiling that wickedly handsome smile that made her weak in the knees. "I guess what I meant to say was is it okay that I'm here?"

She shrugged and focused on her computer screen in an attempt to seem indifferent.

"I wanted to bring you this," he said, holding out a folded cloth to her.

She knew instantly without taking it that it was her mother's mantel scarf.

"Living with two children, I had no choice but to learn how to sew. I'm not an expert, but I tried."

She rose from the desk without stepping out from behind it and reached for the scarf. She wasn't sure what to expect. Velvet was so tricky, and although she'd spent years researching vintage fabrics and living among them she had decided that keeping the rip in the scarf was probably the safest bet. She'd decided to cover the rip with an ornament or a photo frame.

Convinced that the scarf was ruined now, or at the very least an eyesore, she unfolded it slowly.

"Your dad had an old sewing kit he said was your mom's. He gave me permission to look for it in his attic. So last night I did and I found it in an old trunk."

As the fold opened up to the embroidered bundle of wheat she was prepared to hold in her cry and smile through the pain, but instead her mouth fell open and she looked up at Reuben in complete shock.

"Your mom had a good supply so I was able to find what looked like a beading needle and cotton thread that was almost the exact colour."

The damage was almost indiscernible.

"The trick is to sew from the back," he said. "And to make sure not to bring the needle up through the velvet pile. If you can pull that off it's barely visible from the velvet side."

"You did this?"

"I did," he shrugged. "After a quick internet search."

She dropped the scarf to the desk and came around to him. Without thinking too much she reached up and pulled his face down to hers. The kiss was gentle and she meant to pull away quickly, but before she even knew what she was doing she'd linked her hands around his neck and, with a little hop, circled his waist with her legs. His hand slipped under her behind to hold her up.

She deepened the kiss, craving to devour him, but she pulled her mouth from his and looked at him. In this position they faced each other perfectly.

His lips parted and he reached forward to kiss her again, but she pulled back in his arms, and instead dropped her forehead to his.

"Okay, I want to say something." She looked at the clock before continuing, "I was actually heading up to see you in about twenty minutes."

"You were?"

"I was. I kept you a dessert, it's in my fridge." She nodded in the direction of the refrigerator. "And, if I could work up the gumption, I was going to apologize for the way I acted the other night."

He dropped his face to her neck, but she wedged her hand under his chin and pulled his attention back to her face. "I'm not finished."

"Can't you talk while I do this?" he asked, dipping his head again.

She caught his chin. "Talk? I can barely breathe."

He caught her lips again and this time he slipped his tongue inside and tasted her. "Oh God, Penny-Laine, don't you dare tell me I can't touch you or kiss you," he said into her mouth.

His hands ran up and down her legs and then back to cup her ass again. His lips moved on hers and then moved down her cheek to lay a neat row of kisses on her jaw line. "I can't get enough of you." He slipped a hand into the side opening of her overalls and circled her waist.

"Reuben," she said pulling away. "I wanted to say I'm sorry. I was so confused and I never meant to let that happen," she cupped his chin in her hand, controlling the intensity of their kiss. "But it did happen, and it was as much my fault as it was yours."

His dark eyes looked up into her blue ones, languid and wanting. He pleaded with her for sympathy.

"You're making me crazy," she said, clamping a hand over his eyes. "Don't look at me like that, I'm trying to talk."

"I'm listening," he said, his voice thick and slow. "Tell me what you want."

"We're adults, but that doesn't give us the right to hurt the innocent." She ran her hands over his broad shoulders and unbuttoned the second, third, fourth, and fifth buttons of his shirt. "I've fallen in love with Ember and Terra, and I don't ever want to see them hurt."

"Well that makes two of us. They are and will always remain my top priority."

"Good," she said, dipping her head to kiss his neck. "We have to be careful."

"I can be careful. He reached up to wind her braid around his hand. With a gentle tug he lifted her head and looked at her. "Are you sure about this?"

"No., but I spent the last thirty-eight hours replaying it over and over in my head and wishing I could do it again."

He groaned deeply and, cupping the back of her neck, crushed her lips to his.

Once again she pulled away. "You understand we can never let this go beyond what it already is?"

He nodded.

"I'm sure you've had lovers since Eve, but you're the first for me since David." She slid her legs from around him. "I think you might be good for me. My threshold, so to speak, out of the waiting room I've been stuck in."

"So I'm your transition back into the world of sex?" He said.

"Sort of," she said moving her hands on his body. "Does that bother you?"

"I think I can take it."

"And one more thing."

"Anything."

"No more Penny-Laine." She held him off, waiting for him to comply.

The twinkle of mischief succumbed to the desire and he relented, "Okay, but for the record, I think it's cute."

"Good for you," she said, "Maybe when you get back to the city you can buy a bunny and name it that, but *my name* is Penny, okay?"

"Okay, Okay," he said reaching for her lips.

She moved her hands to fiddle with the clasp of his jeans, but he abruptly stopped her.

"No," he said, "not like this. Not rushed."

He grabbed her hands in his and laced his fingers with hers. "The crew is waiting for me right now, so I have to go," he leaned forward and breathed in the scent of her. "Tell me you won't change your mind before tonight."

She shook her head, "I won't."

"Good," he said looking around. "Do you have a bed down here?"

"No, but I know a safe place we can go. What time can you meet me?"

"I usually tuck the girls in but I could make an excepti—"

"No." She pressed a finger to his lips. "Never compromise where they are concerned. You said it yourself, they are your top priority, and we can't do this if that changes."

"Okay, okay, I understand."

"When do you tuck the girls in?"

"Eight-ish."

"Okay," she said. "I'll meet you at eight fifteen at the edge of the trees just past dad's house. Do you know where I mean?"

"Where the wheelers gather in the morning before take-off?"

"Yes," she said. "If you're late I'll understand, I'll wait, but come out as soon as you can."

She went to the fridge and pulled out the container. Turning back to him, she pressed the container into his chest, keeping him at bay.

"Can I kiss you goodbye?"

"No. It's not that type of relationship, remember?"

"God, you're a hard nut to crack," he said, taking the container from her.

"A hard nut to crack? You've been here less than a week and you've already managed to get into my pants."

"You've got a point," he said, smiling. "Does that make you easy?"

"You don't even know when you're being played, do you?"

She poked a finger in his chest, and lifted on her toes until her lips were mere inches from his. "That makes *you* easy, not me. I've been seducing you since I woke up with you over top of me and you didn't even realize it."

She swung out of reach just as he made a move to touch her.

"You little cock-tease," he jeered, reaching for her again, and this time he caught her around the waist. She let him pull her to him, and moaned when his lips claimed hers.

"It's gonna be a long day," he groaned.

"Go," she said against his lips.

He moved to the door, but stopped to readjust himself within his jeans before he buttoned his shirt and walked out.

~

When Penny knocked at the door of her cottage at 7:20, it was Gyla who opened the door. The capris and detailed embroidered t-shirt Gyla wore were both in neutral colours and she'd pulled her hair into a neat chignon at the back of her head. Tiny pearl earrings were the only accessory she wore.

Her smile faltered when she came face to face with Penny. Although she tried to hide her disappointment, Penny knew her face was not the face she was expecting.

"I'm sorry, Mrs. Lafford, is this a bad time?"

"Not at all." She stepped back and gestured for Penny to enter.

"I have to admit I am completely clueless as to the typical schedule of children."

"You and me both," she said, and then continued when Penny looked confused. "They're four, it isn't until preschool that they get suckered into a schedule. Although they are usually up by seven of their own volition, today is not one of those days." She looked down at the baskets. "You're here for the children?"

Penny smiled. "I was going to bribe them into spending the day with me. Trying to pretty up child labour."

Gyla laughed. "I don't think you needed the bribe. They already love you."

Penny couldn't deny the happiness that overtook her at those words. It was important that the children at least *like* her, especially if her Dad intended to marry Gyla and make them a permanent part of the family, but *love* was a strong word, and that was why she had to be careful with Reuben. His daughters were not pawns in their game. She would love them as an aunt would and they need never know about her relationship with their father. It was a moot point. Not worth intertwining two innocent children in the middle of it.

"I think they're pretty special, too," she said, setting the baskets on a small table inside the sunroom and following Gyla through the dining room and into the kitchen.

"I was about to have tea," Gyla said. "Can I get you some?"

Gyla moved to the stove where Penny could see she'd already set out two mugs, and suddenly knew she was intruding. "Are you expecting my Dad this morning, Mrs. Lafford?"

She blushed. "Please just Gyla. And, yes, he'll be popping in for a few minutes."

It was cute how giddy she seemed to become at the mention of Spencer, and Penny smiled at her discomfort. "For tea?"

Gyla clasped her hands in front of her and begin to wring her fingers. "May I ask you a question, Penny-Laine?"

"You can ask me anything."

"I like your father a lot." She wrung at her fingers even harder. "But the last thing either of us want is to hurt you or your brother."

"And I appreciate that." Penny stepped closer to her. "Can I make a suggestion?"

Gyla shook her head, a spear of dark hair falling down over her face. Before she could tuck it behind her ear, Penny reached to do it for her.

Then she took Gyla's hands and stopped the wringing. "Take the tea to go."

"What?"

"I'm capable of taking care of the girls while Reuben's at work. I don't have children of my own, but I know enough not to give them bourbon before five and to make sure they wear their ski-pants when the sun hits its peak at three this afternoon."

She watched as Gyla's creased brow smoothed and a genuine smile spread across her face.

"Reuben's lucky to have you," Penny continued. "Not too many grandmothers would move right in and help take care of their grandchildren and at the full schedule of a parent, no less."

She released Gyla's hands and moved to the cupboard. She pulled out two travel mugs and poured the steeped tea into them. She began to prepare her father's as she knew he preferred. "You need a day to yourselves."

Gyla moved to stand beside her, adding sugar and cream to her own tea.

"As for my goofy father," Penny said, "he's equally as lucky to have you."

Gyla stopped stirring. "Thanks for saying that," she said and Penny could hear her voice become thick with emotion.

"I'm a good judge of character, and the vibes I pick up from you are good ones. Plus, my dad likes you a lot, and he's a good judge of character."

"I hope you mean that."

"I do."

"What I mean is I hope you *are* a good judge of character," Gyla fitted the top on her mug and turned to Penny. "I know young women nowadays need to be extra careful, and they want to be independent and expect men to treat them equally, and I am okay with that."

Genuinely confused Penny squinted at Gyla. "Am I missing something?"

"It's just Reuben. He tries to come off as a rough and tough kind of guy, but I promise you it's just because of the hand he's been dealt. If he feels threatened he goes into full-on armour mode."

She took Penny's hands. "I can feel the hostility between you two, and I don't have any right asking what that's about so I won't, but I just want you to know that underneath all that hoorah he throws around he truly is an old gentle soul. He tends to coddle people he cares for, and to someone who doesn't know him, he can come off as a bit of a hard head at times."

She took the cups to the table, and turned back to Penny. "It's important to me that you two get along."

Penny swallowed the horror that rose within her. What would Gyla say if she told her that right where her hand rested she and Reuben had gotten along just fine?

She resisted the urge to dampen a tea towel and wipe the table down. Surely Reuben had cleaned up after she'd left that night, and not just the strawberries.

She let her gaze fall to the floor. When they'd finally parted, and Reuben was no longer within her, and she'd bent to retrieve her leggings from the floor, she'd felt a trickle. She could remember feeling it run down her thighs before she pulled her leggings up, and then later when she'd squatted to tie her shoes and Reuben still stood before her she'd caught sight of him out of the corner of her eyes and could distinctly remember the moist head of his manhood still dripping and pulsating even as it slowly deflated.

As soon as her dad whisked Gyla out the door she would run a damp mop over the floor and clean the table, just in case.

"Reuben and I are adults, and as such surely we can put our differences aside and learn to get along," she said. Then, because she just couldn't stop imagining this same conversation going on between Reuben and Gyla, she said, "I'm willing to try, but I can't speak for Reuben. You'll have to get assurance from him yourself."

"I'll do just that," Gyla said.

Both Gyla and Penny turned at the sound of Spencer in the entryway.

"I come bearing crumpets," he shouted exuberantly.

The two women looked at each other and a smile spread across Gyla's face.

"I told you," Penny said. "He's a goof."

Spencer stepped into the kitchen with a basket in one hand and a mason jar in the other. "And jelly," he declared with gusto.

He wore jeans, a plaid shirt, and a McCalla Potato products cap, and stopped dead in his tracks when he saw Penny.

"And just think, you chose him," Penny whispered, and the two women burst into gales of laughter.

~

Penny had cleaned the kitchen floor, paying close attention to suspicious spots near the table that were probably just her imagination or just innocent drops of milk, and had cleaned the table with disinfectant kitchen spray. She'd just sat down with a cup of tea when the pitter-patter of footsteps sounded behind her.

She turned to see Terra rubbing her eyes and yawning as she came across the kitchen to the dining room. She looked all crumpled and cute, her curtain of dark hair hanging loose and untidy around her face.

"Nana?" she called, her voice getting a little weepy. Then she caught sight of Penny setting at the table.

"Mrs. Wise," she yelled, her sleepy eyes suddenly wide awake and she started across the room, to throw herself in to Penny's arms. "What are you doing here?" she asked, grabbing the long golden braid that hung down Penny's shoulder.

"I asked your Nana to go out for the day so I could have some time with you and Ember," she said, planting a kiss on the end of her upturned nose.

"Weally?" she asked excitedly.

"Really." Penny squeezed Terra and lowered her back to the floor.

"I wake Ember up," Terra said.

She bounded across the room before Penny could stop her. She followed behind at a slower pace and stopped at the door to watch the interaction between the sisters.

"Ember, Mrs. Wise is here to spend time whiff us," Terra said, bouncing on the bed.

Penny watched as Ember slowly came awake. When her sister's words got through, Ember's whole face lit up and she struggled to look past Terra to Penny standing in the doorway.

"Mrs. Wise," she said pushing off the covers, and then she too bounded across the room and into Penny's arms, a doll dangled from one hand, while Terra clapped and squealed excitedly behind her.

"Now, what do you sleepyheads want for breakfast?" she asked.

9

Reuben tied off red tape around the last tree, using five trees as corner points to totally encompass a small plot of land. Red meant stop, and although it messed up the trail's already plotted path, he planned to stake his case for the small spot just the same. As they'd been instructed, the guys would not bother anything marked red until it had been discussed, and Reuben had front stage when it came to such matters. He just wondered if his case for the *cypripedium reginae*, more commonly known as the showy lady's slipper, would have any bearing on the group of men or, more importantly, Spencer.

He hopped back on the idling four wheeler and kicked it into gear. He was the last one out of the woods tonight. The sun had dried up most of the rain from the night before, but the heavily pine needled ground around the bed of lady's slippers was cushiony and moist. At least forty blooms grew among the lush greenery and stood at least two feet high. Most of the heads were pink, but the odd white bloom grew here and there.

The needles crunched under the tires when he pulled away from the red taped area and headed towards the brook's edge.

He glanced at his watch when he reached the edge of the brook. It was nearing 6 pm. He needed to hurry.

It took mere minutes to tie a rope around the three black ash trees and hitch them to the four wheeler, and then he made his way out of the woods, stopping just before the open field to drop the trees in the small pile he'd accumulated.

He unhitched the trees and then hopped onto the wheeler again. The lights of the big house shone through the thicket and laughter poured out from the deck.

He pulled around to the back of the house where he knew the other men were gathered and parked the wheeler next to the other three already parked under the deck.

Although he doubted it was possible, he hoped he would be able to avoid the men and head down to the small cottage to clean up before he met Penny at the trees' edge. Sure enough, as soon as he stepped out someone called to him.

"Reuben, come join us for a drink."

It was Kyle, and although it had been less than an hour since he'd left the woods he already seemed tipsy. Reuben had no intentions of tipping back anything with the guys tonight, but he did want to talk to Spencer.

"Is Spencer up there?"

Kyle turned to scan the deck. "Nope. Tim says he's not inside, either."

Spencer hadn't joined them in the woods for the past two days, and although Reuben appreciated that the man had other irons in the fire, he knew that Spencer's presence was needed. After all, this was his oasis. Didn't he want to oversee its creation?

"I'm going to get cleaned up a bit and see my girls," he called back to Kyle, "but I may join you later." He knew it was a right out lie, but he doubted Kyle would miss him or even care.

Although he'd heard some offhanded remarks about Spencer's beautiful daughter, they seemed like a good lot of men. It didn't stop him from worrying a bit. He wondered if Penny were at the big house, or maybe still working in the distillery, but as he neared the house he didn't see lights on below.

His worry was unfounded. She'd survived this long unscathed, and he would be seeing her in two hours. In two hours he'd be able to check her from top to toes. That thought put pep in his step.

The house was unnaturally quiet and smelled of cleaning agents. The curtains in the sun room were pulled closed. A dim light from the kitchen lit the entryway and he could see a small light from the girls' bedroom. The rest of the house was dark.

Assuming the children must have fallen asleep early for a change and that his mother had taken the opportunity to do the same, he tiptoed to their room to at least get a goodnight peek. Pulling the shirt from the band of his jeans he started unbuttoning it as he crept closer.

He reached the doorway, his fingers undoing the last of the buttons, and stopped short. His daughters were sleeping, all right, but he hadn't expected to see Penny wedged between them, an unfinished book lying open across her chest. Lacey, Ember's doll, had slipped to the floor.

He moved closer, replacing the doll in the crock of Ember's arm. Penny wore overalls, dirty and splashed with paint. Her hair was mostly in a braid, but some had loosened and spears shot out around her face. The tips of one section of bangs were splashed with green and a second shade of green was smeared on her cheek.

Ember and Terra curled into either side of her, their cheeks sun-kissed and their hair still damp from a recent bath. The book lying across Penny almost gave him a chuckle. He wondered how she'd enjoyed the tales of

Miss Lovewright and her purrless cat. As for himself? He had just about enough of the batty old lady. Unfortunately his girls were relentless.

He hooked a finger under the spine and lifted the book off her, closed it and placed it on the night stand. Then he reached out and gently touched her cheek, the spot with the paint. It didn't tarnish her beauty at all, if anything it made him want to scoop her up from the bed and carry her up to his own even more, and for a second he debated on doing just that.

Where was his mother, anyway? Maybe with Spencer? That would explain Spencer's absence. He wondered if Penny had been asked to watch his girls or if she'd volunteered?

"I've fallen in love with Ember and Terra, and I don't want to see them hurt."

Somehow he suspected she'd volunteered. His heart squeezed in his chest, and he shut his eyes tightly, pressing the L of his index finger and thumb into them. Then he leaned over, cupped a hand over each of the girls' eyes and pressed his lips onto Penny's.

She stirred slightly, licked her lips and sucked the bottom one between her teeth, but didn't wake. Still leaning close to her he watched as she relaxed again and the lip sprung free from her teeth, moist and pink and oh so tempting.

Damn, where was his mother? He wanted to whisk Penny away and make love to her, but he couldn't do that with no one to watch the twins.

Instantly the guilt set in. His mother already gave too much of herself. Oh, but God forgive him, he needed her to give just a little bit more.

As he wrestled with the need to taste Penny again, he pictured lying with her in the bed upstairs. He pictured falling asleep with her in his arms, and waking up to see her beside him. Would he even be able to get up the next morning and leave her behind? God, he needed to have her. He needed his mom to come back, or stay away, or whatever it took to give him the time he longed to have with Penny.

He needed a shower, and now, before he gave into temptation and scooped her up into his arms. Maybe by the time he finished his mother would be back and Penny would be ready to meet him at the trees' edge. And if not? Well he'd have to seriously consider the alternatives. He'd waited all damn day for eight o'clock, and if that time rolled around and he was no closer to getting what he wanted, he was going to have to take it. If that meant taking her upstairs while his daughters slept downstairs and the threat of his mother returning hung over them, then so be it. He was a grown man, and if he wanted to make love to a grown woman who wanted him, he had every right to do so.

He slipped from the bedroom and up the stairs, taking them two at a time, and as he stepped under the shower and the water washed over his body his thoughts rationalized. He was a grown man, and if he wanted to make love to a grown woman there were ways to hide it from others in the house. No one had to know she was here.

But it wouldn't come to that, he told himself. His mom would be home by the time he went back downstairs and Penny would be gone, and then at eight he'd meet her as they had planned.

All this hypothetical drama was pointless. Things would work out. And if not, well, there were ways around it.

Moments later he slipped down the stairs again. His hair, towel-dried as much as possible, still dampened the grey t-shirt he wore. His mother still hadn't arrived, and Penny still slept.

It was just barely 7 pm. and his stomach was getting the best of him, and so he went to the kitchen to scrounge up some food. Just something quick and filling, so he settled on a bowl of oatmeal with a handful of raisins and nuts thrown in for good measure. If things panned out, he would need his stamina at top-notch ability.

He placed the bowl in the sink and crossed to the family room with a coffee. Setting it on a coaster on the end table he stretched out on the couch.

It was the sound of the door opening and the hush-hush of voices that woke him, and it took a moment to place where he was. He stayed there for a second, listening to his mother's girlish giggle and the wooing tease of Spencer's voice, but when the solicitous banter seemed to be getting too heavy for his ears he decided he better make his presence known.

"Mom? Is that you?" He called out, and swung himself off the couch.

As soon as he stepped into the dining room his eyes flew to the clock. 9:15. He resisted the urge to bolt into the girls room to rouse Penny.

"Oh, Reuben," Gyla said, pulling away from Spencer. "Penny's gone, then?"

He poked a thumb towards the girls' room. "She was sleeping when I got here, I didn't bother waking her." He wiped the sleep from his eyes, and stretched. "I only meant to lay down for a second myself. I told Kyle I'd have a drink with him."

"They're still at it," Spencer said. "I just wanted to walk your mother home." He turned to the door.

"Ah, Spencer you don't need to leave yet. I'm gonna go have that drink with the guys anyway."

"Well," Spencer pivoted nervously, "I could have a tea with you, if you're feeling up for it, Gyla."

Reuben tried not to laugh at the coyness Spencer was trying hard, and failing, to master.

"That would be great," Gyla said. "Go enjoy yourself, Reuben," She waved him towards the door. "I'll just wake Penny up and let her know we're back."

Reuben walked out, but instead of heading to the big house he slipped out of sight and waited.

It was less than ten minutes later when Penny stepped from the house. He watched her release her hair from the braid as she started towards the tree-lined path, and as soon as she stepped between the trees he reached out for her.

Giving a little squeal she jumped, but he managed to catch hold of her before she bolted away.

"You're late," he said.

"You scared the bejeebers out of me," she said slapping at his arms en-circling her waist.

"I'm sorry," he said dipping his head down to nuzzle her neck. "Let me make it up to you."

"Change of plans," she said pushing away from him. "I can't open the garage doors or Dad will wonder what I'm up to. So I'm going to take a quick shower, and you bring your vehicle instead."

She moved toward him and pressed her body into his, reaching up on her tiptoes as though she intended to kiss him. He leaned down to kiss her, but she twirled away just before their lips touched. "I'll meet you at the trees' edge in fifteen minutes," she said and took off up the path, skipping.

~

Reuben couldn't believe she'd made him relinquish the wheel of his jeep, and he pretended to sulk as he slid into the passenger seat beside her.

"I spent the day with Ember and Terra," she said, throwing the jeep into gear.

"I figured as much," he said, and clarified when she looked confused. "I saw you sleeping with them. What did you do to tire them out so early?"

"You wouldn't believe it." She reached into the pocket of her jeans. "So I took pictures." She brandished her phone. "Just go to gallery and take a look."

The first picture filled the screen, Terra in coveralls, knee pads, garden gloves, and a sunhat, covered head to toe in dirt and grass stains. "You mean this?" he asked, turning the phone to her. "Because *that* I believe."

"Can't you even tell your daughters apart?" she jeered. "That's *not* Terra."

"What?" He spun the phone around again to get a better look.

"Flip through the next few pictures. I swear I did not Photoshop any of them. That is truly Ember on her hands and knees in the dirt."

Penny watched as he flipped through the photos, loving the shocked expression on his handsome face. "And the best part? She had a blast."

"I can tell."

"Did you notice the small lavender plants on the deck?"

He lifted his head. "I didn't."

"I told them they could take them home when they leave. I hope you don't mind. The good news is that, should you decide to get a pet bunny, they don't tend to like lavender."

"My Penny-Laine will probably be the exception to the rule, considering her namesake."

"Just keep flipping," she said and he reactivated the blackened screen. "See that?" She pointed to a picture. "You now have new swear jars."

"Oh thanks for that," he said sarcastically.

"According to what the girls tell me, if it weren't for you and your potty mouth you wouldn't need the jars at all."

"My daughters have been gossiping about me?"

"According to Terra, nana said that every third word out of your mouth is filthy. Well, she called it filfy," she chuckled. "And Ember said nana's afraid daddy's sworing will rotten our brains."

"I don't swear that much," he said. "But according to mom every once in a while is too much. She would not want to be in the woods with us."

She slowed the car and turned into a narrow driveway marked by reflectors.

"This is my friend's," she said as they came to an opening where a little cabin lay nestled at the side of a lake.

"Does she know you plan to do bad things in it?"

"She's the one who suggested it." Penny turned off the engine and turned to him.

"You told your friend about me?"

"Just this much," she said, lifting a hand to indicate a small space between her thumb and index finger.

"Wasn't it you who said we can't speak of this to anyone else but ourselves?"

"But she's my best friend."

"Oh you didn't add that little stipulation in the original rules."

She unhooked her belt and scooted across the seat to straddle him. "It's in the fine print. Don't blame me if you didn't take the time to read it before agreeing."

She slowly began grinding herself on him, her wet hair fanning down over their faces to tent them.

"Where is this fine print written?" He worked his hand up her t-shirt. She wasn't wearing a bra and he easily cupped one of her breasts as he pushed her back against the dashboard.

"Here?" He slid the t-shirt up and dipped his head to flick a tongue over one taut nipple. "Down here?" he slipped his other hand down the front of her jeans and found the band of her panties.

Keeping her arched back against the dashboard, he slipped his fingers inside her and felt her muscles tighten around them. She quivered beneath his hands and moaned, arching her back and pushing into his hand.

He had to get her inside quickly, before he took her right here and now. This time he would make love to her the way he longed to.

It took all the willpower he could muster to remove his hands from her, and he reached to open the door. With her still straddling him, he stepped from the jeep and let her slide down the length of his body until her feet hit the ground. She turned in his arms and together they looked at the cabin.

Built at an angle to take advantage of the view, the cabin was simple, with a small porch attached to the front. A wooden swing, aged from time and the wear and tear of the elements, hung from the porch rafters. Tall pines towered around the cabin; some overhanging branches shaded the roof. The moon, and its reflection from the lake, danced together. The air was still and not a ripple disturbed the water. A lone rock dove cooed from the trees and moths flew about, coaxed from their perch by the beam of the headlights. A fire pit lay dormant at the waters edge. Old tree stumps, wedged into the ground from time and weight, circled it.

Several clapboards hung drunkenly from the cabin wall, and the timber railing of the deck had splintered in several places. One baluster was broken, and now the rail at that corner sagged almost to the porch flooring.

To the casual onlooker the cabin looked deplorable, but to the careful observer the cosmetic appearance could be forgiven. A bit of time and money would spruce the place up at a fraction of the cost it would take to remove and rebuild, and a new cabin would not have half the character this one did.

"It's perfect," she said, snuggling back against him.

"That it is."

He wedged a hand into the front pocket of her jeans and removed a key, which he dangled in front of her face. "What do you say we check out the beds?"

"You have a one track mind," she said swiping the key from his hand.

"And it's been in the gutter all day."

Reaching behind her she grabbed the hem of his t-shirt and pulled him forward. "The gutter, huh?" she asked stepping up onto the porch.

The boards creaked as they walked across to the door, suddenly in the dark but with the natural light of the moon to help them navigate. Moths fluttered about before coming to rest on the clapboard wall.

She fiddled with the key in the lock. "And did you find me in this so-called gutter of yours?" she asked twisting his shirt in her fist as she turned to face him.

The door creaked open behind them. "Oh you were most definitely in the gutter, in fact I wonder if you're as agile as my mind imagined you to be."

He stepped closer running a hand down her hips, and around to cup her ass.

"There's a rule in this cabin," she said, reaching behind him to pull the elastic from his hair. She held it up between them. The light from the moon reflected in her eyes, her hair fanned around her casting shadows on the honey glow of her skin. "It's a place to relax and as such one must always let their hair down." She tossed the elastic over his shoulder before lifting her foot and kicking the door open behind her.

"I think I can remember the basic layout of the cabin," she said, fumbling in the dark. He followed her lead. The place smelled musty and damp.

"I don't think anyone's been here in years."

"No one has," She said, releasing his shirt and finding his hand instead. "It's been neglected ever since Bill Larkin passed on four years ago."

Reuben allowed her to pull him along, her fingers intertwined with his own. Her other hand reached forward, disturbing the dust on furniture she touched.

The dust circled up around them, sending her into a fit of coughing. "I wish I'd thought to bring a flashlight," she said between coughs, "and a blanket, too, I doubt there's anything clean here."

A thud sounded in the dark and she cried out before keeling over. He bent down beside her and heard the string of curse words under her breath.

Rolling her back onto her bottom he pulled her canvas shoes off, kneading her toes between his hands. He lifted one foot to his lips and brushed a kiss across her toes. They curled in his hands and he smiled. "I made your toes curl," he whispered in the dark.

She hickled. "You're crazy," she said but her voice, in the shadows, had a trill to it that vibed with the trembling inside him at just the mere touch of her skin.

He blew lightly on her toes and she hickled again. He reached forward and grasped the back of her neck, hungrily seeking her lips.

Their tongues crashed into each other, flitting in and out as he devoured her mouth. Then he cupped her face and pulled his lips from hers. "I have a flashlight in the jeep," he said, his breath coming out in huffs between them. "You wait here. I'll be right back."

Retracing their steps out into the night, he scrambled to the jeep and riffled through the glove compartment for the flashlight. He hadn't used it in a long time, so it took several strikes against his palm to coax it on. In the back hatch he found a folded blanket and within seconds he was back in the doorway of the cabin.

The light sliced through the darkness, particles of dust dancing within its beam, and came to rest on Penny, still sitting on the floor. She'd stubbed her toe on a small side table slightly askew from the wall.

With the light to guide her now, she hoisted herself up and made her way to the kitchenette. After scavenging through several drawers she came up with two candlesticks and a book of matches and turned to him.

Everything was lined with a thin coat of dust, and there she stood amidst it all looking as pristine and perfect as he could ever remember anyone looking. He ran the light down to her feet. A trail of tiny footprints connected the space between them.

Their eyes met over the small distance, and she held out the candles bashfully. When she made a move towards him, he held out a hand to halt her.

"Don't move," he said, travelling the beam slowly down her body again. "You're beautiful and I just want to look at you for a minute."

She wore a white t-shirt, crumpled from his roaming hands, and blue jeans that hugged her hips and legs. Her dainty feet were bare, her toenails painted mauve.

He ran the beam up her legs again and tilted the light away just before it reached her face. In the shadows her blond hair fell over her shoulders and down her breast, cloaking her in a veil of golden splendour.

When she lifted a hand to the hem of her t-shirt his breath caught. It was a slow deliberate move that captivated him as she slowly lifted the t-shirt, candles still held in her palms, and slipped it up and over her head. Her breasts were perfect and perky, nipples rigid, the soft velvet of her areola a deep pink in comparison to the paleness of her skin.

He felt himself harden as he drank in the sight of her. For this moment in time, she was his to devour. His to touch. To have. To hold. He wanted nothing more than to watch her undress before him, but when her hands went to the clasp of her jeans he scrambled forward to stop her.

She deserved to be undressed, unwrapped like the gift she was, to have every inch of her touched and equal attention given to each gift she offered up to him. She deserved to be worshipped, and he wanted to do just that.

But not here, not amidst dust and grime inside a cabin not yet swept for pests and possible squatters. She deserved much better than a stranger's abandoned cabin in the middle of the night, but if it was all he could offer, then he at least owed it to her to make sure the premises were safe.

"I've waited too long," she pleaded, relinquishing the candles and matches into the nothingness. He heard them fall to the floor, and felt her tug at his t-shirt.

He tried to bend to retrieve the candles, but her hands were on the band of his jeans and she was pulling them down despite the rock hard resistance fighting against the downward thrust. But she was adamant and soon his jeans were down past his hips and his penis was standing erect between them.

In the next ten seconds, a few things happened in quick succession. She dropped to her knees, her hands closing over him, his flashlight hit the floor and went dark, and he fell back against the wall as her mouth closed over him. A groan erupted from deep within his chest and his hand instinctively reached out to cup the back of her head. Still tucked up under his arm, the blanket unfolded and rolled down the length of him to drag onto the floor.

With her lips rolled in over her teeth she applied pressure to the base and slowly pulled out, and the blanket gave way altogether and fell down around their feet. Her tongue flitted out with tender flicks probing at the taut flesh of the head, sending elastic sparks down the base to tighten his groin and then, before he had time to recover, she slid the whole length of him within the hot moist cavern of her mouth and moaned around him as he spasmed, nearly releasing himself against her uvula.

Reuben bent slightly at the waist, closing a fist over his throbbing cock on her outward draw, and it might have been the hardest thing he ever did in his life but he caught her face before she took him within her mouth again and lifted her to him. "God, woman, what are you trying to do to me?" he asked, his voice heavy and thick with want.

She flattened herself against him. Her bare breast pressing into his chest. He folded her neatly into his arms and kissed her long and hard.

"We have to do this right this time," he said, his voice languid. He drew in long deep breaths trying to steady himself, and ran long tan fingers through his thick black hair.

He unbuttoned his jeans and pulled them up, not bothering to rebutton them. He'd almost finished. He'd almost ruined everything. Christ she was making this damned hard for him. He felt around on the floor for the matches and struck one. In the glow her face looked flushed and perspiration glistened on her breasts.

He ignited the wick of the candle and lifted the blanket to her. She took it and bundled it up into her arms. He reached for her hand and slowly moved across the cabin to the bedroom, making a sweep of the place as he went.

In the bedroom he used the candle to light the lantern on the night stand, then he blew out the candle's flame. A large, white sheet protected the mattress on the bed and he carefully removed it trying not to disturb the dust too much. Then he took the blanket from her arms and spread it over the mattress.

And only then did he turn to her. In the flickering glow of the lantern she stared at him, a languished look filling her eyes. She pulled her head backwards as he neared her and breathed unsteadily, and when he reached for her and slid her down unto the bed the most intense sigh reverberated from her and the demeanour of her face crumbled. A low mournful sob tore from her throat as he dragged off his shirt and stretched himself out on top of her.

She arched her head back on the bed, the soft column of her throat inviting to his mouth as he ran his lips down it and over her collar bones. Moving on top of her he used his tongue to tempt and tease every inch of her. Her cries echoing through the cabin as his tongue flicked over her stomach and dipped into the soft indent of her navel, and as his head dipped lower to the mound of golden curls her fingers closed around the locks of his hair in gentle encouragement.

Penny's stomach muscles had not had a workout quite like this in some time. As soon as she allowed her muscles to relax a whirling sensation coursed through her again and she was once again as clinched and uptight as piano wire, and then suddenly she was unstrung again and threatening to puddle.

Reuben lifted his head and began the searing path back up to her lips. She could taste herself on him, and could feel his heart beating overtime. He lifted from her and kicked off his jeans. In the light of the lantern she could see his erection rigid, and hear the deep groan in his throat as he stared down at her stretched out before him.

As he leaned down to take a nipple in his mouth she could feel the tip of him brushing along her thigh and twisted beneath him trying to coax him to give her what she longed for. But he didn't comply with her wishes. Instead he flattened her hands above her head and explored her mouth once more.

"You're perfect," he whispered against her lips. "Beautiful, and delicious." He kissed her long and hard, before dragging his mouth away and groaning loudly. "Mm, so delicious. Beautiful. Perfect," he repeated over and over, kissing her face, her jaw, her neck, and her lips.

He shifted atop her, urging her legs to open with his knees and positioned the head of his penis between her legs. His forehead pressed into hers and their eyes locked as he let the head of his cock press into her.

She thrust forward and he pulled back again, the tip right there at her opening, teasing. Their breath mingled, their fingers intertwined above them, forehead to forehead. She let her eyes flutter closed in anticipation.

"Look at me, Penny," he whispered. "I want to see you. I want to watch you when I enter you."

He moved forward a fraction of an inch and when her eyes lowered again he pulled back. "Look at me," he said, his words heavy and laboured.

The very tips of his lips lightly grazing the tips of hers, he spoke into her mouth. "Tell me what you want."

"I, I," she tried to speak, but the need was so heavy that her lungs re-fused to emit the air needed to complete the words.

"You what?" he asked, flicking his tongue out to moisten her lips. "I don't know how much longer I can wait."

"Please," she cried, her lips opening on his.

"Yes?"

"I, I," her voice was a deep alto, a sob cracking on the edges. "I want you," she managed.

She could feel him twitching between her legs, the head of his cock tight and hot.

"Please Reuben," she pleaded.

"For God's sake, tell me what you want Penny," he pleaded in return.

"I, I," she thrust her hips against him. "I want you inside me," she breathed, her voice a long sob.

She felt his fingers relax and then slowly and deliberately he inched himself forward until every last bit was buried within her and his hips closed down on hers. She saw his eyes close then, and his tongue darted into her mouth coaxing hers into his.

"Oh Penny." He slowly began to rock within her. He pulled out slowly and thrust forward, groans punctuating each word he spoke. "You're not supposed to be this perfect. I'm not supposed to want you this badly."

He thrust himself in and out. His fingers no longer intertwined with hers, he ran his hand down past her hips and lifted her knee to better thrust within her. "God, you feel so good. Too good. I want to make love to you all night."

His hips slammed into hers as his thrusts became quicker. "I want to make love to you forever. Your perfect body on mine," he squeezed into her, his arms encircling her, bringing her even closer. "I've never met a more beautiful woman than you. I knew from the moment I saw you that I had to have you."

He cradled her face, his dark brown eyes searching hers. He dropped a row of kisses along her jaw line and buried his face into her hair. "Oh Penny," he said pulling out and giving himself a moment to calm down. "Oh God, you're driving me crazy." He slid back inside her and slowly began the rhythmic thrusts again.

She met him thrust for thrust, clawing at his back, pulling him closer. They melded together, blending perfectly. Their bodies entangled, his dark hair mixing with hers. They clung to one another, both saying things that would never hold up in the light of day. Making promises that could never be.

And as together they crashed into each other, two waves perfectly timed to converge, all the emotions and feelings overtook her and she cried, "I love you. I love you. I love you."

Ragged and spent he rolled onto his side, pulling her up against him. She panted in his arms, hot tears rolling down her cheeks she sobbed against his chest.

He didn't release her. He didn't question her need to cry. He just tightened his arms around her and soothed her, and as her sobbing subsided he made love to her again. Gentle and easy, filling the room with soft cries of pleasure, and pretending for now that love was an afterthought, that love did not equate into any sum they tallied up between them. They were merely bridging the gap between lost loves and heartache, creating stepping stones out of the jungle of sadness and lovingly bidding farewell to loneliness.

I love you stood between them. The elephant in the room that they both pretended wasn't there. He held her wrapped tightly in his arms, the tips of his fingers gently grazing the centre of her back.

Penny had one arm slung over his hips, her head burrowed into his chest. She didn't want to move, afraid he'd break the perfect spell that had fallen over them. In the shadows a clock was frozen in time on the wall, perpetually 9:45, but Penny knew it was well past midnight in real-time.

Still she lingered, breathing in the scent of him, her heart filled to capacity, and her commonsense trying really hard to void it all. She screwed her eyes closed tightly, trying to push reality away.

"Penny?" He brushed the hair away from her face as he bent to look at her. "We have to go. The girls will be up extra early tomorrow morning, and there's nothing they love more than catching me sleeping."

At the mention of Ember and Terra her head began to level, as they'd already decided the girls were top priority in all this. She would not begrudge them the joy of climbing into bed with their dad, or bouncing on him as he slept in an effort to rouse him.

She slid out of his arms and reached for her panties on the floor. As she stood to pull them up he rounded the bed to stand before her.

"Are you okay?" he asked. He cupped her face in his hand and lifted her chin, their eyes meeting.

"I'm fine," she said forcing a smile. "Why wouldn't I be?"

"I know, I know," he said. "I guess I'm feeling guilty, is all."

"Guilty? Why?"

He dropped his hands to her shoulders, sliding them down her arms, and cupping the sides of her breasts. "Oh, shit, Penny," he looked down at her, half dressed. "You deserve better than this."

He stooped to plant a kiss on her shoulder. "You deserve a forever, someone who's ready to give you that." He dragged his teeth over her shoulder, and pulled her closer to him. "You don't deserve to be used."

She stepped out of his arms. "Used?"

"Isn't that what I'm doing? Just using you, no promises or commitments, just a late night rendezvous and in the morning we don't speak about it, or even pretend to like one another?"

He pulled on his underwear, and reached for his jeans. "That's not fair to you. You deserve better." He pulled his jeans up, and closed the distance between them where she still stood in her panties. He reached for her.

"Don't tell me what I need," she said swinging away before he could take her in his arms. "I have more than enough," she stabbed each leg into her jeans and yanked them up over her hips. "This is all I ever wanted from you."

"Penny, I heard you. I was there, remember," he pointed to the bed. "You said you loved me."

She closed her eyes tightly and squeezed her hands into fist. "I know what I said. That's what I do, I say a lot of stupid things in the moment that I don't mean."

She wheeled around searching for her t-shirt and then remembered she'd removed it out front. As he pulled his own t-shirt on, she stood there feeling exposed and fragile before him, and hating it.

His eyes softened as he watched her, and he reached for her. "Okay," he said, pulling her to him. "I'm sorry. I shouldn't have mentioned it."

She allowed him to hold her. "No, you shouldn't have. It would have just gone away with time."

She lifted her arms out from between them and circled his neck, pulling his mouth down to hers.

"I wonder," he said, pulling down one of her hands to place it on his hard-on, "how many times I'd have to make love to you before this stopped happening every time I held you."

"I'm half-naked. You're just being a typical man," she said, trying to lighten the mood. "Now look who's reading into things."

He took up the lantern and followed her from the room. She slipped her t-shirt over her head, and turned to him, now as clothed as he was.

"Was this enough?" she asked.

"Was what enough?"

She tilted her head, thrust out a hip and nervously tapped her feet. "This." She wagged a finger at the space between them.

"Do you mean do I want to fuck you again?"

She shifted hips, her other foot nervously tapping, too. "Yeah," she said. "I guess I'm wondering if you're a one trick pony, or if you want another shot at the prize." She lifted a thumb to her mouth and nibbled on her nail while she waited for his response.

He jabbed a thumb over his shoulder. "Oh, that, what we did in there, wasn't the prize?" His eyes danced mischievously.

"God, Reuben," she said, sucking her cheek between her teeth. "Are we doing this again, or have you had enough?"

He took two steps closer. "I think we both know the answer to that," his voice was slow and deep. "Do *you* want to do this again?"

"I do," she said. "I just can't promise every night. I do a lot of my online business at night."

"That's reasonable. I am going to have to sleep sometimes, too."

"I'll tell you what," she said, digging in her pocket for the key, and stepping out onto the porch. She looked around and then crossed to a log stool at the corner of the porch. "See this?"

She kicked the log stool, and he nodded. She bent down and with some straining lifted it. She held the key up for him to see and then slipped it beneath the log stool. "There," she said, swiping her hands down her pant legs. "That way we don't make this a promise and no one gets hurt. No more meeting at the edge of the trees. Now that you know where the cabin is, just meet me here. We can use Dad's ATVs to reduce the risk of being caught. If I show up and you aren't here, I'll just leave, and the same goes for you."

She entered the cabin again and went to slip her feet into her shoes. "But only after eight," she reminded him. "The cabin is only ever open to us after eight, okay?"

"Just stop for a moment," he said, setting the lantern on a table. "If you ever decide you've had enough, take the key away. No questions asked. I'll just know."

"And you?" she asked. "What happens when you've had enough?"

He stared into her eyes for a long time before he spoke, "I'll be gone."

She tried to ignore the chills that cascaded down her spine, but as they drove in silence the chills became more unbearable, and when she slipped into her bed at the big house she let them percolate and boil over, soaking her pillow.

10

Penny awoke the next morning to unexpected news.

Although she was certain she'd overslept she'd risen at her normal hour. Her body was craving nourishment, so instead of skipping breakfast she pulled ham, spinach, and cheese from the fridge and was in the process of chopping it into small pieces when her dad strolled into the kitchen.

They exchanged good morning pleasantries and he planted a kiss on her forehead. Then he spread his hands helplessly and said, "After all my careful planning, she up and did it herself."

Penny looked up from her chopping and eyed him suspiciously.

"She asked me to marry her."

He held up his hands to show thin cuts on his fingers. "I've been slicing myself to pieces trying to twist paper into roses, thinking I need to make it all fairy tale perfect for her, and she just blurts it out over tea last night."

Penny set the knife down and turned to him, taking up one big hand in her own to study the tiny wounds. "You can make roses out of paper?"

"Well, yes," he said pulling his hand away. "Or at least I use to be able to."

She leaned back against the cupboard and studied him as he added water to the Keurig and selected a k-cup from the carousel. "In my younger days I was an origami guru. But now I have these big ol' sausage fingers."

He popped the k-cup in and closed it, the machine made a popping sound as it punctured the foil, and he chose his settings before turning back to her. The machine spit and sputtered behind him and then a slow trickle sounded spitting drops of coffee over the cupboard as it poured down into the drip tray.

"Oh, shit," he said, grabbing a dish towel and slipping his cup beneath the flow all in the same motion.

"She's really doing a number on you," Penny laughed.

Spencer wiped up the drops and tossed the towel toward the cupboard. "I feel like my head isn't screwed on right Just now in the bathroom I almost spread toothpaste on my razor."

Penny tried to keep a straight face but she couldn't. She burst into gales of laughter. "I'm sorry, Dad," she croaked when she saw the frustrated expression on his face, but before she knew it he had joined her and they were both laughing so hard tears rolled down their cheeks.

Behind them the espresso machine gave a funny slurping sound like it was clearing its throat, and beeped.

They both dropped to nearby chairs and spent several seconds trying to regain their composure.

"I'm making an omelette," she said dragging the underside of her thumb over her eyes to wipe the tears away. "I'll make you one too if you'd like. Maybe you can grab your toothbrush and help me chop up this ham."

As they resumed their laughter Kyle stepped into the kitchen. He looked from one to the other, confused, but the laughter was contagious and soon he was laughing as well.

After a few minutes all three had somewhat composed themselves, and Penny returned to the cutting board. She pushed Spencer away as he neared her, prepared to help. "Go away, Dad. You're in no shape to be around knives."

Spencer pulled his mug from the Keurig and dropped back down in his chair, still hanging on to the last ripples of laughter, his big shoulders still occasionally shaking. Penny cast a glance over her shoulder at him. The goofy smile on his face melted her and she put down the knife to go to him. Taking his head in her hands she bent to kiss his forehead. "Congratulations, Daddy."

"Thanks sweetheart."

"Uh, aspirin?" Kyle said.

Penny pointed him to the medicine cabinet in the corner. He opened it and dropped two pills onto his palm. "What's with the congratulations?"

Penny pushed the chopped up ham to the side and set to work on the spinach. "He and Gyla are tying the knot."

"What? No way." Kyle slapped Spencer on the back. "I guess that explains why you've been M.I.A. for the last couple days."

He shook Spencer's hand and then turned to Penny. "If you're looking to beat him to the altar, I'm free on Saturday."

"Oh, darn it, I have to weed the garden on Saturday," she said.

"No poached eggs this morning?" he asked, coming to stand beside her.

"Omelettes."

"Without bacon and tomato? That's blasphemy."

"You take ham and spinach or nothing at all." She pointed towards the fridge with her knife. "Grab the eggs for me."

"Hey, hey, watch where you're pointing that thing, lady."

A tap at the patio door made all three of them turn. Reuben filled the doorway.

He wore a cap and had pulled his hair back into a braid. His jeans were loose-fitting and he wore a red plaid shirt, a couple of buttons undone at the neck. The sun was rising behind him, and he looked like the perfect start to a beautiful day.

Kyle fidgeted beside Penny at her sharp intake of breath when Reuben came into view and she chanced a glance at him, a weak smile playing on her face.

"Weeding the garden Saturday, huh?" he said, handing her the carton of eggs. She shifted awkwardly and he threw her a wink.

"Reuben!" Spencer said as he threw open the patio door and ushered him inside. "Come join us, Penny-Laine's making omelettes."

"Dad," she said, going out of her way to avoid looking directly at Reuben. "At this rate I'm never going to get out of here."

"I'd love an omelette."

She wondered if she were the only one in the room who heard the underlying mockery in his voice, and she looked up quickly.

"With lots of cheese," he continued, his eyes locking unto hers. She shot silent daggers at him.

"Help yourself to some coffee," Spencer said.

Reuben stepped to the cupboard. Giving the carousel a spin he selected a Colombian coffee from the pods and popped it into the Keurig. He took a mug from the mug tree, slipped it into place, and stepped aside to wait.

He stood too close to her. The clean scent of him circled around her like a lasso

"I didn't get to bed until late, and when I did I had a hell of time getting to sleep," he said, his voice husky.

"It's this heat," Kyle offered, finally popping the pills in his mouth and washing them down with a glass of water. "I had the window opened full on and I still had a hard time settling."

"I'll get you both a fan from the garage later," Spencer said.

"You keep this up and your train just might roll in to the best friend station before noon," Reuben said. He slid into the seat opposite Spencer.

"From what I hear," Kyle said, removing his own mug from the Keurig and setting at the table, too, "best friend isn't what he's aiming for."

"I heard that, too," Reuben said. "My mom was up bright and early, beaming from ear to ear."

"So she told you?" Spencer said.

"I think she got up early especially to tell me. I couldn't be happier for the two of you. And look on the bright side," he said, sitting back. "Not only do I get a great guy for my new Dad, but I scored a brother and a sister, too."

He eyed Penny mischievously over the rim of his mug. "Speaking of that, I haven't had a chance to meet Warren yet. Maybe *he's* in the market for a best friend." He let his mug hit the table a little louder than was necessary. "If so, I'll have to let him know I'm accepting applications."

"Reuben," she shot at him and all eyes turned on her.

"Yes, Penny?"

"Why don't you whisk up the eggs and shut the hell up."

"Penny," Spencer said in surprise.

Before he could reprimand her she reached forward and clamped a hand over his mouth. "No, Dad. If I'm going to be his sister, then I need to start treating him like my brother."

"Does that mean I get to pull your pigtail?" Reuben said.

She shoved the carton of eggs into Reuben's chest. A crack sounded from the carton but she paid it no mind. Instead she leaned down until her face was level with his. The bill of his cap touching her forehead. "Make your own damned omelette."

She glanced up to see Tim walking into the room. "Oh, and look, another potential best friend. Maybe *he* can help you."

She spun on her heels and walked out.

Penny wrapped Gyla in a hug.

"Welcome to the family."

"Don't be too hasty. He might high-tail it out of here when he realizes what he's agreed to."

"If his smile this morning is any indication, I don't think you'll have any worries." Penny accepted the mug of tea Gyla passed her and added her own milk.

"You do realize I'll be moving here with him," Gyla said.

"Of course you will. Where else would you live?"

"And he's asked my opinion on the woods oasis. He wants to take me for a ride around the area later this afternoon."

"Naturally," Penny said, sipping her tea. "Your opinion's important. I wouldn't expect my father to just go ahead with the plans without consulting you, especially in light of recent events."

Her face lit up as she remembered something and she reached for Gyla's hand. "He didn't give you an engagement ring?" She stared down at the ringless hand in horror.

"Well, the whole thing *was* a little unorthodox. I caught him off guard."

"But he's been planning a big proposal for you so I thought he must at least have a ring."

"We're older now and things we once thought were important aren't anymore," she said. "I had an engagement ring when I married Steven, and it stayed on my finger for about three months after we married, and then I just grew tired of it. I baked a lot and I was forever having to remove it and then I'd misplace it and waste hours searching for it, or if I forgot to take it off it would need to be cleaned, and it fetched up in everything, and so I stashed it in a jewellery box and never thought of it again."

She stared off into space. "This time around, I want to be more practical. I want to focus on what truly matters. So I've told Spencer that aside from the wedding band he'll place on my finger on our wedding day, I don't want a ring."

With both hands wrapped around her mug, and her elbows up on the table, she sipped her tea. "I really love your father, Penny. He's a great man with a heart of gold." Her whole face lit up. "I never suspected to find anyone I'd want to spend the rest of my life with." She shrugged. "When you get to be my age, all the good guys are either gone or taken, and no one seems to take you serious anymore. And then one day I was on the computer and I got to thinking about high school and my younger days, so I searched up my graduating class. 1975. And I was thinking about a friend I had who I haven't seen in forever, Joanna Marshal. I wondered about her life, and so I did what what the cool kids do."

"You have Facebook?"

"I didn't, but I do now."

"That's *not* where you met my dad."

Gyla beamed and her eyes twinkled. "I sure did. Your father had no idea how Facebook works, and he'd written a message he'd meant to be private right out on Joanna's wall, telling her to keep the whole conversation between them."

Penny's hand flew to her mouth. "He did not."

"It was the sweetest letter of apology I'd ever seen."

"What was he apologizing for?"

"Apparently they'd met in town and he'd asked her out, but things didn't go quite like they'd planned, and they found themselves in an awkward situation where he had no choice but to go home with her. Then they started to, well," she made sweeping gestures with her hand, "you know? He got a little frisky with her, and she went ballistic on him. She accused him of being like every other guy and only wanting one thing from her. She kicked him to the curb. So the next day he wrote her a 'private message' explaining why she was wrong about him."

Penny dropped her head in her hands, and looked out from between her fingers. "Oh no, I'm almost too scared to ask what happened."

"It went something like this: 'I wanted to clear up our little misunderstanding. I thoroughly enjoyed spending a lovely meal with you last night, and I regret losing my keys and having to call a cab. I was however very grateful that you let me accompany you home, and did not intend to kiss you or even touch you. I pride myself at being a gentleman, and I am sorry if you thought my intentions were impure. Although I am not one to broadcast my issues, I feel compelled to tell you that although I am still able to perform—'"

"Oh. My. God."

"—'I am not able to do so without the aid of medication.'"

Penny couldn't decide whether to cover her eyes or her ears.

"'I had no medication on me last night and, even if I did, I would re-quire at least thirty minutes—'"

"No no no no!"

"'—for the medication to take effect. Please keep this message privately between us, and contact me should you feel it in your heart to give me a second chance.'"

"Please tell me Joanna deleted that."

Gyla laughed. "The one good thing your dad did was to sign up with a variation of his name. So no one knows Spencer McCalla, of the ever successful McCalla Potato products limited has any trouble functioning whatsoever."

Penny mimed wiping her brow.

For a few minutes the two ladies sipped their tea in quiet, each contemplating how their lives were about to change, and both of them smiling softly.

"I have a confession," Penny said, breaking the silence.

"Okay," Gyla said, suddenly very serious, and Penny knew she was expecting the worst.

"Our kitchen at the big house was a little crowded this morning, so I really came down here for something to eat."

Relief flooded Gyla's face and she pushed from the table, "why didn't you say so sooner." She pulled a frying pan from the pot rack. "Let's see, I have eggs, bacon, tomatoes, and cheese. Are you in the mood for an omelette?"

11

That afternoon everything and everyone cooked under the heavy blanket of the blistering heat. Not a wisp of air could be felt, and the forecast held no promise of relief.

Penny gave in to the heat and moved into the distillery to bundle some freshly harvested lavender for hanging. She opened the double doors and rolled her hanging cart inside, and tuned the radio to a local station as she worked. She'd received a large order for lavender tea and pure lavender essential oils, and wanted it to be as fresh as possible since it was for a new customer in the city who was opening a business called *Spa and Sip,* and was in the market for a permanent supplier. Behind her, three medium-sized copper stills hummed quietly as they worked, in their last half hour of the three-hour distillery process.

She had already downed three bottles of water in a bid to combat the heat, and was going for a fourth when a chime sounded from her computer. She twisted the cover off the bottle as she made her way around the desk.

It was Facebook: one message was pending. She opened it, and her heart leapt. It was Reuben. His message was simple.

Join us for ice cream at 3?

She tapped her fingers on the desk as she stared at his message. She could just ignore him, but Facebook always stamped messages as seen once they'd been opened so he'd know she'd ignored him.

Us? she typed.

His reply was quick. *Me and my two tiny bodyguards.*

What was he doing? Hadn't they talked about this. Hadn't they'd made promises around the twins. She typed her reply angrily. *Remember top priority and not involving anyone else in our little game?*

It's just ice cream.

It's false hope.

False hope?

We don't want to give them any idea that there could potentially be a me and you.

It's just ice cream.

No.

Suit yourself. Home made vanilla bean, with the option of strawberries on top, but that's okay, I'll eat your share.

Ok

You're seriously rejecting me.

I'm seriously rejecting you, Romeo.

What if I say the girls are sleeping.

She strained her ears to listen. She could faintly hear voices above, but she wanted to be certain before she replied, so she ran to the back of the room and climbed the stairs quietly. She pressed her ear to the door and listened. She could hear them. If she had to guess they were playing in the bedroom.

She rushed back to the computer. *I call bullshit.*

You need a swear jar.

I'm in the basement, genius, and I'm not deaf.

He didn't reply.

Do me a favour? she typed a few seconds later.

I don't have a webcam.

Very funny. Favour?

What?

Bring me ice cream?

But the girls will read into that too won't they?

I'll meet you at the basement door.

And can I kiss you?

Her stomach did a flip flop, and she typed her answer slowly, a soft smile on her lips. *Yes.*

Five minutes. Strawberries?

No strawberries.

Four minutes.

I'll be waiting.

Over the hum of the stills she could hear Reuben call to his girls, and the patter of feet running, and she slowly made her way up the stairs to wait.

She heard the lock turn and stepped down several stairs to allow for the inward swing of the door, and there he stood in jeans and a t-shirt, and a bowl of ice cream in his hand. He reached for her hand, pulling her up the stairs, encircled her waist and pulled her to him.

Pressed into him, she felt the heat of the day go up a few degrees even as chills made a quick sweep of her skin. She could taste ice cream on his lips.

He turned her from the stairs and flattened her against the wall at the landing, his kiss deepening and his free hand roaming up and down her side, lingering beside her breast.

When they finally pulled away, Penny reached for the ice cream, but he held it out of reach.

"I'm sorry about earlier," he said.

She reached for the ice cream again.

"I can be something of an ass sometimes."

"Sometimes?"

He leaned in to her. His hand came around to cup her ass, and he pulled her close again. "Do you feel what you do to me?"

A beeping sounded from the basement: her stills completing. "Can I have the ice cream now?"

"Will you meet me tonight?"

"That's not how this is supposed to work."

"I know. But can't we break the rules just once?"

"Fine," she said, grabbing the bowl from his hand.

Penny closed up shop by 4:30. An hour later she had showered, eaten a light supper, and loaded cleaning supplies, water, a cordless hand vacuum, and bedding into the four-wheeler.

Two hours later and she was sitting in a mostly-tidy cabin, eating a granola bar and sipping tea from a thermos. When she heard Reuben pull up in front of the cabin a few minutes later, she went to the door.

She watched as he pulled himself from the four wheeler, long legs quickly eating up the distance between them. At the bottom of the steps he paused to pull the elastic from his hair and toss it over his shoulder. Within seconds he was in front of her, his hand cupping the back of her head and his lips on hers. His hand caught the end of her braid and he gently pulled the elastic from her hair too, tossing it from the porch, and then he swung her up in his arms, kicked the door closed behind them, and carried her to the bedroom.

~

Penny slept beside him. Her cheeks flushed from their lovemaking and perspiration glistened on her chest and shoulders. A thin white sheet stretched taut over her breasts, a cotton bridge across the valley.

This time things had been less hurried, and they had barely spoken. They'd risen and fallen together, each in perfect accord with the other, their bodies and minds in sync.

And now, lying beside her while she slept in his arms, Reuben could barely get enough of even the sight of her. The clock on the wall was still stopped at 9:45, and the lantern was on its last possible combustible wick. The shadows danced in and out as the flame contemplated obliteration. Reuben didn't dare move to blow the lantern out of its misery or to light a candle, but the thoughts of the darkness eating up his view of her was an unwelcome thought.

She twisted against him, the sheet slipping down over her breast, and the tips of her nipples lightly grazed his skin.

What time was it? If he had to guess it was nearing midnight, but she was sleeping on his arm and so he couldn't check his watch.

She'd been exhausted. He saw that the second she stepped out on the porch to greet him. Her day had been busy and then she'd cleaned the cabin to make things more comfortable for them.

He'd liked the thought of her waiting for him a little too much. Truth be told, it scared him. He didn't want to expect anything of her, least of all her waiting. Someday she'd wait for another, and he had no right letting himself expect any waiting from her on his behalf.

He brushed back her hair gently and she twisted her head deeper into him. Not just anyone would do for her, he decided. He saw how Kyle looked at her, and although Kyle had done nothing to him personally, he would not do. Penny would need someone better. Someone who complemented her completely. Someone with an equal amount of brawn and compassion, with integrity and a good sense of family and togetherness. Not qualities he saw or even imagined in Kyle. Sure the man was okay to work with, and he'd even shared some laughs with him, but at the same time he had a longing to punch the teeth out of his head.

Why was that? He searched his mind for a reason, but all it ever came back to was Penny. He hated Kyle wanting her, and that was all the man had ever done to Reuben that could warrant such thoughts.

Reuben shifted uneasily and closed his arms tighter around Penny.

Kyle would not do, but in reality he didn't think anyone would. She was just too perfect right where she was, but that wasn't fair to her. He could not ask her to put aside the human need to nest and have a family, or to live without the closeness of a husband, and for what? Interpersonal jaunts in a cabin with him from time to time? She deserved something lasting and forever, promises of completeness and faithful companionship all through her trek of life.

She doesn't deserve this, he thought just as the flame petered out and died. He stared into the darkness, and could see nothing. A perfect omen to what her future would be if he didn't let her go.

Just as he was about to make a move to rouse her, his eyes adjusted, and the white face of the clock punctuated the dark. The hands of time still frozen, but it was a small ray of hope nonetheless.

He settled back down, pulling the sheet up around them. He knew they couldn't stay here, but for a few minutes more he wanted to pretend that they could.

12

Ridgeville is known locally as the belt of Digby County, and the weather tends to be more extreme there than in the rest of the county. If it is snowing lightly in neighbouring communities, it will be a near blizzard there. If it is comfortably warm across the region, it will be unbearably hot in Ridgeville.

Today was a windy day in the county, which meant it was a near hurricane in Ridgeville. The only thing saving Penny's lavender gardens was the surrounding trees. She'd made sure to keep a comfortable number around the garden to take the brunt of the wind, but removed just enough to let the sunlight in too.

She'd hung random wind chimes in the trees, and today's wind was thrashing and twisting them so much that their usually gentle percussion sounded more like a wildly furious irato, and some had been tangled so much that their song had been silenced altogether.

Claire was coming to visit today. If Penny had access to her own cottage, she would have planned dinner for them in the sunroom, but instead she'd rolled out a couple of Spencer's Plexiglas privacy panels to a corner of the deck and situated them so they blocked out the wind for the most part, but still allowed them to enjoy the warmth of the sun and a pleasing amount of breeze.

She intended to take Claire on a tour of the oasis that afternoon, although she had not taken a moment to enjoy it herself yet. She'd see the progress for the first time today, so she would not be able to talk Claire through the plans. Of course, she did have some idea of what her dad had wanted before the work begun, and had even offered up requests and suggestions of her own. But she wasn't aware of the changes, deletions, or additions to the plans since then.

It would be a nice stroll nonetheless, and Claire would no doubt have her camera with her. With any luck at all she would at least get some beautiful shots to add to her collection. Although Claire was a doctor, she could have been successful with her photography. Her pictures were beautiful and haunting, and had an artsy feel to them, but she didn't share them with the world. She shared them with close friends and family, and Penny even owned several framed prints herself, but Claire had no desire to stretch her talent to anything beyond a hobby.

In accordance with Ridgeville's tendency towards the extremes, the same could be said for its residents. They took the term good neighbour and kicked it up several notches. So it was no surprise when Claire showed up on the back of Cooper O'Neill's four-wheeler.

Cooper was an elder in the community, from a long line of O'Niells, and owned at least half the pastures and woodland lining Ridgeville and its surrounding roads. It was his cattle and sheep that dotted the countryside, and although his success was obvious it had not done anything to lessen the goodness of his heart. It may have helped that he'd known Bill Larkin all his life, but Penny doubted it. His generosity stretched to everyone, and the only differences he would have shown to an acquaintance as opposed to a stranger was the path of his conversation and the mention of family.

"Hello," he called up at Penny from the drive, his big hand lifted above his head and his wave a huge arch in the air above him. The smile that plastered his face was contagious and Penny matched him, her own hand flapping wildly above her head in greeting.

"I have fresh lemonade," she called.

"Oh that's okay. I need to be getting back anyway. I just wanted to deliver Bill's beautiful daughter to you safely. Couldn't have her tearing up the bottom of that pretty little car of hers."

He settled back down onto the four-wheeler. "You tell Spencer I'll be dropping in to see him soon."

"I'll do that."

She watched him take off down the driveway before she turned to greet Claire on the steps. "Roads still bad, huh?" she asked circling her friend in a hug.

"They are, but I did see the grader so I think they're fixing them today." The wind lifted Claire's hair and whipped it around her head. She tried to control it but it was no use.

"It's uncommon for the roads to be so bad this time of the year, but we have had lots of rain this summer."

"From what I hear there are less people with dry wells this year, too, so even though it's wreaking havoc on the roads, it's doing good elsewhere."

"That's one way to look at it," Penny said, laughing as a wisp of Claire's hair fell across her eyes. "Come on inside."

"No rain in the forecast today," Claire said, following Penny into the cottage. Her black hair fell around her face, silky and shiny, and looking no worse for wear.

"Isn't that great?" Penny pulled open the refrigerator and removed the pitcher of lemonade. "Can you grab a couple tumblers from the cupboard?"

"I do enjoy the rain, though," Claire said. She selected two vintage tumblers. "I can *not* believe your dad still has these." She traced a finger over the etched picture of the loon. "I remember my mom only going to that one specific garage for gas, and if the man at the counter tried to stiff her even one sticker she'd be right there to let him know."

She followed Penny back out on to the deck. "She'd fill one card and then start working on filling another because she was determined to get four loon glasses, her favourite of the eight designs." She placed the tumblers on the table and turned towards the house again. "Do you think Spencer would care if I grab one of his caps from the peg just inside the door? I keep forgetting just how crazy the wind gets out here, and I really need to tame this beast."

"Go for it," Penny said. "Oh, and grab that bag of chips from the cupboard while you're at it."

Within seconds Claire was back with the chips and a McCalla Potato Products Ltd. cap on her head. Just as she was about to slide into the chair opposite Penny, she looked out through the Plexiglas and squinted, cupping a hand over her eyes to shield against the sun. "Is that Number Seven walking up the driveway?"

Penny had to stand to see, but sure enough it was Reuben coming up the driveway. "That's odd," she said, sitting down again. "Wouldn't it have been quicker to just drive out?"

"So is it?" Claire asked, searching Penny's face for a clue.

"Yes, that's Reuben." Penny tried to hide a smile. "Stop looking at me like that.".

"He's really done a number on you. You're actually giddy." Claire half-stood to look at the man approaching. "He certainly looks okay from here."

Then her glance turned into a stare. "Just wait a second," she said, standing fully,.

Confused, Penny stood, too. "Do you know him or something?"

"It looks like he's bleeding."

Penny tossed her napkin on the table and circled the Plexiglas panel. At the railing she stopped to get a better look.

Reuben was cradling one hand in the other, and the hem of his shirt was wrapped up under his fingers to catch what was obviously blood.

She bounded down the stairs towards him, with Claire on her heels. "What happened?"

He stopped and she circled his hands with her own, prising open his fingers to take a look.

"It's just a little cut," he said. "I nicked myself with a pair of pruning shears."

She looked down at his palm filled with blood. "That's not just a nick, Reuben."

"Let me take a look," Claire said, squeezing in between them and taking Reuben's hand in hers.

"Claire's a doctor, Reuben," Penny said and reluctantly moved away.

She watched as Claire pulled the hem of Reuben's shirt up over his palm, gently sopping away the excess blood. The other side of his shirt flapped in the wind, lifting up over his belly-button and exposing the subtle chisel of his abdomen. A six-pack, Penny knew, their definition made less obvious with the light dusting of hair. Penny's fingers itched at the thought of that body beneath her fingers.

"It doesn't look like it needs stitches, but it will definitely need to be cleaned and bandaged."

Inside, Claire guided Reuben in to the bathroom, and ran warm water over the cut while Penny retrieved the first aid kit from the closet just outside the bathroom. From there she could hear their conversation.

"You must be Reuben."

"That I am."

"I'm Claire, Penny's best friend."

"Are you the friend who owns the cabin down the road?"

"I am," she said, a smile in her voice. "Have you been to my cabin?"

Penny knew Claire, and she had a way of prying the most intimate details from anyone. If she didn't get in there quickly Claire would have him spilling out all the sordid details of his time within her cabin.

She scrambled around the shelf above the closet and located the first aid kit. Rushing back into the bathroom she thrust the kit into Claire's hands. "Here you go," she said and the two women's eyes met. Claire ignored the warning in Penny's eyes.

"It's a great little cabin," Reuben said. "Are you looking to sell?"

"Oh no, it's been in my family far too long." Claire opened the kit and found an antiseptic spray. "Besides, I co-own it with my sister, so I couldn't sell it even if I wanted to."

She turned her hat around backward so she could see better, and set to work on his cut. "I thought the cabin would be broken into by now. Was everything okay inside?"

"I couldn't see that it was bothered at all." Reuben turned to Penny. "Could you?"

She melted under his gaze, her stomach doing flip flops. They were all acting like the whole world knew that they were intimate, and that it didn't matter. Unable to speak, she just shook her head no in response.

"It does need a few repairs outside, but it doesn't appear to be leaking yet," Reuben said to Claire. "I wouldn't want to chance it for the winter, though. It looks pretty rotted in the back." He winced a little as Claire applied ointment to his wound.

"Back where the trees are overhanging? I hate to cut the trees down, but they've been nothing but a nuisance."

"They just need a good trimming and the roof fixed under them," Reuben said.

She finished off the bandage and gently pressed the edges of the tape down. "There. It'll be tender for a couple of days. Just keep an eye on it, but I think you'll be fine."

Reuben stood and adjusted his shirt. "Thanks for that. I didn't mean to spoil your day."

"No problem at all," Claire said. "Now if I could scoot you guys out of here I'll clean up and go pee-pee."

As soon as the bathroom door closed, Reuben took Penny's hand and pulled her out to the kitchen. "You look pretty today," he said, slipping his bandaged hand around her waist.

"I look the same as I always do."

"True, you're beautiful every day," he said brushing his lips over hers. "But you look different."

"Just windblown," she said.

He nuzzled his head in her neck and inhaled deeply. "I think it's the pink. I've never seen you wear pink before."

She pushed him away, "Stop, Claire's in the next room."

"But I thought you said you told her about us."

"I've told you a hundred times already there is no—"

"Yeah, yeah, yeah, I know there is no us."

"Then stop saying it, if you remember."

"I do remember," he said pulling her closer, "but I think there *is* an us. Not every *us* has to be permanent you know. We are a form of *us*, even if it's not forever."

He cradled her, his chin resting easily on top of her head. "And the *us* we form is just perfect."

"No," she said. "I don't feel comfortable with that. There is no us, just me and you, okay?"

"What scares you about that?"

She squirmed within his arms to get her hand between them, and cupped her hand on his rising member. "I'll twist," she threatened.

His eyes widened. "You wouldn't dare."

"Oh I dare," she said, tightening her grip. "Now repeat after me: there. Is. No. Us."

"It's just a simple word. It doesn't mean anything," he said and winced when her hand tightened even more. Then his face relaxed and he beamed down at her mischievously. "You know you're actually turning me on a little."

"Oh really?" she said, tightening even more." There is no us."

"Okay, okay, there is no us," he said, and her hand loosened on him. "But you don't have to move your hand."

She slid her hand away from him and circled his torso with her arms, stretching her head up for a deeper kiss, and then quickly pushed out of his arms when the bathroom door opened.

"You're not going back to work, are you?" she asked just as Claire stepped into the kitchen. Reuben had turned towards the door in an attempt to hide his growing erection. She could see him breathing deeply and knew he was mentally talking his little friend down.

When he finally turned only someone aware of it would have realized that while his mental pep talk had worked, the message hadn't completely sunk in yet. She bit the inside of her mouth to keep from laughing.

"I might just duck in to get the wheeler after I change, and let Spencer know I'm calling it a day." He stepped out on the deck behind Penny, and she knew the subtle brush of his hand on her behind was intentional.

"Thanks for this," he said to Claire, raising his bandaged hand. "It was great meeting you." He turned to Penny, "See you later."

Although she could tell by the tone of his voice that he was trying to pass it off as a casual statement she heard the underlining question. "Claire and I are heading for a hike in the woods after we eat. If you want us to we can pick up the wheeler for you and let Dad know you're staying out."

"Are you sure?"

"Oh yeah," Claire agreed. "The wheeler will get us around quicker, and we can close more distance and still have time to hang out a bit before I leave at five."

Reuben looked from one to the other, and then rested his eyes on Penny. She knew the burning question in his eyes without him even asking. "I imagine we'll be pretty tuckered out after this," she said. "I'll probably call it an early night."

She saw the flicker of disappointment in his eyes.

"Well, you two enjoy your day." On the steps he turned back to them. "I didn't see your car, Claire. Did you arrive by taxi?"

Claire laughed, "my limo's around back," she teased. "No, a neighbour drove me, I left my car in his driveway."

"Will he be picking you up at five?"

"No, I thought someone from here might give me a ride out." she glanced at Penny.

"Well, seeing as Penny will be too exhausted by the end of the day I'll meet you here at five and give you a lift if you'd like."

"Yeah, I'd like that," Claire said, and turned to Penny. "That's okay with you isn't it?"

"Of course it's okay," Reuben piped up. "Spencer's my boss. Penny and I are just Penny and I, right Penny?"

She looked him squarely in the eyes, "right, Reuben."

"Besides it's the least I can do. If it weren't for you I'd probably be off getting my hand amputated right now."

Claire laughed. "I don't think it would have come to that."

"It's a great idea," Penny said, "And maybe, if you have a minute that is, Reuben can even stop in to the cabin and show you what needs repairing."

"Sure, my whole night just opened up, so I could definitely do that," Reuben said.

Penny's eyes narrowed. He was deliberately taunting her now. She'd refused him one night, and he was making her pay. Well she wasn't going to give him the satisfaction of thinking she cared.

She moved around the Plexiglas and sat down at the table, busying herself by adding way too much mayonnaise to her sub,. Then an idea hit her. She lifted the pepper dish and uploaded half of its contents on top of the mayonnaise. Then she quickly went about preparing the sandwich.

Just as Reuben called his goodbye, she leaned over the railing and handed it to him. "One for the road?"

13

The internet is notoriously bad in the early evening, a small disadvantage of living in a rural community, but Penny was attempting to surf nonetheless. Anything to keep her mind off the time. After a long loading period she managed to get on her website and was tweaking things that didn't need tweaking, rechecking order statuses and tracking packages she'd sent even though there was no need, as all this was already worked into her morning schedule when the internet was at its peak. She was surfing on a wireless laptop in the bedroom at the big house, so she was getting more timed-out messages than usual.

The driveway wasn't visible from the bedroom, so she'd left the patio door open in hopes of hearing any approaching vehicles. It was nearing 8 pm and so far she'd heard nothing. She wished she hadn't turned him down. It had been silly and childish, she knew, but it was too late to take it back now.

Reuben had sent her a friend request already and she'd accepted it the day he'd made her ice cream. Although they had already decided they would never be a couple, and she didn't think they could ever be friends in the traditional sense of the word, they would definitely be family now that Spencer and Gyla were engaged, so she'd accepted his request with that in mind.

Now, as Facebook loaded and he came into view on her screen she wondered if it had been a mistake after all. He was not hers to fret over, they were both free agents...but seeing him now tagged in a picture less than thirty minutes old, with his arms wrapped around a pretty brunette, her stomach clenched and her heart ached.

"Ran into tall dark and handsome tonight," the photos caption read.

Penny's cursor hovered over the brunette's name, and her profile picture popped up. Janine Newberry was drop dead gorgeous, with a soft cloud of perfectly pampered hair, a beautiful mouth with brilliant white teeth and full lips, and big brown eyes with dark lashes. Standing together, she and Reuben did nothing but complement one another. She looked like she belonged beside him, and for that Penny grieved.

Reuben did not belong to her, and that was just how she had wanted it. It was what she'd demanded before she propositioned him for a no-strings-attached affair. She had no right to care whether he saw other women. They were free to do what they wanted, with whomever they chose.

Janine was perfectly perky and downright beautiful, and she was obviously enjoying the company of the tall, dark, and handsome Reuben Lafford. Maybe he'd had enough of Penny. And what if he had? Wouldn't that be okay? Hadn't they laid out the ground rules already, had even gone so far as to decide on parting ways to end their affair without words.

I'll be gone, he'd said. She had assumed he'd meant that he'd pack up the girls and leave Ridgeville. Had he meant something else? Gone from her, but still very much here? Gone from the shack? Gone from their bed?

Their bed? There was no *us*, and by extension no *theirs*. Reuben was his own man, and if he chose to be with Janine tonight, that was his prerogative. Should he decide to spend the rest of his life with her, that was his right, too, and she would have to be okay with that.

She'd spent more than three years being alone, and had coped just fine. Nothing had changed. Having loved Reuben was a happy distraction from the loneliness for a while, but that was it. It was not a forever kind of situation, but it had told her all she needed to know about herself.

She did not have to be lonely. She was not required to mourn indefinitely. Three years and then some had been enough time to put her life on hold. David was dead. Marriage vows ended at death. She knew that and so had he. They'd spoken it in their vows, had signed their names on the dotted line in agreement of it. *Until death do we part.*

She would love him for the rest of her life, there was no doubt of that, far beyond her last breath even, but that did not mean her heart could not love again. Reuben had proven that to her. He'd taken a stalled heart and awakened it. And now here she was in love, and still alone.

Closing her eyes she shivered as the realization washed over her. Her heart already knew what her mind was just barely willing to admit. She loved Reuben. In the most cliché of ways she was pretty sure her heart had gone against her better judgment, and she'd fallen in love with him that first night, when he'd pressed his finger to her lips and cautioned her not to scream. *Love at first sight.*

She opened the drawer of the night stand and removed the mended mantel scarf. As she traced the area he'd sewn, she tried to picture his fingers holding the needle. Although she knew how competent his fingers could be, she also knew how large they were. He'd chosen the finest needle, he'd told her, something smaller to better sew delicate fabric. She knew the careful precision it would have taken to mend something like this and not leave behind a bulging seam.

She traced the thin velvet scar and wondered about the new gaping wound on her own heart. Who would mend that? And would the scar be as fine and delicate as this one? Somehow she doubted it. She expected the hole in her heart to never heal completely, but it would heal nonetheless, just as the wound left at David's parting had healed. That didn't mean that from time to time a memory wouldn't reach out and caress the scar, stirring up a reminder of days gone by, but she would heal. She would cope. She would go on.

She needed a distraction. Something with enough gusto to drive her mind away from Reuben, and there was only one thing she could think of that gave her that much passion.

She keyed in her favourite vintage fabric website and waited for it to load. She'd been toying with the idea of new cushions for the French Victorian parlour suite, but all the fabrics she liked were far outside her price range. She'd been eyeing up a couple yards of vintage Manuel Canovas toile linen with a pretty orange botanical print, and she wanted to take a moment to dream of fabric.

Auld Antique Geezer's website had a scrolling marquee across the top, announcing the business's participation in the *Maritime travelling Antique Expo.* Penny clicked the marquee for more information, and then the link for the expo's official website. The next stop would be in Halifax the following weekend.

She returned to *Auld Antique Geezer*, located the contact page to get their email, and brought up her email system. It was spur of the moment, more spontaneous than she usually would have been. Her normal protocol, before she planned time away, was to check with her dad first, make sure he would be okay alone, and contact Warren to plan for a check-in.

This time was different. Her dad had Gyla now, and although some of the crew did leave for the weekend, most usually stayed behind. Plus it wasn't like she was slipping away tonight. She'd have all day tomorrow to tell him before she left the next morning.

Penny sent an email to Joe, the owner of the antique shop, to ask if it were possible for him to bring along several different vintage fabrics for her to have a closer look at, including the Manuel Canovas piece.

After quickly making reservations for a two-night stay at her favourite hotel in the city, she closed the laptop and pushed off from the bed. If she was going to do this then she would need to set her alarm for earlier the next morning and try to get Saturday's chores finished as well, or at least the pressing ones that couldn't wait for Monday.

Even with an early morning ahead of her, and the promise of a weekend getaway, it wasn't enough to get her through the night. It would take something stronger than herself to shut off her thoughts and make her sleep.

It was quiet. She couldn't hear the men chatting on the deck at all, which was their normal after-hours behaviour. It had been an overly warm day despite the wind, and the heat had probably tired them out and driven them to their beds earlier than normal. The one night she could have used the company.

Penny slipped from the bedroom and tiptoed into the kitchen. She pulled an ice bucket down from the cupboard, added a little water to it, and held it over the ice dispenser. The ice clattered in its descent and splashed water out onto her arm as it crashed into the bucket. She selected a bottle of Fine Old Canadian Ruby and slipped it into the ice water. The wine had been a gift to her father, but he wouldn't miss it. He'd told her once that if he drank wine it would be Osoyoos Larose Vqa or nothing; besides, tonight just felt like a Ruby kind of night to her.

With the wine bucket wedged into the crook of one arm, she pulled a block of cheese from the fridge and a strip of crackers from the cupboard. What she really wanted was cheesecake. Nothing tasted better than cheesecake and old Ruby, but with this being spur-of-the-moment and all, she hadn't really had time to plan ahead.

"Drinking alone?"

Penny turned, the crackers dangling from her teeth. Kyle stood in the doorway, fresh from the shower. In its dampened state his blond hair looked darker. He wore green plaid pyjama bottoms and a white t-shirt, his feet were bare, and a bottle of Alexander Keith's dangled from his fingers.

Unable to speak anything outside of a grunt, she nodded.

"Can I join you or is this a solo gig?"

She eyed him suspiciously, and cocked her head towards the bottle he held.

"Oh, this?" Raising the bottle to his mouth he drained the last few drops, then tossed the empty bottle to the trash. "Gone." He held his hands out for proof.

She jutted her chin out and garbled instructions to him. Without hesitation he stepped forward and took the crackers from her teeth.

"You understood that?"

"I did."

"Impressive." She handed him the cheese as well so she could retrieve a knife and plate.

"I'm more than just a pretty face," he said smiling and batting his eyes.

She laughed, "I can see that."

"So, are we taking this to your room or mine?" A mischievous twinkle danced in his eyes.

"You're not much of a Casanova, are you?" She held the bucket out to him. "Take this to the deck and I'll grab wine glasses."

Kyle had chosen seats where the setting sun was most visible, turning the chairs at an angle to take advantage of the view, and had opened the wine. He took the glasses, filled them, and handed one to her.

They sat, quietly looking out over the deck as the sun sank lower in the evening sky, sipping Ruby in all her full-bodied goodness.

"Thanks for this," Penny spoke into the quietness.

"Oh, the pleasure is all mine." He reached for the bottle to refill his glass.

"I didn't take you for a wine man."

"I'm not really," he said, smiling at her. "But I could be. Consider this my audition."

Penny laughed and lifted the bottle. Condensation circled around the base and plopped down on to the deck floor. "I'm auditioning for this part, right here," she said, poking the bottom of the bottle.

"What a coincidence," he said, "So am I. You better get on it. I'm already one glass ahead of you."

"But you're doing it all wrong."

He chuckled. "I am? How so?"

"It's not how fast you get there." She lifted her wine, swirled it, and brought it to her mouth, pausing for a second before taking a sip. "To truly appreciate it you have to savour it, smell it while you drink. You're guzzling it like its water. Give your tongue and taste buds time to fall in love."

"Seems like a waste of time to me."

She watched him as he lifted his glass to his mouth and breathed deeply, and then took a drink. He closed his eyes for a second, and she waited with bated breath for his verdict.

"Well?" she asked, when he finally opened his eyes.

He stared at the glass, his brow furrowed. "Nah," he said and downed the rest of the wine from the glass.

She laughed.

"Would you be offended and kick me off the deck if I ran inside and got something decent to drink?"

"Decent? Now *that* offends me." She yanked the glass from his hand. "Go get your bottle of cat piss if you must."

Penny made her way to the edge of the deck and looked off towards the path leading to her cottage. Unless his vehicle had somehow managed to get past her without her realizing it, Reuben hadn't even returned to tuck his children in for the night. He was entitled to a night off, but the idea of him not being there left a bad taste in her mouth. They were top priority' she'd made him promise that. No, she'd made him promise that in regards to their relationship. The stipulations he and Janine had laid out between them were their business. She had just hoped that Ember and Terra were important factors in any relationship he chose to partake of.

Kyle came up beside her and set a glass on the rail. He set an unopened bottle of beer on the deck and then popped the top on a second. "This is for you."

"No thanks." She raised a hand in protest.

"Yes thanks," he insisted. "I let you pretty up ol' ruby for me, and I gave her a chance. Now you have to let me do the same for good old faithful Keith." He gestured towards his bottle, "I've grown to love him, so I don't bother with glasses and head and all the fancy shmancy stuff, but if I want you to fall in love with him too I have to do this the right way."

He lifted the glass and tilted the bottle to pour, not letting any drops fall until he got her approval. "I'm not going to push him on you. You have to give me the go ahead before I do this."

Looking at the bottle and back at Kyle, she bit the inside of her lip as she contemplated the idea. "I don't hold beer well," she said.

"You have to decide fast. If you want the full effect I need to pour this soon. The longer I hold it the quicker my fingers warm up the bottle, and the beer loses some of its zing."

"Fine," she said, reaching out to tip the bottle.

"Ah ah, let me do this." He held the bottle firmer, resisting her tip. "This takes a fine art to get the perfect head."

The amber liquid's first stream swirled against the inside of the tulip glass in a wave that petered out into a frothy bubbling pool. A bitter pool. Which was exactly where she was at tonight, and in that moment it seemed like the perfect pool to dip her feet into.

"You stop pouring at riiiight abooout..." the glass upright now, the stream was a near trickle as he eyed the bottle, "there." He stopped about two inches from the end, upended the remainder into his own mouth, and handed her the glass. "Hold it by its stem as much as you can, so your hand doesn't warm it up quicker than it ought to be. You get the most bang for your buck when the beer is cool."

She took the glass with more care than she thought it really warranted.

"You don't have to treat it like it's going to shatter in your hand, just don't be all handsy."

As she raised the glass to her mouth, he shot a hand out and tugged it down by the foot. "Ah ah, let's do this right. You're trying to fall in love, remember?"

He popped the top on his own bottle. "Now swirl it gently, it'll open up the flavours for you."

She swirled it, some of the foam clinging to the sides of the rim.

"Now close your mouth and smell it."

She obeyed.

"Now smell it again, only this time open your mouth a bit and allow yourself to inhale while you do."

She closed her eyes, let her lips part slightly, and leaned into the glass again. Her eyes shot open in surprise as the bitter smell took on a malty taste in the back of her mouth even though she had yet to actually sip it.

"Ahhh, see what I mean?" He smiled and nodded encouragingly, pleased with her reaction. "It's like foreplay."

"Interesting," she said. "Now what?"

"Now go ahead. But don't swallow right away. Give your taste buds time to consider it."

She took a sip and would have lowered the glass had his hand not shot out to hold the glass to her lips.

"A little bigger sip than you would with Ruby."

She deepened the pull and the bitter liquid filled her mouth.

"Now move it around a bit, let it coat your palate and the insides of your cheeks, and then, when you think you're good and satisfied, swallow it."

First there was bitterness so strong it shook her core, but then sour pangs shot along the sinews of her jaw, plucking each cord with a different level of sour, and then it all merged together with sweetness, saltiness and something deeper she couldn't quite put her finger on. Soon a whole umami of tastes she had never tasted before danced within her mouth, and then she swallowed and a whole litany of fumes wafted up into her nasal passage, intensifying all the flavors she'd just discovered.

"So what do you think?"

"Amazing," she answered, going in for a second sip.

"Look at that. You're drinking cat piss like a pro. You don't have to take as long this time, but just keep doing a quicker version of all that and the flavours will just keep opening up." He watched her, a satisfied smile spreading across his face. "It's good, right?"

"I don't mind a cold beer once in a while, but I've never been a huge fan. You have opened my eyes, although I don't know if it'll be a daily drink, I'll certainly be less hesitant to accept one. I bet you could sell beer to a teetotaller."

"I tended bar in the city a few years ago and I've turned a lot of beer virgins into beer-o-crats," he said. "Lots of people would come in on cold days and buy fruity drinks, spritzers, or a margarita to combat their thirst, but I can't think of anything more refreshing than a cold beer with a perfect head on it."

"You were a bartender? Imagine that."

He chuckled, "Oh, that was many moons ago."

"And you lived in the city, too. Do you still live there?"

"Hell no. My wife's father owned the bar I worked at, and as soon as I exed his daughter he gave me the boot. So I moved back to Annapolis, started up at Waldman Construction and I've been there ever since."

He leaned in to her, nudging her shoulder with his. "But enough about me. I'd rather talk about you."

"There's not much to tell."

"It's no secret I think you're beautiful." He held his hand out to touch her arm when she shied away. "Now, now, no need to put your guard up. I know a taken woman when I see one, and I'm not about to try to sweep the rug out from under Ol' Rue's feet, but I have to tell you if he leaves you in the lurch I plan on making my move."

"Aw, you're sweet," she said.

"I'm not aiming for sweet."

"I know." She allowed him to drape an arm around her shoulder. "But Reuben hasn't taken me."

"No, maybe not. But he has you nonetheless, doesn't he?"

Her breath hitched. It had been little more than an hour ago that she'd finally admitted it to herself, but there was no way she could speak it aloud. That would just validate it and give it room to run rampant. She meant to contain it. For now, anyway.

"Nobody has me," she said.

"Well, prove it."

"How can I prove something like that?"

"Let me kiss you?"

She turned her face up to look at his. Maybe this was what she needed, a nice distraction from Reuben. And although it felt like betrayal on every scale imaginable, she answered, "Okay."

He dropped his arm from around her shoulder, placed his bottle on the rail, cupped her face with one hand and drew her to him with the other, his lips seeking hers. As his mouth moved on hers her insides crumbled and her face contorted as tears pushed at her eyelids. And as his tongue probed for entrance, the tears let go and dripped down to break the seal between them.

He moved away, still cupping her face in his hands. "Our first kiss," he said, pushing the tears from her cheeks. "It was nice. You tasted as sweet as I thought you would, even with beer on your lips."

He pulled the sweater up over her shoulder, his hand lingering a moment longer than necessary. "And it wasn't too bad for a last kiss either, if I do say so myself."

He ran a friendly hand down her arm to take her hand. "It's okay. I wasn't expecting you to enjoy it. When you're already taken it's hard to give to someone else, isn't it?"

"I'm sorry," she said, moving away from him.

"Don't be. I already knew the outcome before our lips even touched. I was just being selfish. I can now say I kissed the most beautiful girl in Nova Scotia."

She smiled through her tears and reached out to playfully punch his shoulder. "You're a perpetual flirt, did you know that?"

"Reuben's a lucky man." Kyle moved to retrieve his bottle. "If he's smart, too, he won't let you get away."

He raised his bottle and clicked it against her glass. "Here's to the two of you." A smile tugged at the corner of his mouth. "And what the hell, here's to me, too, because even if you don't think so I'm pretty darn cute."

She laughed, loving the lighter mood he was bringing to a heavy situation.

"Now let's go eat some of that cheese and get shit-faced drunk."

~

Reuben heard a crash. Not a glass breaking kind of crash, more of a thud, and then something tumbling. It was loud enough to wake him, and when he fumbled in the dark for the lamp beside the bed his knuckles smashed into an abrupt wall instead. Where the hell was he?

He turned in the bed, groping for the lamp on the night stand, but instead he hit something and sent it clattering to the floor.

His eyes adjusted to the dark and he caught the brilliant white of a clock face, and the shimmer of the moonlight playing on the wall at the foot of the bed, and it all came flooding back to him. He was in the shack.

He'd only meant to stay for thirty minutes in the hopes that she'd show up, even though she'd already told him no. He had hoped that she'd miss him, and want to be with him. Admittedly he'd been weak; he craved her like an addiction.

He'd tried to stay away, but then Janine kissed him and although his usual protocol would have been to fall into bed with her, he couldn't. He didn't think she would satiate him any longer. Janine's kisses were stale and lifeless; they didn't spark that yearning in him that Penny did.

He hadn't meant to fall asleep. He was just giving her thirty minutes. If she didn't come to the shack he would leave. What time was it anyway?

He held his wrist up the window and squinted to make out the time. 12:38 am.. He flicked the elastic on his wrist, and combed his fingers through his tousled hair.

What had he heard? Swinging his legs out over the side of the bed, he rose, and fumbled his way to the door.

The low rumble of a motor idling sounded. He heard giggling and then, "Whoops."

Although the voice was slurred and more giddy than normal, he recognized it. More awake and aware of his surroundings he went to the night stand, opened the drawer and removed a flashlight. In the beam he could see that he'd dropped a candle to the floor, but he didn't bother picking it up.

Just as he reached the front door and was about to open it, he heard a male voice. "Ah Penny, I think someone's here."

"No one's here. It's pitch black in there. Now help me, would you?" she said, giggling again, her voice straining like she was tugging on something.

"Then what's that vehicle?"

"Help me get this board off the—"

Reuben could hear the abrupt end to her sentence and knew she'd spied his jeep. He'd parked among the trees rather than up close to the cabin so as not to draw attention to it.

He heard something drop and then the crunch of gravel under feet and knew she was moving towards his jeep.

He opened the door, shining the beam of the flashlight into Kyle's eyes.

Across the lot Penny was close to the jeep. "What the hell?" she spat, and kicked the front tire of the jeep. "That bloody asshole brought her here."

She circled around, her steps uncertain. As soon as her eyes locked on to his he saw her face change, and she bounded up the steps to slam her fist into his chest.

"You brought her here?"

"Brought who here?" he asked, blocking her fists as best he could.

"Move," she ordered. "I want to meet her."

"Meet who?"

Penny stopped, her chest heaved with every breath, and her eyes misted over. "This is my friend's cabin, not yours. I didn't give you permission to bring anyone else here."

She tried to put her hands on her hips, but her coordination was off and they kept slipping. "Go get her," she said raising an aimless hand in the direction of the bedroom. "Take her out of here. This was our place. You could have found somewhere else, instead of being a heartless asshole and bringing her here."

Her gesture threw her off balance, and she stumbled backwards. With a quick sure hand Reuben reached out and caught her, twisting her around in his arms so that her back was against him.

"I've got her, Kyle."

Penny thrashed in his arms, but he held her fast.

"She'll be okay, you can go now. Go get some sleep."

"No," Penny yelled. "Leave me, Kyle, don't," she slurred.

Kyle twisted the handle of the wheeler, but didn't leave.

"Just go," Reuben said. "She'll be fine. I'll take care of her and make sure she gets back okay."

"Pen, you'll be okay, right?" Kyle said. Penny just stared at him with glassy eyes.

Kyle lifted his eyes to Reuben's. "You be good to her."

"I'm not the one who got her drunk."

"Ah, trust me, she was going to do that all on her own. I just supervised is all." He revved up to leave. "See you tomorrow morning, Penny," he said and pulled off.

With the two of them alone on the step, Reuben surveyed the damage. She'd crashed the wheeler into the railing and the whole right side had let go. The floor had given way and the log stool had fallen, the railing wedging it and the deck floor tight into the ground.

Her once high ponytail now slouched down crooked on the back of her head like a deflated balloon. He turned her in his arms. "You're a bad drunk."

"I'm not drunk."

She began to wiggle again. This time he let her go, and she bounded off the step to the fallen corner of the deck. She bent awkwardly and wrapped her arms around the log stool, trying to tug it loose.

"What are you doing?"

"The key," she spat, tugging harder.

He watched her fight with the log stool a while longer. "The door's already unlocked."

"I'm taking it," she yelled regaining her strength. He saw the log stool move a bit, and knew if she weren't careful the whole right side of the deck was going to come down on her arms and wedge her under it.

"Taking it? Why?"

"I'm done," she said, sweeping her arms out loosely. Her strength had ebbed away and the arch she meant to make failed into floppy wrist sweeps instead. "I've had enough of you."

He reached into his pocket and pulled out the key. "You're not going to find the key under there. Look."

She looked up at him, her tear-stained cheeks blotchy in the moon-light, and her beautiful blue eyes glistening with unshed tears.

"You want it?" He jiggled the key in the air.

She nodded and reached a hand out.

"Then come get it." He slipped into the shack and killed the flashlight.

"Reuben," he heard her shout as he made his way into the bedroom. He retrieved the candle and secured it in its holder. Locating the matches inside the drawer, he struck one and lit the wick. The soft glow filled the room, and he waited for her.

"Reuben?" She sounded less crazy, her gusto all but gone, and she sniffled.

"If you want the key you have to come get it."

"I can't," she said, her voice tiny.

"Why?"

"Is she in there with you?"

She sounded so fragile and he wondered how much of this she would remember in the morning. "I'm alone, Penny. Now come here."

"Was she in there with you?"

He smiled in the dark. "Who?"

"Janine Newberry," her voice slurred and cracked. "Did you make love to her?"

"I did not bring Janine here."

"Did you make love to her?"

"No. Now will you come here?"

"I can't."

"You can't?"

"I can't walk."

He went to the door. In the shadows he saw her crumpled to the floor.

Crouching beside her he lifted her in his arms and walked her to the bed. He lay her down with as much tenderness as he could, and began to unbutton her jeans. The tiny protest that came from her made him stop.

"You'll sleep better," he said and she dropped her spaghetti arms. He eased the jeans down over her hips, pulled the sandals from her feet, and dropped the jeans to the floor. Then he removed his own jeans and slipped in beside her.

Pulling the blanket up around them, he drew her close and gently slipped the elastic from her hair, adding it to the one already on his wrist.

"Did you ever make love to her?" She asked in a whisper against his chest.

"Never," he whispered, stroking her hair and letting her meld into the contours of his chest, and then because he doubted she'd remember in the morning he said, "I'm holding the only woman I ever want to make love to."

He heard her deep sigh of relief and the unmistakable smile in her voice. "Good," she said, and settled down for sleep.

14

Reuben was no stranger to morning wood. It came with the man suit he was born in, but waking up with a beautiful woman beside him had become a foreign concept, and his morning wood seemed a bit too happy to have her there.

Immensely happy was more like it as it throbbed against Penny's ass, loving the warmth and softness of her body. Usually he could mentally talk himself down, but today the mental coaxing was acting as an aphrodisiac and he could bounce pennies off the taut skin at the tip if he so desired.

Penny wore a zippered cardigan, and he slowly inched the zipper down so he could let the cardigan fall open. She wore a green tank top beneath, and a lacy beige bra peeked out from the top of the tank.

He tucked his hands around her, and gently tugged her closer, burying his face in her hair, groaning deeply. He wanted her to wake up and comply with his advances.

Would she even remember how she'd gotten there? He doubted it. It didn't matter; all that mattered was that she was here, rather than in Kyle's bed, where she could very well have ended up.

That thought made his blood boil, which didn't help his erect condition. He flicked his tongue out tasting the skin at the nape of her neck, and then closing his lips down over his tongue, drew the damp skin up into his mouth.

She stirred in his arms, but didn't awaken, just turned slightly, breaking the suction of his lips on her skin, and he caught her lips with his instead. She didn't respond as he kissed her, but the soft whimper that escaped her throat set him even further on eruption's edge.

He had never made love to her in the morning light and the blood thrummed in his veins at the mere thought. The shack was flooded with sunlight now, and a streak stretched across the bed to lick at her neck and kiss her face. It was a different atmosphere and he wanted to make love to her in all the atmospheres the earth had to offer. This morning he wanted to see the sunbeams dance over her naked skin, and watch her move atop him in the full glow of the day, the streaks of the sun washing over her naked breasts and kissing the soft velvet tips of her nipples.

And he would be jealous of the sun and follow its lead. Kissing, licking, and suckling every inch of her skin that the warm morning reached. Ravishing her like he'd never ravished her before.

She'd come last night for the key. Would she wake up with that same mind set? Would she still want to be done with him? Or was that just the drink talking? Did her obvious jealousy for Janine make her do rash things that she would never have done otherwise? He hoped so, but he had to keep an open mind nonetheless, just in case.

He'd sort of lied to her. Sort of. Although he and Janine were lovers he'd never made love to her. She was just a friend who helped him on long nights when he was in the Valley or she was in the city, it was an unspoken rule: they fucked with no strings attached, and that's all it ever was for him. She was a means to an end.

The thought didn't make him happy. He'd used Janine, but it had went both ways. She used him, too. She never expected anything more, and she was blunt enough to tell him so if she had.

Penny was different. He tried to pretend otherwise, but he knew. Deep down he knew. This was not a game for her, even if she tried to tell herself it was. She just wasn't the type to with-benefits anything. She was a keeper, and she gave to get.

He knew that, even if he tried to tell himself it would all work out in the end. It wasn't fair to her, and it made him feel like an ass. On top of that he couldn't just hurt her and walk away forever. She would be family now. His step-sister, even if they both swore they would never be step-anything no matter who married who.

She shifted in his arms and rolled unto her back, one arm tossed up over her head. He shifted too, lacing his fingers with hers. She was a delicacy he had no right to tarnish. Everything about her was perfect. The way her fingers slid perfectly into the webs of his fingers. The soft golden skin of her hand against his darker skin just seemed so perfectly matched. She was too much for him. Her softness against his hardened body balanced him. Did he want to be balanced? Was balanced so great? He'd been doing fine living slightly askew, and then there she was, and everything about her made him a better person.

He rolled the blanket off her, letting the sun wash over her. Leaning up on his elbow he looked at her. Her hips jutted out under the band of her panties and the hem of her tank top stretched taut against her rib cage.

Shifting against her, he lifted the tank and strummed his tongue softly against her ribs. *A delicacy he had no right to tarnish.* Those words rolled over and over in his mind as he allowed his mouth to slip to one hipbone. He closed his teeth over her hip with a slight pressure but felt her move under him. *A delicacy he had no right to tarnish.*

He lifted his head and let his eyes take the exotic trip up over her hips, across her taut stomach to the gentle swell of her breast, along the graceful slope of her neck and chin line, to her parted lips. And then up to her eyes.

He hadn't expected then to be open, but his brown ones met her blue and he inhaled deeply at the intense pull.

"What are you doing?"

"Looking at you," he said, a smile toying at the corners of his mouth. He felt her fingers tighten on his. "Is that okay?"

She shook her head no.

"No?"

"No."

"Why?"

"I'm done." She didn't bother to move.

"Seriously?"

She just stared at him.

"Well, I'm not."

"It was never supposed to be a mutual agreement, Reuben, remember?"

"Why now?"

"And we were never obligated to give a reason why, either."

"I want one anyway."

She shrugged. "Things changed."

"What things?"

"Just things, is all."

"Kyle?" He hated the anger that surged in him and punctuated his words.

"Kyle?" She laughed. "Kyle's my friend."

"Tell that to him, I'm not sure he knows it."

"Jealousy isn't very becoming on you," she said and lifted her free hand to wipe the sleep from her eyes. He moved to take it, pushing it above her head, as he positioned himself over her.

"Are you going to force me now?"

"No." He looked down at his throbbing member, stretching against the cotton of his briefs. "Don't do this to me Penny," he hated that he was begging, but he was aching for her, and he really needed to end this.

"Just because you want me doesn't mean I want you, Reuben," she said and he hated how straight and even she managed to keep her voice.

"You want me," he said, pushing in to her. "You're just on some stubborn high ground, trying to act tough."

"It's not an act." She bucked against him, trying to put space between them.

He repositioned his hands so that both of hers was in one of his, and moved his free hand down between them to slip beneath her panties. He didn't even have to dip inside her to feel how wet she was for him. The juices had already spilled out of her and soaked her panties.

"Oh, you want me," he said, tracing a finger over her opening gently. He felt her quiver beneath him, and laughed. "You want me."

"I don't."

He returned his hand to its original position, the wetness on his fingers making it easy to slip her fingers within his.

"Don't do this to me," he said reaching down to place his forehead to hers. He moved his legs to spread hers open. "Please."

"So what are you going to do now, fuck me anyway?"

He flinched, her callousness piercing like a dagger into his heart. "Don't say that."

"Don't say what?"

"It doesn't sound good on your lips."

She gritted her teeth, and bucked her pelvis into him, trying to push him off. When he didn't budge she sneered up into his face, lifting her head from the pillow, "Fuck, fuck, fuck."

His movements were quick as he released her to grab her head in his hands. He hadn't meant to kiss her so hard, but his lips moved roughly on hers, crushing her lips into her teeth. She took advantage of the situation and before he knew it she'd whipped him around so she was straddling him. She shimmied down the length of him and pulled his trembling member from his underwear. Her curtain of blond hair fell over her shoulders and tickled his abdomen.

He looked down at her, positioned over his groin. He throbbed in her hands, and for a second she just let him. Then slowly she closed her hands around him and began to move them up and down.

"No, not like this," he said, reaching for her, but she increased her hold and her strokes and he fell back against the bed, writhing, until he couldn't hold back any longer and released his load against her palm, spilling out unto his stomach.

And then she released him, reached up and wiped her hands down his t-shirt. She slid from the bed, retrieved her jeans and quickly slipped them on. Lifting his jeans from the floor, she rooted around in the pockets until she came up with the key.

He watched her from the bed, anything but satiated. "Don't."

At first she just stood there, looking at him, her breathing a little heavier than it should have been, and her shoulders slightly shaking. When she spoke her voice cracked. "I'm done." She bit her trembling lip and shook her head. "Kyle says after this weekend, you'll no longer be needed. So I guess this will be the last time I see you like this."

She sniffed and ran her knuckles under her nose. "When I return, you'll be gone, and that will be a good thing. Dad and Gyla probably won't marry for at least another month or so, that will give me plenty of time to get use to being without you."

"Where are you going?"

"Away."

He set up, reaching for her. "But I wanted to show you something first."

"What?"

"In the woods. There's something I want to show you."

"I've been all through the woods, Reuben. I've seen it all."

"But not this, I promise, it's too far off the path. You'd have to be looking for it to actually find it."

"You found it."

"Because it was my job to find it." He slipped from the bed, adjusted his underwear and grabbed his jeans.

"I don't want to do this anymore."

"Then tell me what you do want."

"I want what you can't give me, Reuben."

She moved from the bedroom.

"You want me to love you?" he asked, and she turned around, sadness etched in her eyes. "Fine, I'll love you. Done. Done."

Her smile was weak, and he knew she was winning.

"It doesn't work like that."

He followed her into the main room, zipping up and hooking the button. "What doesn't work like that? I'm fucking trying, Penny."

She turned at the doorway and bent to fasten her sandals. When she stood again her eyes were brimming with tears. "You shouldn't have to try."

She opened the door and stepped out unto the slanted porch, then turned and stared at him for a long time. For a moment he thought she was going to bolt, but she rushed back to him and reached up to plant her hands on his shoulders.

"I have to do this, because having *this*," she motioned to the bedroom, "And not *this*," she laid her hand over his heart, "just isn't working for me. And while you're trying to love me, I'm busy trying *not* to love you."

Hot tears rolled down her cheeks. "I broke my promise to you when I said I would never love you, because I do. I don't want to, because you're pigheaded and heartless, but I do. I got a glimpse of who you really are, if you could throw away that asshole cape you insist on wearing, and I fell in love with you against my better judgment. But I've loved and lost before and it didn't kill me."

She reached up to plant a kiss on his cheek. "I'll be fine." She sniffled, wiped her eyes and pushed the tears from her face. And then she tried to stand tall, tried to look tough for him. "I'll be fine, I promise, and so will you."

She reached up on her tiptoes and touched her lips to his. He moved his mouth to deepen the kiss, but she moved away. "I suspect I'll see you at the wedding. You take care of yourself," she said, standing ramrod straight. "But please stay away until then, please."

"That's it?"

"Please?"

"Okay," he said.

She smiled half-heartedly.

"So that's it, then?"

"Yeah." She moved to the door, and didn't stop as she ran down the steps, threw her leg over the wheeler and started the engine. "I love you."

He couldn't hear her over the engine, but he saw her mouth the words. And then, just like that, she was gone.

He wanted to scream at her that he loved her, too, but he didn't. She was right, he was an asshole, and *she was a delicacy he had no right to tarnish.*

15

Certain that everything was successfully taken care of, Penny locked up the distillery and palmed the keys in order to better juggle the three empty dessert bowls she carried.

Her steps faltered as she neared the front door of her cottage, and she contemplated leaving. Regardless of the silent scream inside her head telling her to put the bowls back in the distillery, she raised her hand and knocked.

Gyla opened the door. "Oh dear, this is your home, you don't need to knock." Gyla gestured her inside, and took the bowls from her. "I was wondering where those were."

"I'm sorry. I should have told you I'd taken them." She scratched awkwardly at her eyebrow to hide her fluster.

There had been three ice cream encounters on the basement stairs. Heated encounters that lasted no more than five minutes. Just enough time to give her the prelude to coming attractions without Ember and Terra coming to look for him. The ice cream was delicious, but it wasn't necessarily the main attraction to her late afternoon trips up the back stairs.

"No you shouldn't have," Gyla said opening a cupboard and placing them beside three identical bowls. "This is your home, you can take whatever you'd like."

"I brought them downstairs the day I watched the girls and I just forgot to mention it." What was she doing? This was not a great way to start a relationship with her father's fiancé. Wasn't it enough that she'd lied, now she had to go and cement the lie, too?

"Well the girls will be happy. They've been playing 'find daddy's bowl' for a few days now. Now maybe they'll stop upturning all the cushions and rummaging through everything in a bid to be the 'winner'." Gyla laughed, "So far neither of them have succeeded. I don't know what got it in their heads that he'd hidden them. They do concoct the craziest theories when something goes missing."

Penny's laugh was stilted, but Gyla didn't seem to notice. "Also I wanted to bring you these." She held the distillery keys out. "The door to the back stairs does lock from up here but I've also latched it from the other side as an extra precaution in case the girls get curious. I don't want them falling down the stairs onto that cement floor. So keep these in case you need to get into the basement for whatever reason."

Gyla took the keys and looked at Penny skeptically. "Are you okay, dear?"

Penny tried to coax her smile into her eyes. "I'm completely fine."

"Spencer told me you were leaving for the weekend. I hope we haven't done anything to scare you away."

Penny leaned forward and squeezed Gyla's hand. "Of course not. You've been amazing, and I've fallen head over heels in love with Ember and Terra."

She looked around. A carton of crayons sat on the table next to a couple colouring pads, and several coloured pictures adorned the fridge. Ember's Lacey doll was asleep on the floor in the sun room, a rolled-up hand towel beneath her head and another draped over her, blank eyes staring up to the ceiling. Small cardigans hung on pegs by the door. From where she stood she could see the new swing-lid swear jars, colourfully designed and decorated by herself and the twins. "Ah, the swear jars really stand out. They did a splendid job on them."

"Thanks so much for doing that," Gyla walked further into the room, crossed to the mantel and lifted Reuben's jar. "You'll also notice Reuben's potty mouth hasn't improved much, either. Just this morning he had to pay for three swears." She shook her head disappointedly. "He's been especially testy these last couple days. Maybe being in the woods has finally driven him stir crazy."

She sat the jar back on the mantel. "But I doubt it, he tells me being here has rejuvenated him, and has made him long to return to his roots, but still something is eating at him that I can't quite put my finger on." She talked more to herself, and as though she remembered she had company she stopped abruptly and looked up, a smile on her face.

"And what of Reuben?" she asked.

"Excuse me?"

"Well, you've told me how you feel about me and the girls, but what of Reuben?"

What of Reuben? That was a far more difficult question to answer. If she were honest she'd tell Reuben's mom how much she loved her son, and that having spent the last twenty-four hours without seeing him or touching him had been pure hell for her. But she wouldn't say that. It was not something anyone needed to know, the outcome would still be the same no matter who she told, and telling others would not help her plans of letting him go.

"We've learned to get along," she said instead.

A huge smile spread across Gyla's face, and she stepped forward to pull Penny into her arms. "I'm so happy to hear that. That's all I could ask for. Sometimes learning to tolerate a person can open up a whole new arena."

She stepped back, her hands still holding Penny at arm's length. "That was my goal, getting you two to tolerate one another." She squeezed Penny gently. "And Reuben's been kind to you?"

Penny stiffened. "Sure," she said and conjured a smile from somewhere.

"He hasn't racked up any debts I need to report to the swear jar minions?"

Penny laughed and shook her head.

"Good. I raised him to be a good man, and although he does some questionable things at times, like any other human on this planet, for the most part he always makes me proud."

Penny's heart swelled at the delight in Gyla's eyes. She herself was fast learning that no matter how much you love a person they don't always do what you want them to do. No matter how much you love them, they don't always love you in return.

"I really have to get going. Are the girls still in bed? I had hoped to say goodbye."

"They're actually up and gone already."

"Really?"

"Reuben put them to bed early last night in order to round them up and have them out the door before seven."

"Oh." Penny tried not to show her disappointment. "Well that's good then."

"They're visiting family in the Valley today."

"Oh," was all Penny could manage. "I'll be going, then. Please be sure to kiss them for me and tell them I'll miss them, but that I'll see them soon."

Even as she said it she felt the tears stinging the back of her eyelids. She turned to leave, but as her hand rested on the doorknob Gyla stopped her in her tracks.

"And what should I tell Reuben?"

"Excuse me?" she didn't turn.

"He makes lovely ice cream, doesn't he?"

She turned to look at Gyla, her brow furrowed and tears hung heavy on her lids.

Gyla's eyes held so much sympathy, and her smile was weak. "It's only been fifteen months for him, and his heart isn't sorted out yet."

Penny pinched her lips tightly together in a bid to stave off the tears, but the shake of her head sent them slipping down her cheeks just the same.

"He just needs more time." She stepped forward and cupped Penny's face in her hands. "I've nursed that boy through far too many hangovers to know that he didn't go out drinking with the boys every night like he said he did."

She spread her thumbs across Penny's face to wipe the tears away. "It took me a moment longer than normal to piece it all together, I'm getting old and my noggin doesn't work as well as it once did, but I watched him, and it didn't take me long to see it. The missing bowls, the sneaking out and lying to me, and then slipping in in the wee hours of the night and sometimes nearly daybreak. And then one morning I saw him go into the distillery and that smile on his face when he came out was all the evidence I needed." She reached up to kiss Penny's forehead. "For what it's worth, I'm sorry he hurt you."

"He hasn't hurt me," Penny lied.

"Honey, it's written all over your face. I knew from the moment I lay eyes on you at that door that he'd hurt you good and proper." She raised a finger. "He's my son, and because of that I am allowed to say that he's an asshole."

Penny snorted despite herself.

"He had no right to do this to you, and I don't mean to give you false hope, and God help me if I'm wrong, but I know my son. I know that when he takes a lover he doesn't go through hoops and leaps to protect her, but he did that for you, and that has to say something."

"I'm fine," Penny insisted. "And I really have to go."

She pulled from Gyla's hold and moved to the door.

"Don't give up on him, Penny-Laine."

She hesitated in the open doorway, unsure what to say, and then she turned around. "You're wrong. He didn't hurt me. I did that all on my own. I demanded a set of rules, and then when I couldn't stick to them, I took it out on him."

"The heart doesn't abide by rules, my dear."

Penny closed her eyes and let the sting of those words wash over her. "I broke the rules. However you'll be happy to know, your perfect son abided by them nicely."

She tried to laugh, but the laugh caught on a sob and muffled out. "And why not? A no-strings-attached-booty-call less than five minutes away sure beats having to drive three hours like he's been doing."

"You are not a booty call," Gyla said sternly. "Do you think this hasn't hurt my son, too?"

"Well I'm sorry for that," Penny yelled and reached to slam the door closed behind her.

She was nearly down the steps when Gyla caught her arm and stopped her. "Don't go like this. Come inside for a moment and take a breather."

Penny let her lead her up the steps, across the deck and back inside the cabin. Gyla bent to untie and remove the canvas shoes from Penny's feet, and then she drew her to a chair at the table.

Penny wept quietly at the table as Gyla busied herself preparing tea, and then she set a steaming mug before Penny. A flower-shaped diffuser sprouted up from the middle.

"Do you know what I learned from you, Penny?"

Penny looked up, tears and snot running together, and took the napkin Gyla handed her.

"The night I stepped from that jeep and smelled all that lavender, I had such a calm come over me. And then I met you for the first time. Do you remember that?"

Penny sniffled and swished the infuser around in the water. She smiled through the bleariness. "You came to the basement to invite me for dinner."

Gyla smiled. "Your Dad told me so much about you. How you persevered after your husband died and had made this great little business for yourself, and in all honesty I was intimidated. I don't know what I was expecting, but when I saw you behind that desk, and you were just a little thing, I knew I hadn't been expecting that. I think I was expecting a female version of Spencer, in physique anyway."

She laughed. "And you were so gracious and friendly, not to mention beautiful. Suddenly Land of Lavendula had a face, and it was you. You were the perfect face for all of this beautifulness and fragrance. A completely perfect example of tranquility."

She looked out the window over the sink, the breeze ruffling her hair. "I looked at you and all of this and I knew that even through the craziness that life throws at us we can weather anything and come out shining all the more beautifully because of it, and on top of that still manage to be humble and gracious. You showed me that. I got all of that from just looking at you. What does that say about you?"

She sat down across from Penny with her own mug of tea and matching flower infuser. "That tells me that you are a force to be reckoned with."

She lifted her infuser up and down in the water. "I'm not sure if you're familiar with the poet Dylan Thomas, but he wrote an especially beautiful poem and when I saw you and how self-assured you were I thought of that poem. You 'do not go gentle into that good night'. Life threw dirt at you and what did you do? You raged on. You made a lavender garden. A business. You persevered."

The two woman sipped their tea, a quiet calm settled over the room and the smell of lavender hung thick between them.

"Now, I want to tell you a little about Reuben, if you'll allow me to."

"Okay." Penny's voice sounded small to her own ears. She hated feeling this helpless. She hated that she needed the gentle assurance of the older woman, but Gyla made it easy to accept it anyway.

"Although I do have a front row seat, for the most part I don't interfere in his private life. At least I try not to, but I have occasionally stepped in when he is spiralling out of control. I don't rebuke him; I just calmly explain to him what I am seeing and suggest ways for him to fix it."

She sipped cautiously from her steaming mug. "I am his mom after all and I can't just sit back and watch him self-destruct. Moms are notorious for their meddling ways. Someday you'll experience that first hand, but for now just take my word for it."

Penny had long ago given up on the idea of a baby, but still the mention of one sent a flutter through her. Would she be the meddling kind of mom? A helicopter mom? Had her own mom been meddlesome? She couldn't seem to remember. She'd ask Warren, maybe he'd remember. Did she dare hope for a baby again?

She'd opened herself up to Reuben. Could she open herself up to another man, too? The thought sickened her. She didn't want another man as long as Reuben monopolized her thoughts.

What would a mixture of her and Reuben look like? She wondered if their baby would look like Ember and Terra, with dark hair and eyes, and dark skin? They seemed to favour their dad. But then she didn't know what Eve had looked like.

"What did Eve look like?"

She hadn't realized she'd spoken that aloud, nor had she realized that Gyla had been talking until the unfinished sentence hung obvious in the air between them.

"I'm sorry," Penny was quick to apologize. "Oh, God, you said something earlier and I just got lost in thought." She clamped her hands over her face to hide her shame. "I'm so sorry."

Gyla laughed. "Stop apologizing, Penny." She reached across the table to urge Penny's hands down from her face. "There. Now where did I lose you?"

"Oh, God I don't know, I'm so sorry."

"Let's back track, I was explaining to you about my strategies for pulling Reuben from the edge."

"It was a baby." Penny's voice was low.

"What?"

"You mentioned a baby, and my mind just took off." Penny settled her chin into the cup of her palm, a blush creeping into her cheeks.

Gyla rolled her eyes trying to back track her conversation to pinpoint the mention of a baby. "I didn't mention a baby, did I?"

"No, you didn't. God this is embarrassing." Penny closed her eyes and shifted awkwardly as she squeezed her forehead, trying to work away the embarrassment. "You said someday I'd know what it was like to be a meddling mom, and zap, my mind just ran with it." She cupped a hand over her mouth and looked up bashfully at Gyla.

Gyla beamed from behind her cup. "Reuben makes beautiful babies, doesn't he? Ember has Eve's personality and every so often I'll see an expression cross Terra's face that looks just like her mom, but those girls are cut right out of Reuben."

She twisted her head to the side to study Penny, and then reaching over she ran a hand down Penny's golden hair. "Reuben was such a beautiful boy and his genes are strong, but I'd take a little blond haired boy, too." She gleamed at Penny. "Whatever you can give me, I can work with, darling."

Penny sat back in her chair. "Oh God, this is crazy. I certainly wasn't implying that I'd have a child with Reuben."

"Weren't you?"

"No" She stood up and circled her arms around her middle. Her stomach doing flip flops, not out of repulsion, but rather out of glee, and she was appalled at herself for letting some silly fantasy work her up like this. "No."

Gyla chuckled. "Don't get so worked up. Sit back down and finish your tea."

Still holding her stomach protectively, as though she expected Gyla to do some voodoo on her that would plant a baby into her womb if she let her guard down, she sat down.

Gyla removed the diffuser from her own mug and placed it on a napkin in order to sip the remaining drops of her tea. "Whether you have babies with my son or not, you are going to be a fabulous mother when the time comes, and it will be a privilege to watch you raise them."

Penny breathed a sigh of relief. "Thank you, but I've already given up on the idea of children. I'm thirty-three, and not getting any younger."

"You've got plenty of time. My mother was in her forties when she gave birth to me." She took her cup to the sink.

"Would you finish your story?"

Gyla cocked her head, "My story?"

"You were telling me a little about Reuben."

"Ah, yes," Gyla sat back down, a far-away look in her eyes. "Now where was I?" She tapped her finger tips together as she tried to remember. "I remember now. I don't interfere with Reuben and his private life. It's called private for a reason. So I am not going to sit here and give you a rundown of his past relationships. I just think that, for you, and I don't say this because I am about to marry your father, but because I can tell you've fallen in love with my son—"

Penny made a motion to protest but Gyla closed a hand over hers.

"I just think you need a little more to help you understand my son a bit better. I have no doubt that in the last three weeks you've gotten to know him on a level I never could. I appreciate that what a mother knows and what a lover knows can be entirely different, and I also understand the rose-coloured glasses mothers tend to wear when viewing their children. I have tried on several occasions to take those glasses off and look at Reuben a little more critically than I normally would. I don't know what's happened between you two, but I sense that he's hurt you. I am not going to pry. I think you are both capable of working things out between you on your own, but I want you to know that the last few days have been rough on Reuben. He's testy and grumpy, and restless, too."

"He's not sleeping well?"

"I was up at two last night and he'd fallen asleep on the couch."

"But he was up early this morning."

"That he was," Gyla said. "I tried to talk him into sleeping a bit longer this morning, but he insisted on sticking with the plan."

"Has he checked in to let you know he's okay?"

"He will," Gyla smiled. "I suspect they've made it just fine, or else his Uncle would have called to check on him by now."

"He's gone to visit family?"

"A few family members on the Lafford side are home from Ontario. They'll have a more formal reunion with the whole lot next weekend, but Reuben wanted the girls to meet their cousins before that. Uncle Bernie's son, Elden, is home, too, with his children. Reuben and Elden were best friends growing up, so Reuben was really looking forward to seeing him again. They'll be back around supper."

Penny wondered about Reuben's family. If things had been different would he have invited her along? If she hadn't screwed the whole thing up by telling him she loved him would he have taken her with them? Of course not, she scolded herself. That would have broken all the rules in one fell swoop.

"That's nice," she said around the lump lodged in her throat.

"When Reuben was a teenager, he had a gaggle of girls flocking after him. I would be lying if I said he didn't like the attention, because he did. What young boy wouldn't love that? But Reuben didn't date any of them. Instead, there was a girl next door who just saw Reuben as a simple boy; it may have been because they'd grown up together. She certainly wasn't the kind of girl I'd have chosen for him, but he liked her. I think it was mostly due to the fact that she didn't make a fool out of herself around him. Instead she fished and hunted with him, and wasn't afraid to get her hands dirty. She had her own dirt bike, and preferred hanging with the boys rather than the girls. They just got along, and she didn't trip over her tongue every time she saw him."

"Why didn't you like her?"

"Oh I liked Janine just fine, and I still do, but I saw right through her."

The muscles in Penny's stomach clenched. How could she compete with that? Reuben and Janine had history; all she and Reuben had were a few weeks of incredible sex.

"Janine was so smitten with Reuben. She loved all those things because he loved them. My hope for Reuben was that he would find someone who could love him and still be true to herself. People have some weird idea that a relationship only works if both people have so much in common. The truth is opposites attract, and they have a way of balancing a relationship."

Penny finished off her tea, and rose to take the mug to the sink.

"Take Eve, for example. She and Reuben were as different as day and night. She was flashy and showy, loud, and very social. Reuben was the complete opposite, but when they were together they just synced up. Everything worked in harmony. She pulled him out and he pulled her in, and the opposing pulls just balanced nicely. Not to mention how much they loved one another. You couldn't walk into a room with them there and not feel it. You could tell this one was going to play out until the end, but the big guy upstairs had other plans. I wish it wasn't so, but when he makes a move you just have to go with it."

"The same was true of me and David," Penny said. "He was very social, and, well, I wanted to live in the woods." She laughed. "He followed me, but he kept me active in the real world, and I kept him grounded. At least that's what he always told me."

Gyla glanced over her shoulder to the wedding picture on the wall. "He was handsome."

"He was amazing. He had such a love for life. He wanted children more than anything."

Penny walked to the picture and ran a finger down David's face. "We'd finished the house, and he'd just gotten a part-time teaching job. I had a meagre half-acre lavender garden then, and the idea of it being success- ful was just a dream. So we thought we should wait until things were a little more permanent."

She swiped her hands over her cheeks and turned back to Gyla. "I wish we hadn't decided that."

Gyla moved beside her and wrapped an arm around her shoulders. "We shouldn't fret over things that are out of our control."

Penny turned into Gyla's arms and let herself be held. "I didn't mean to fall in love with Reuben."

Gyla laughed. "The tension between you two at dinner that first day was sharp enough to cut glass, and Spencer had already told me about the coffee incident on his deck. I thought I was going to have my work cut out to get you two to even tolerate each other."

She held Penny at arms length. "I should have known. Love works in mysterious ways."

"He's already told me he can never love me," Penny whispered.

"Of course he did, because that is what Reuben does." Gyla smiled warmly, and shook her head. "He lies."

16

Penny ran a finger over the fine stitching. The raised green fronds and brilliantly-coloured fuchsias had caught her attention even before Joe pulled them from the tote. She hadn't come here for new drapes, but by the way these were flirting with her she was almost certain they'd be going home with her just the same.

"Those are late 1920s and unhung," Joe tempted her.

"They're beautiful."

"Well, you can't beat the price." Joe reached behind to take another swatch of fabric from the tote.

It was like being in heaven, and Penny's eyes danced over the swatches, bolts, and bundles. She flipped through a swatch book and fingered the tiny squares of beautiful textiles.

"Everything's beautiful," she said running her hand down a silk fold of green and yellow fabric. "It always makes me wonder why they were just stored and never used, especially the mint pieces like this." Her fingers traced the fronds and fuchsias.

"Did I ever tell you the story of how I come to have such a lovely collection of fabrics?"

"Oh, Joe, don't bore the young lady." The woman arranging things on the tables swatted Joe playfully on the shoulder. "She came here to browse and shop, not for one of your story hours."

Penny smiled at the gentle banter between the two. "No, that's okay. I'd love to hear the story."

"You just keep arranging this mess and let me get on with my business, woman," Joe said, and then turned to the side to pull more fabric from the tote. "Don't mind Margaret. She's spent the last forty-seven years trying to make me shut my mouth and it hasn't worked yet."

"Forty-eight years," Margaret said.

"It's forty-seven," he whispered to Penny. "The first year she was actually a nice person."

"I heard that," Margaret hissed. Then she turned to Penny. "I thought I was marrying a man, he had me good and fooled for about a year. I had no choice but to treat him like a child after that. Crazy man frolics around everyday like he's a prized stallion and it's show day at the farm."

Penny loved the easy camaraderie between the two. It made her heart happy. She'd seen this kind of comfortable love before between her mom and dad. It was a rare kind of find. Rarer still than the beautiful fabrics covering the table before her. Her dad had Gyla now, and although Gyla would never take the place of her mother, she couldn't deny that their love seemed like the comfortable kind of love too.

Joe continued rearranging fabric on the table while he talked, his thin hands giving each swatch and bolt the utmost attention. "My dad bought all the old stock from several fabrics and notions stores that sold out during the great depression."

Penny looked at him, unable to hide the doubt in her eyes, and he lifted his palms upright. "I swear that with God as my witness. He did it because he could. He'd already been very successful with his own business, but with prices plummeting no one was spending money any more, and a lot of little businesses went under. My dad had the money and he saw a chance to invest. He was of the mind that although times were hard, they wouldn't stay that way forever, and in the meantime he was getting by better than most without ever having to touch his savings. What little money people were spending on clothing they were spending at Harris's Haberdashery. Makes sense, if you think about it. Those new business had yet to make a reputation for themselves, but Harris's was already a name people knew and trusted. He was looking to double or triple the payback on his little investment."

Joe laid a hand on a bolt of cloth as if touching something sacred. "My dad was a lifesaver for some of them, although, truth be told, he was taking them for pennies on the dime, but a bail-out's a bail-out is how they saw it. Rather than fold in with the banks they wanted to walk away with good names and their pride as intact as possible."

Joe raised a finger and shook it as he pounded the point home, "Pride is as loud a beggar as want and a great deal more saucy." He dropped his hand again and straightened out a silk narrow cloth along the side of the table. "It was Ben Franklin that said that, and truer words have never been spoken. A man's pride can sometimes make or break him. So my dad bought them out, lock, stock, and barrel."

He bent to fish around in the tote again. "But he didn't live to see the return on his investments, not fully anyway, and although mom handed the shop reins over to my Uncle Si she kept a lot of the stock my dad had bought."

He lifted a bundle from the tote and set it gently on the table, working at the ties binding it. "But she had no use for it and it just sat there, and then when she passed on I inherited the whole kit and kaboodle."

The ties fell aside and he carefully began peeling away the paper protecting the bolt of cloth. "I believe, young lady, this is what you're looking for." He pulled back the last sheet of paper, presenting her with the Manuel Canovas Toile fabric she'd been eyeing on his website.

Penny's heart skipped a beat. The orange popped out from the fabric much more vibrantly than she had expected. The pictures on the website did not do it even a quarter justice. There was much to be said for good lighting and, truth be told, the pictures on Auld Antique Geezer's website were dull and lifeless.

He placed the fabric in her hands as gently as if it were a newborn baby. "Now this bolt of fabric right here is not from my father's collection. I bought it at an estate sale. I thought it was ugly as sin, but that's where my Margaret comes in handy."

The old man reached back to squeeze his wife's hand fondly. "She was born into a farming family, but you'd think, of the two of us, she was the one born to a haberdasher." He pulled his wife to his side and hugged her gently. "This caught her eye. She recognized the work instantly, and she insisted we buy it. She did take five yards of it for herself and sewed up a pair of curtains from it, and that left me with the twenty you see here."

"And your website says you won't sell by the yard. Can I convince you to change your mind?"

The old man scratched his head and looked the bolt up and down. Margaret coughed beside him and Joe looked up. Penny caught the warning look even as the older woman feigned another cough into her upper sleeve.

"Well, I'd much prefer to sell the whole thing straight out if I'm honest."

"At the price you're asking that's just under one hundred eighteen a yard. What if I buy five yards at one hundred thirty a yard? If you continue to sell it at one hundred eighteen a yard you're still going to get a good chunk of pocket change, and you get the added bonus of not having to wrap it or ship it."

"That's one thirty plus taxes, right? I still have to pay taxes even if you don't."

Penny looked at the drapes as she rolled the figures around in her head. "Okay, I'll do the plus-taxes for the fabric, but you have to give me the drapes for two fifty. Two fifty, taxes in. That'll put us at an even thousand. Deal?"

Joe's eyes lit up, but she quickly saw him tone down the excitement and look at Margaret for approval.

"I came here all the way from Digby County just to see your collection, but I want to shop around at the other vendors too. If you make me blow all my money here at your table, I'm not going to be able to give the others a fair chance, and I'm eyeing up a pair of crocheted floral square pillow tops a few tables down." Penny pointed across the room. "Depending on your price and how much money I've been swindled out of after I make my rounds, I may return and buy that swatch book from you. No wheeling and dealing, just a straight-out buy, asking price plus taxes."

Joe chanced a sideways glance at Margaret and she nodded, giving Joe reason to light up again. Penny suddenly realized that Margaret was probably the backbone of the business. She was like the silent partner, the bigwig hiding in the background while Joe did all the talking. It made sense because Penny had noticed that Joe's eyes grew a little wider at the mention of any kind of money, and without Margaret he'd probably take low ball offers on everything without waiting for the high rollers.

Joe extended his hand. "You've got yourself a deal."

The place was bustling already despite the early hour, and Penny found time slipping away as she became so engrossed in the vintage displays. She was nearing the end of her circle-round when she spotted a table adorned with First Nations knickknacks. It was the vegetable dye rug with subtle band colourings and simple geometric figures that caught her eye.

As she fingered the rug, she noticed a child at the end of the table with a shallow wooden dish. Inside the dish were six disk shaped dice. In the child's hand were a series of sticks. He gently moved the bowl, and the disks moved from side to side, but didn't flip, just gently rocked on their rounded bottoms.

Penny watched as the woman behind the table demonstrated the game to the child by thumping the dish down hard on the table. The disks bounced and danced and when they settled four lay upturned, their rounded ends facing up. She took the sticks from his hand and thumbed through them, removing two rounded sticks from the pile. The child smiled hugely and the woman beckoned for him to do the same. The dish came down with a wild thump, and only 1 of the rounded bottoms pointed upward. The little boy clapped in glee when the woman presented him with a stick with arrow fletching.

It didn't take the child long to lose interest and move on, and when he did the lady took the game and placed it further back on the table to discourage too much exploring by eager hands.

"That was interesting, I've never seen this game before," she said to the woman.

"It was popular among the mi'kmaqs many moons ago," the woman said. "But it's making a comeback now. My grandchildren have taken a shine to it since the last Aboriginal day festivities."

"Does it have a name?" Penny lifted the shallow dish and ran her fingers over the decorated dice.

"Waltes."

"How do you play it?"

"It's really simple. You slam the bowl down hard, then count the dice that are decorated side up. Any die facing up is worth a point, you get a simple stick for each die pointing up, but for five pointing up you get a feather stick, and for six you get an arrow."

Penny wondered about Ember and Terra. Had they ever played waltes? Sure, she'd sworn off a sexual relationship with Reuben, but he would be her family now by marriage whether she liked it or not, and that meant she would get to have a relationship with his girls.

It was a highlight of the joining of the McCall and Lafford family. She'd fallen in love with the girls from the first time Terra wrapped herself around her leg. And better yet, the feelings seemed to be mutual. Even though she would never be a true step-sister to Reuben, she already knew she'd be the perfect aunt to the girls.

She suddenly really wanted to buy the game. After a long passage of polite dickering over the prices, she left with the game and the rug. She was grateful she'd brought along a personal shopping cart.

The cushions she'd purchased took up most of the room, but she still had room for the swatch book, so she ended her walk-around at Joe and Margaret's table and purchased that as well, full price plus taxes, as promised.

She'd almost reached her car when her cellphone rang. Her brother Warren's name lit up the screen.

"Hi."

"Hi Pen. Just making sure you made it okay."

"I'm okay, it's my bank account that needs rescuing," she said as she opened the trunk of her car. A long blue tote box filled the trunk and she used her free hand to pop the lid.

"We truly are as different as day and night."

"Different is a good thing, Warren. Plus, I couldn't picture you fawning over doilies and wearing anything other than jeans and a t-shirt."

"I guess I just don't get your obsession with fabrics and laces and that sort of thing."

"Just the same way as I don't get why you've never grown up enough to stop playing hide and seek."

"Geocaching, Pen, it's called geocaching."

"That's just a fancy word so grown-ups feel better about playing hide and seek."

"Don't knock it 'til you try it, little sis. I'm going to take you with me one of these times," he said.

"Let's not, and say we did."

Warren laughed. "I miss you. When are you getting back?"

"Are you at Dad's?"

"I am. Decided rather than just check in, it was high time I came and had a look at the oasis, and visit the old man and our up-coming step-mom."

"That must have made dad's day."

"I barely registered a ten-second greeting, Dad's got his eyes on a bigger prize," Warren said. "In fact it turns out his bride-to-be has your cottage alone for the weekend and they're taking advantage of that."

Penny cringed. "Ugh, Warren, I do not need that picture in my head, and in my cottage no less." And then his words really took hold. "So by alone, you mean, Reuben and the girls have left already?"

"Oh no, Reuben left, but the girls are still with Gyla."

Penny stopped short, the waltes game in her hands. Why had Reuben left the twins behind? And how gone was he? "I thought Reuben would be finished this weekend and be gone by Monday. That's what I was told."

"Duty called, I guess, and the bit of work he has left on Dad's oasis will just have to wait."

"Duty calls?" she said coldly. "What kind of man just up and leaves his children in the care of his mother?"

"The kind of man who has to make a living to care for said children," Warren said, just as coldly. "I met the guy before he took off to the city, and he didn't strike me as the kind of man who would pawn his children off if there wasn't a really good reason for it."

There was pause, then Warren laughed. "And his children were having a ball of fun when I left your cottage so I don't think they're suffering from separation anxiety. Geez, when did you become so judgmental?"

Penny put the last of the items in her trunk, collapsed the shopping cart, and wedged it in beside the tote box. She huffed a bit as she worked.

"You okay, Pen?"

"I'm fine, and I'm not being judgmental. I just know he took off for a whole evening a couple nights ago and left the girls, so how much free time does one guy need?"

"I can't speak for that, but I do know those girls are having a lot of fun and they're getting tons of love."

"They're great, aren't they?"

"They could grow on me," he said.

Penny groaned. "Ah, I just wish you hadn't chosen this weekend to finally tear yourself away from the McCalla Corp. I miss you, and I could really use a hug from my big brother right now."

"Are you sure you're okay?"

"I'm fine. I just spent about two thousand dollars. and I think I'm suffering from buyer's guilt."

"I doubt two thousand will break you, Pen. You rarely get away and there isn't a whole lot to spend two grand on in the woods. You want my suggestion?"

"I have a feeling I'm going to get it either way so you may as well spill."

"Go spend a thousand more on meaningless food and drink, and upgrade your basic room at the Marriott to a suite, book an extra day or two, and live a little. If you're not willing to let some new man wine and dine you, then wine and dine yourself."

She didn't speak.

"It's been three years Penny. Three years. You've been stuck for three years."

She sniffled into the phone, and would have corrected him had he not continued.

"There's no denying David was a great man, and I'm sure if he'd been given the option he would never have chosen to leave you, but he didn't have a choice, Pen. It was shitty that that happened to him, and you, but it did, and now he would want you to move on."

Penny was inside her car now. "If he didn't have this crazy idea that he needed to go in early to familiarize himself with the curriculum, this would never have happened," she choked.

"No one can know that. If we could, we'd all be living in a bubble pretending to live."

The line was silent for a long drawn out moment, and then he continued. "It's okay to step out of the bubble, Pen."

"I—" she tried to talk but tears overtook her. "I tried, Warren," she choked through her tears.

"Yeah, this is a step in the right direction, you're away for pleasure and not business and that's a great step. Heck, for you that's a leap, and I'm proud of you for that. But, and I may be a shitty brother for saying this, I want more."

"Warren?" Penny's voice shook with unshed tears.

"Pen?"

"Reuben."

"Yeah, I know, you're pissed at him for leaving his girls, but I'm—"

"No, not that, Warren. Reuben…" she took a deep breath and sniffled, "I… he…he and I…oh shit!"

"Did he hurt you, Penny? Cause if he did—"

"No, no, I…" She allowed a sigh to wrack her core, and a small squeaky sob constricted her throat. "I love him," she managed to say in a whisper.

"What was that, Penny? Speak up." She could hear the macho aggravation in his tone and knew he was ready to plough down anyone who dared to lay a hand on his sister. "I swear to God, if he's hurt you in any way, I'll tear him limb from limb."

"Wait, wait." She pulled a tissue from the box on the passenger seat blew her nose loudly, and then tried to regulate her breathing.

When she finally could speak, small hiccup sounds punctuated each word. "I've fallen in love with him, Warren."

17

The humidex was so high that Reuben didn't have to check the weather reports to know that thunder would be on the agenda for the evening.

The next few weeks would be busy for him. He'd accepted a job transfer with the Department of Natural Resources and before the end of August he would be working out of the Cornwallis office. Which meant he needed to give his notice to his landlord and find a new place in or around the Valley before the end of July. That gave him less than a week to get his ducks in order.

Ember and Terra wouldn't see much of their father for the next couple of weeks, but he hoped the sacrifice would result in a better situation and a better lifestyle for all of them.

He was thankful for his mom. Over the last year and half she'd been the glue that kept them all together. Even before Eve had lost the fight his mother had been there. She'd taken his denial and turned it into hope, and then when hope was lost and Eve left him, she let him rebel, but only for so long, and then she pulled him from the brink and told him in no uncertain terms that she would never allow him to give up.

She deserved some happiness herself, and Spencer was it. Now he had to man up and stop depending on his mother to make the tough calls.

Being in the country for the last two weeks had been an eye-opener for him. He was not cut out for the city. That had been Eve's lifestyle of choice and he'd gone along with it because as long as she was there, the city was his choice, too. It was time to get back to his roots. Time to delve his hands into nature and show his daughters what they were made of.

And what about Penny?

Well, Digby County would have to be big enough for both of them. Their families were about to converge. They would both have to learn to get along.

In hindsight he knew he should have left her alone. He certainly hadn't helped their chances of an amicable relationship. Even if they did learn to behave in each other's company, he would not be able to sit in the same room with her without wanting to smell her hair or taste her lips. He wondered if he'd ever be able to sit at family meals again with her across from him, and not want to push plates and cutlery aside in order to have her on the table.

And what of her future lovers? Would he be able to watch them together and not want to knock the teeth from the man's head? He'd forever wonder what went on between them behind closed doors, resent the man who strummed his tongue down the cords of her ribs, and wonder if she gave the same whimper when he nibbled on the delicate skin at her hipbone.

His stomach turned violently at the thought, and he swayed for a second as he fought the urge to retch.

Where was she? He'd tried to work the conversation around to her when he'd met Warren, but it was too hard to do without casting a spotlight on his intentions.

And what *were* his intentions? He didn't even know. All he knew was that he wasn't finished yet. It had been too abrupt.

He'd expected a gradual decline in his desire for her, or to feel the decline on her end, in which case he'd have slowly pulled himself away. But this was too quick. They'd still been on fire. He had felt it. She'd seemed okay with their arrangement. She'd been enjoying the heat as much as he'd been.

Then she pulled the rug out from under him. She'd broken the most important rule of all. She'd fallen in love with him. With *him*, of all people. The most callous man on earth. She'd fallen in love with someone who was unable to love in return, and because of that she'd ended what they did have.

Now the only thing he could do was accept it, and try to form a relationship with her based solely on family ties.

With his daughters still in Ridgeville, the apartment was quiet. He'd tossed several empty boxes at the foot of his bed with the plan to fill them. He didn't even have a new place yet, but when he did he'd be glad for the head start. For now he'd just pack the non-essentials.

There was no knowing when he'd be this alone again, and with that realization he'd resigned himself to the unthinkable task of sorting through his life with Eve. It was time to face the demons from his past.

Half bending, he lifted a box and tossed it to the corner. It hit the closet door, and the door creaked open.

He had a reflex reaction to lunge forward and slam it closed again, but just as quickly he stopped himself.

Maybe that's what it needed. Just for a moment. A little air. A small sliver of his present world swirling around into its darkness, getting him use to the idea.

He dropped to the edge of the bed and looked into the small slit of darkness afforded him. He couldn't see inside no matter how he twisted his head, and that was as it should be. He needed a couple of minutes to get used to the idea anyway.

He laughed at his own cowardice. It was a closet, not a ticking time bomb. The damage had already been done, almost fifteen months ago. The hard part was over now. Wasn't it?

He'd been through all the dreaded firsts. The first Christmas without her. The first anniversary, and Thanksgiving, and Valentines day. He'd already survived his birthday, and the twins' birthday, and, hardest of all, her birthday. He even managed to make it through the first anniversary of her death. What could hurt him now?

Kneading the tight muscles in the back of his neck, he tried to massage away the worry. Her whole life was in this closet. Even to the things she'd kept around the bed in her final days had been placed in this closet at his request. Until he could get himself to deal with it, he'd said, but he knew he'd never truly be ready. He wasn't entirely sure that moment was now either, but it was as good a time as any.

Pulling his hair up into a loose bun, he walked to the closet and wrapped his hand around the doorknob. He could smell her. Even after fifteen months her smell still lingered on her things and in her space.

Leaning forward he pressed his face into the crack of the door and inhaled deeply. Oranges. That was the first smell that hit him. And then a sweet undertone of soft vanilla wafted out. She always smelled intoxicating, and the orange and vanilla matched her flirty and sunny disposition. She was a ray of sunshine and so the combination of the two scents always made him think of a sunny day. She had the ability to put a sparkle in his gloom and show him the silver lining in his cloudy day. She filled him with love at just a mere smile, or the slightest touch of her hand.

Just as he was about to step back and pull the door open further, the memory of lavender filled his senses. As quickly as the lavender pervaded his memory, the deep organic smell of balsam and nature mingled with it and he knew the scent he was remembering. His body intertwined with Penny's emitted such a pleasing mix of sweetness and spice, and was fast becoming his favourite scent.

She had no right to be here contaminating the memories of his dead wife. She didn't belong. She needed to stay out of his head while he reminisced about Eve and the love they shared. There was no place for her here.

The orange and lavender clashed together, and swirled around in his mind's eye. He doubled over with nausea even as the thoughts filled his head, and stumbled backwards, tripping over the boxes and landing on the bed.

Tears pooled in his eyes, spilling down into his hair and onto his pillow. There was no one there to see his weakness, and so he allowed himself to break into a million pieces.

His hands fumbled for the picture frame on the night stand, and then there she was before him. His beautiful Eve smiling out at him from the silver frame. Her hazel eyes and olive skin a perfect combination.

She and Penny were as different as day and night. Penny's eyes were blue. Except blue seemed too subtle a word for them. They were the truest form of blue he'd ever seen, and they seemed to take on a life of their own. Like tiny bulbs were infused behind the irises and her emotions were hardwired to the dimmer switch.

Her eyes were dark the last time he'd seen her, shiny with tears, but dark. It had not been his intention to kill the light, but he had.

"You would be ashamed of the man I've become," he whispered to Eve, and then he dropped the frame to his chest and squeezed his eyes closed.

He wanted tonight to be about Eve. He wanted to sort through her things and give her the solemn respect she deserved, but no matter how much he tried he couldn't push thoughts of Penny from his head, and so she would have to remain. He would find a respectful way to keep her at bay. Or at least he would try.

Pushing from the bed he reached for the doorknob and pulled the closet door open. A million things demanded his attention at once: a silver belt, black stilettos, a pleather jacket, and the red silk robe she wore after a bath...

Up against the wall, as far away as she could get it, Eve had placed her unlucky seafoam cardigan. The cardigan she wore so much, with its oversized pockets and snagged rows of cable-knit, that it had started to look like her even when she wasn't in it.

She'd been wearing it the day the doctor told them she had cancer, and she'd been wearing it the day the same doctor told her that the treatments weren't helping. To Reuben it had become her bad-news cardigan, and he hated it. He pulled it from the hanger and stuffed it into a box.

He needed a happy thought to push out the bad now, so he reached out to trace the salmon-coloured blazer only she could wear so beautifully. He wasn't even sure Penny could pull off that look.

Of course she couldn't, and weirdly enough he didn't want her too either. She was not the blazer kind of woman; it was too stiff-upper-lip for her, and he found himself smiling as he slipped the blazer into a box to toss out.

And then there were the brocade swing shoes that for some odd reason his fun-spirited wife loved, turquoise and wing tipped and so insanely loud he always questioned her love for them and secretly hoped at any moment she would tell him that, 'yes, of course, they were a joke', but she never had. Although he just knew Penny would appreciate them she would not be caught dead wearing them in public, but all the same he wanted to see her in them. They would be far too big, but he longed to see her try them on just the same. He knew she would laugh at their boldness and flop around in them for a moment before she'd take them off and wipe them down and set them neatly in the corner for show.

He searched out the tight black jeans and white blouse Eve always wore the shoes with. As he fingered the clothing he smiled as a memory of her dancing flashed into his head. He wanted to see Penny dance, except he wanted to be squished up against her while she did so and feel her tiny hips and rounded ass as she gyrated to the music, but he also wanted to watch from a distance, let her tantalizing rhythm tempt him and make him count down the moments until he could have her beneath him.

He dropped the shoes into the box along with the jeans and blouse, and swallowed around the lump in his throat. This was not working out like he'd hoped.

He needed to get Penny out of the room. To force her out of his head. To give him some time alone to sort through Eve's belongings in a respectful manner. These thoughts of another woman were not appropriate. It was bad enough he'd let Penny crawl under his skin; he couldn't have her eating up all his memories of his wife, too. Eve was the mother of his children, and she deserved respect.

He pressed the palms of his hands into his eyes in a bid to rid her from his memory, but it was useless. He needed a cold shower. Something jarring to rudely awaken him.

He shed his clothing and stepped under the water, but as the coldness washed over him it did anything but cool him down. It was useless. She had a hold on him and it didn't look like she was letting up anytime soon.

Even beneath the cold downpour his manhood ached for her, and as his hand circled its girth he allowed his mind to fill with images of Penny, her curtain of golden hair, the intoxicating way her hips swayed when she walked, her crazy laughter, her rounded bottom and shapely legs. As he spilled his seed into the cold shower he leaned into the wall and closed his eyes. She was making a wanton of him, and although he knew he shouldn't, he liked it.

As he adjusted the shower for a warm spray, he pulled the elastic from his hair and watched as it slipped onto his wrist. It was white as opposed to his normal black one, and he'd been wearing it for a couple of days now. Perhaps it was half the reason he couldn't get her out of his head. He doubted it, but at this point he wasn't ruling it out either. He lifted the elastic over the shower rod and let it drop to the floor.

Under the warm spray he let his body relax, enjoying the warmth on his uptight muscles. He worked his hair into a lather and was about to rinse when he heard the distant ringing of his cellphone.

"Shit." He turned his head into the water and began rinsing away the shampoo. The ringing stopped, but then soon started up again quickly after. "Shit, shit, shit."

He threw back the curtain and grabbed a towel. As he rushed through the doorway he spread the towel to wrap around himself, but he'd chosen a hand towel by mistake. "Fuck." He tossed the towel to the bed.

Reaching for his phone he activated the black screen. Six missed calls from Penny Weis. Why the hell was she calling his cellphone? He had all kinds of scenarios springing alive in his mind. Someone was hurt. She needed help. But his all time favourite was the one where she told him she had been wrong, and she was waiting for him at the shack. He'd rush back to Ridgeville, right now. He'd beg her to wait, and in three hours he'd be at the shack panting like a dog.

The phone rang in his hand and he jumped. As he slid the answer bar to the right he lifted the phone to his ear and asked, "What's wrong?"

"If I'm going to help you, you have to let me in."

What the hell was going on? He rushed to the doorway of his bedroom and strained his ears. In the distance he could hear the light rapping at the door. He was naked, and he couldn't very well answer the door in that state.

"Just give me a second."

He dropped the phone and reached into the open closet for Eve's robe. He jabbed his arms into the arm holes and pulled it closed around him, holding the flaps together as he rushed from the room.

"I'm coming," he said into the phone.

As soon as he opened the door their eyes met. Then she lowered hers to take in the rest of him. A mixture of emotions flashed across her face: surprise, love, disbelief, hurt, and betrayal.

In a quick motion she turned to leave, but he caught her arm and pulled her inside. Closing the door behind her, he pressed her against the door and dipped his head to claim her lips, Eve's robe falling open between them. The effect she had on him was not even human. Just seeing her outside his door in a simple grey t-shirt and denim shorts, cell phone to her ear, sent him over the edge.

She struggled against him seeking release, but he swept her up into his arms and strolled across to the bedroom. Without stopping he kicked the boxes aside and took her to his bed. He placed her tenderly on the bed, her hair fanned out beneath her and his wet hair dripping down to speckle her t-shirt.

He only just realized how much he wanted to see her there, among his sheets and his things. He just wanted to stand back for a moment and take it all in but he couldn't get himself to move from her side.

"Stop," she demanded pressing against his chest. "I didn't come here for this."

He allowed her to twist out from under him and she bounded from the bed. "God, how many women do you have anyway?" Her accusations were a sneer, her eyes following the opening of the robe he wore. His erection apparent against the silk material.

"Oh this?" he asked. Lifting from the bed he pulled the robe off, and let it drop into a box on the floor, standing naked before her. "This was my wife's."

"And in there?" she asked, tilting her head towards the bathroom. "Is that your wife in the shower, too?"

For a second he wondered why the water was even going, and then it hit him. "Oh shit," he said rushing to the bathroom.

He closed down the shower, yanked a bath towel from the cupboard, and caught her just as she was about to step from his bedroom. "I was in the shower when you called. There's no one in there, I promise." He tied the towel around his waist and gestured to the bathroom. "Feel free to look for yourself if you don't believe me."

"I actually don't give a shit."

But he could see that she did. It was written all over her beautiful face.

"Why are you here?" he asked and then reached out to press two fingers against her lips. "No wait, don't tell me. I don't care."

She clamped a hand over his wrist and thrust his hand away from her mouth. "Kyle called me."

Now it was his turn to be pissed. Kyle was a thorn in his side, or a malignant tumour that was hell bent of making his life a living hell.

"He made it sound like some sort of emergency. He claimed Gyla asked him to call. She said you were here and that you were dealing with some tough things that you shouldn't deal with alone. She wanted me to come and lend a hand." She raised her hands out at her side. "So here I am, fool that I am."

"You're anything but a fool."

"Did you put him up to this?"

"Hell, no. But I'd love to have you, if you'll stay."

"So there's no emergency?"

"None that I'm aware of."

He tugged her closer. Eve's memory paled in comparison to the vivid being before him. Her sweetness enveloped him, and his body yearned for hers.

"What is this?" She gestured to the boxes strewn on the floor.

"Nothing," he stammered, and began a quick gathering of boxes, piling them against the wall atop one another.

Her voice was soft when she spoke again, "are these your wife's things?" Penny stood within the closet running her hand down a long scarf that hung from a peg on the back of the door.

He nodded in agreement and she leaned down to retrieve the pair of brocade swing shoes from the box. "These are great shoes," she said, running a finger down the intricate pattern. She looked up at him, her eyes soft and understanding. "Can I make a suggestion?"

He shrugged.

"Keep these for Terra."

"Terra?" He laughed, "you haven't forgotten my daughters already, have you?"

She didn't laugh with him. "I haven't, but I know girls, and these will never be Ember's thing. She'll probably always love the softer side of life, and although she may give leather a try, and," she reached out for the pair of stilettos, "black stilettos, she'll never go this route. But Terra? I think there's a day coming when she'll appreciate the risqué allure of these. They'll help her be feminine without losing her funk. And shoes like these never go out of style."

He stared at her for a long moment. He'd thought the ordeal of going through Eve's things needed less of Penny, but now he could see that it needed more.

A slow smile spread across his face. Of course his mom would know that, she had a way of coming through for him even when he thought he was okay. "You say Mom sent you?"

"According to Kyle, but I think he's pulling my leg. Gyla would never do this."

His expression softened as he looked at her, brocade swing shoes in one hand and black stilettos in the other. She was like a breath of fresh air. He was already feeling better. "Yeah she would," he said stepping closer to take the shoes from her hand. "She has a knack for knowing just what I need and, if she has to, she'll move heaven and earth to give it to me."

Pulling her to him, he folded her in his arms. This time she didn't pull away.

"Gyla knows how angry I am with you," she spoke against his chest. "Plus, I hate you."

"You don't hate me." He tilted her chin up to him and brushed his lips lightly over hers.

Penny blushed and smiled up at him wanly.

"She knew I needed you." He spread his fingers along her jaw line. "Mothers know everything, didn't you know that?" He kissed her gently. "They have a sixth sense or something. Even science doesn't have an explanation for it. It's just a known fact."

He felt her arms tighten around him, her hands splayed on his back, and then she turned her head into his chest and inhaled deeply. "You're my favourite smell," she said.

He bent to hook his arms under her bottom and raised her from the floor, then he walked the few feet to the bed and lay her down with ease. As he positioned himself atop her, the knot in his towel came loose and fell away.

"But things haven't changed," she said as he leaned into her. "You already know how I feel about you, and you should also know that I mean to be true to myself."

He fell to the side of her, propped up on an elbow, his arm still hugging her middle. "I wouldn't want you to be anything but true to yourself."

"Thanks." She cupped his face with her hands. "So can you put some clothes on and let me help you?"

"Help me?"

"You're sorting through her things, aren't you? I assume that's what Gyla meant when she said you needed help dealing with some tough things."

"Shouldn't we talk first?"

"About what?"

"About the elephant in the room that we're both trying to ignore."

"What is there to talk about?"

He moved to lie on his back beside her, tugging the blanket up to cover himself. "Can I try to explain to you where I'm at?"

Neither of them moved.

"I'll make us a coffee, and we can set at the table while we talk," he urged.

Out of the corner of his eyes he saw her turn her head to look at him. "Is there really any need? I mean, you're not required to fall in love with every girl you fuck."

"I know that."

"Then we don't need to talk about it."

"I think we do."

"Why? What difference will it make?"

"Three things," he said, turning to her. "We're about to become family, whether we like it or not. In fact we are family already, unofficially. Two, you may have rushed over here to my aid, but that doesn't mean you're not still pissed at me, and most important of all to me, is I like you. A lot."

"And why is that most important?"

"Coffee?" he urged, rolling from the bed.

18

From Reuben's fourth floor apartment the lights over the Halifax Harbour shimmered in an iridescent blur. The rain had started, just a light drizzle, but enough to take the still warm air and stir it up a bit. It made everything damp and sticky.

When Reuben returned from the café with coffee and muffins, Penny was on the balcony taking advantage of the occasional breeze the rain offered, a small reprieve from the stuffy atmosphere.

He'd hurried as fast as he could without running. It was almost laughable the way things were. Jodi served him every day at the corner café, and every day he flirted a little with her, and every day she brushed him off. Today she'd given him a little, she'd actually seemed interested.

A few weeks in Ridgeville hadn't turned her into a troll, but it had taken his desires and wants and set them on a different path. Penny was in his apartment and although Jodi's eyes told him tonight just might be his lucky night, he still preferred a sexless night with Penny.

What the hell had she done to him?

He watched her from the doorway. The tip of her ponytail flitted on her shoulder as the slight breeze danced across her. She'd left the patio doors open and stood at the railing. Even though the balcony had a roof, a light sheen of rain clung to her. He had a crazy desire to taste the rain on her skin, and his tongue twitched in his mouth at the thought.

As quietly as he could he placed the coffee and bag of muffins on the patio table and came up behind her. Even far from the country the smell of lavender clung to her. It mixed with the warm petrichor of the rain and left an intoxicating aroma.

As much as he wanted to touch her, he couldn't. They needed to level out the playing field. She was armed with love and he couldn't tamper with that. He was not a talking man, but that didn't excuse the fact that they needed to talk. They needed to lay everything out on the table and see if anything could be salvaged of their relationship.

"I got coffee and fruit explosions," he said, and she turned. The rain had peppered her grey t-shirt, causing her nipples to push against the fabric, and she looked sexier than ever.

She'd let him go, and whether he liked it or not he had to abide by her wishes.

Reuben liked how Penny looked in his kitchen as she pulled two plates from the cupboard and placed a muffin atop each of them. He wanted to go up behind her and wrap his arms around her middle, pull her back against him and kiss the back of her neck, but he'd promised to be a good boy and talk.

His thoughts were anything but talkative. The path she sent his thoughts down was what one might call a gutter, but the feelings she evoked didn't feel dirty to him, they felt celestial. They felt right.

"Do you want a pat of butter for your muffin?" he asked instead and walked to the fridge to retrieve the butter.

"It's a fruit explosion. The butter will ruin the explosion."

"If you say so, but to me a few seconds nuked and then spread open with a pat of butter, *is* the explosion," he teased. If he were honest he'd tell her about the explosions going off inside him at just the sight of her standing in his kitchen, but he was too chicken.

"You do your way and I'll do mine, but I will get mine *nuked*, as you put it."

He grabbed up the plates and placed them side by side in the microwave for 40 seconds. She sat at the table and waited. He placed her warmed plate in front of her and sat opposite her at the table with his own. The butter spread out on the muffin, mingling with the explosion of fruit in the centre.

"I'm not good at this," he said.

"Eating?"

"Talking."

"Well, it was your idea."

"Yeah, because it needs to be done, but that doesn't mean I like doing it." He pulled a piece of muffin loose and popped it in his mouth. "Falling for someone isn't easy for me. I like you, I like you more than I have liked most people."

He wasn't doing this right, but it was hard to form a coherent sentence when his head was screaming words like love and forever at him in conjunction with her name. He didn't care what huge plans his heart wanted to conjure up; he was not ready for a commitment. "It was a short trip from the altar to the grave for me...in fact less than three years. The trip from falling in love with Eve to burying her was not much longer than that, and I don't really think I'm over her yet."

"You're never going to get over her, Reuben, so if you are waiting for that to happen, you have a lifetime of waiting to do. It's never going to happen."

"I know that, but there *has to be* a quiet lulling between missing her so fiercely and being okay to move on, and I just haven't gotten there yet."

"Are you going to miss me?"

"We're going to be family, so having you right there under my nose every time I turn around is going to take some getting used to."

"But are you going to miss me?"

"I'm going to miss making love to you, if that's what you mean. And I doubt I'll ever be able to pass the shack without thinking of you."

"But will you miss me?"

There was so much more he would miss about her. He would miss the knowledge that she was waiting for him. He would miss coming to her. But what it all boiled down to was yes, he would most definitely miss her. Telling her that was another story.

"I can't be in a relationship right now, Penny. It just isn't time for me."

"And you've told me that far more times than I care to hear. I heard it loud and clear the first time, so why is it that we have to talk now?"

"I just want to explain to you my reasoning."

"I understand that, as well. You aren't ready to move on. You're not over Eve, I understand that. I heard that, too, so what more is there to say? I say let's do what I came here to do and be done with it."

"I don't know," he said. "I guess I just owed you the time and the explanation."

"You don't. I knew what I was doing coming in to this. Did I expect to fall in love with you? I certainly didn't, because I am still in love with David, and I always will be. But loving you doesn't mean I can't still love him. It just means I can honour him by loving you, because I don't think he means for me to be lonely for the rest of my life. How unfair would that be? That is why the wedding vows stop at death, Reuben, because a human needs a physical being to love on earth, and I know David would expect me to do that and he would be okay with it."

"And so would Eve, but I have to be okay with it, too."

"That's your right. No one is telling you that you need to love anyone ever again. If you choose to stay single for life, that's your right. I don't need to be pep talked, I don't need soothing. I'm a grown woman and I knew straight out that we could never be. I just fell for a split second, but I'm over it now. I promise. Everyone we meet is for a reason and maybe that reason for us was for this exact thing." She gestured between them. "You showed me I could love again. You helped me. Does that mean I'm going to rush right out and find a man to marry?"

He felt his breath hitch. He couldn't imagine her being with anyone else. Was there anyone good enough for her? Anyone he could justifiably give the okay to? He doubted it, but maybe she was right. Maybe in time he would be okay with it. Maybe they were just meant to be in each other's life in this fashion as a metaphorical stepping stone.

"Probably not. I don't think I'll marry for some time, to be honest. But maybe, because of you, I will say yes to the next man who asks me out. " She hickled. "Maybe Kyle."

His stomach lurched. Kyle was not good enough for her.

"He's already told me he's interested. Maybe I'll let him take me out sometimes. You never know, right? After all, I would never have thought that I would like you as much as I ended up liking you, so miracles obviously do happen. And we've already gotten the first kiss out of the way, so that awkward moment is gone."

Reuben stiffened, the explosion of fruit soured as he swallowed it and he coughed. "He kissed you?" he asked when he was able to speak again.

"He did. He was a complete gentleman, though. He did ask my permission first, unlike you. You manhandled me."

"I don't recall you complaining."

He wondered how she'd feel if she knew how badly he wanted to crush her against the fridge behind her and claim her lips. How badly he wanted to lay her on the table and have his way with her.

Still, the thought of Kyle kissing her was disconcerting. It didn't sit right with him. It made his skin crawl. If he were honest he felt cheated on. It was an idiotic way to feel, but he felt it just the same. Even though she wasn't his, she *felt* like his, and the thought of anyone else kissing her made his blood boil.

But hadn't he just told her that he wasn't interested in a long-term relationship?

So what right did he have to deny her one, when she had just announced that *she* was ready. He couldn't ask her to wait for him; that would be too unfair.

There was the slight possibility that he might never be ready, even though she had him contemplating the thought. She'd almost convinced him. He'd almost let Eve go. Even though Penny with anyone else didn't seem right, letting himself be faithful forever to another person other than Eve didn't feel right to him, either.

"Does that bother you?"

"What?"

"Me kissing Kyle."

He pulled his chest in and took a swig of his coffee. "You get to kiss whomever you want." He tried to sound convincing, but he could hear the condescending tone in his own voice.

"Yes, I do. It was sweet, too. It was one of those kisses I had to think about, but I'm thinking maybe I liked it more than I put on."

He took a huge swallow of the coffee, unintentionally, and tried to swallow it despite the sting on his tongue. "That's good," he said around the scalding. "I'm sure he wouldn't complain."

"Probably not. He's already told me that should you toss me aside, he'd be interested in taking up the slack."

The scald on his tongue was nothing compared to the burning in his veins as his blood threatened to boil. He was not going to let her taunting get the best of him. He would be as nonchalant as possible, and see if he could turn this seething rage around and make it back-fire in her face. She was not going to make him feel threatened. As much as he craved her, he only wanted her, there was no *need* involved. He could make do without her, he could make do with her being with someone else.

But Kyle? There was something that irked him about Kyle. Maybe because Kyle was here, in this moment. Maybe any man in any space of time would have his blood boiling, too.

"I didn't toss you aside."

She didn't reply. Instead she popped the last of her muffin in her mouth and soaked it with a swallow of coffee.

"Did I? Do you feel like I tossed you aside?"

She looked up at him from over the rim of her mug, but didn't answer.

"Because, if you recall, I was anything but ready to toss you aside."

"So, basically, you want to toss me aside, but pick me up whenever you're in the mood?"

He started to protest but she held up a hand and stopped him. "Oh, but no one else is allowed to pick me up, either. Or to even stop and look at me with any sort of interest. Oh no, I have to stay tossed, until you decide to totally discard me altogether."

"That's not fair. I was liking what we had. You're the one who decided that we ought to end it. So basically *you* tossed *me* aside."

"You must be so hurt," She mocked.

"Not hurt, just sort of hanging."

She set her cup down and looked at him. "I don't think you'll mope around for long."

She was so wrong. He'd already been moping. He'd already envisioned a mad dash to the shack to meet her. He'd already wished she'd let him touch her the way he longed to touch her. He'd definitely mope around a bit. She was not an easy transition point. He didn't want to transition. Not yet.

"You're not as easy to get over as you think, Penny."

She laughed. It was an awkward laugh, and although he didn't want to lead her on he didn't want her to think she meant nothing to him either.

"I have to say this summer has been one of my favourites." He stared across the table at her, waiting for a reaction. "I don't think I need to tell you that right now all I can think about is taking you to my bed."

He watched as the colour crept up into her cheeks, and he loved how vulnerable it made her look. But he knew she was as tough as nails. She could stand ramrod straight in her beliefs and even if she wanted him right now, and he had no doubt that she did, she would not bend. Once she made her mind up about something there was no changing it.

But then, hadn't he thought the same thing weeks ago when she swore there would never be anything but contempt between them? She'd relented then. But it had been at her own accord. No amount of flirting would make her change her mind until she was *ready* to change her mind.

"Is this how our talk is going to be?" she said, taking her plate to the sink. She ran it under the water to wash away the muffin crumbs, and reached over his shoulder to take his.

As quickly as he could he caught her hand, pushed his chair back from the table and pulled her down onto his lap.

"This is how I'd like to talk," he said, slipping his hand under the curtain of hair to cup her neck. "We always seem to agree when we are like this."

He pulled her down and lightly touched her mouth with his, his tongue probing at her lips for entry.

She moaned against him, and he felt himself harden. He speared her tongue with his own, tasting the fruit amidst her natural honey taste. The combination was intoxicating, natural wine on tap.

She shuddered against him. He felt it. The shiver of her body against his as his lips softly worked on hers.

"This isn't talking," she whispered against him.

"Shhh," he said, pulling his lips from hers for a mere second. "You just have to listen."

Their breath mingled together, the scent of coffee heavy between them. "Can you hear that?" he asked against her ear, his lips brushing against her earlobe.

The blood thrummed in his ears, the need for her was the most prominent feeling he'd ever felt in his life.

He held her around her waist. His fingers spread out along the band of her shorts. The hem of her t-shirt lightly brushed his fingers. His senses were already heightened, and the soft brush of the fabric sent his breath in shaky rasps against her mouth.

He wanted to devour her. The small sips he was getting did not satiate him. He wanted to leap in head first and take until she could no longer give. And if she would let him he would do just that.

Every atmosphere...he wanted her in every atmosphere and space his imagination could conjure up. Right now he longed to see her amidst his sheets, on his bed, draped with his favourite quilt. He wanted to make love to her until dawn approached, and then he wanted to make love to her again. He wanted to wake with her in his arms, to see the last shadows of night lift from her eyes.

But none of that would be okay for him if she didn't want the same. None of the taking would be enough if he couldn't give to her as well, and right now what she wanted he couldn't give. How could he? It wasn't his to give.

Dragging his hand slowly up from her waist he let it consider all the soft contours of her figure, his fingers lingering a moment longer than necessary at the slight curve of her breast.

He released her other hand and gently cupped her face in his palms, pulling his lips away from hers. They sat there, forehead to forehead, eyes closed, and he willed his heart to stop pounding, and his need for her to subside.

And right when he felt himself calming, she whispered, "I hear it; it's deafening."

And everything he'd just worked to control hydroplaned on the slippery surface of her voice and, once again, he lost all control.

19

David's passing had not only left Penny lonely, but in more ways than one she'd lost herself. Not all at once; it was a slow process at such a gradual pace that she wasn't even completely aware that it had happened at all, until she'd finally found herself again. For a moment she'd been tricked into believing her life was all that she wanted it to be. The only place she'd focused any energy on at all had grown exponentially, and that success had tricked her mind and heart into believing they too were full.

And now here she was, on the brink of losing herself again, and ironically in the same spot she'd found herself: in Reuben's arms.

It felt right to be in his arms, and for a moment she had forgotten how wrong it actually was. He'd stepped into her life without any sugar coating. He had promised a quick release from the physical wants and needs that every human has, and he'd followed through. She'd told him that all he was to her was a way to move from the stalemate position she'd found herself in, and then she'd made a complete three hundred sixty degree turn on him and declared love. Had she really expected him not to cower and shy away?

But he hadn't run away. Instead he'd opted to live a lie. He'd wanted to pretend to love her so that things could continue as they were. That would never do for her. She could not continue making love to him knowing that was all it could ever be. Although the love-making was top-notch and she would miss it, in fact was actively missing it now, she couldn't just pretend either.

She matched him kiss for kiss, her hands slipping beneath his short sleeves to squeeze his biceps. It was true what he said, that their bodies together had the best communication, that everything was in sync, each in perfect harmony with the other. They just worked in perfect unison, each giving and taking, and both of them left satisfied but still wanting.

But no matter how right his lips felt on hers, and how perfectly their bodies melded together, they were not singing the same song. She'd discovered herself again and liked what she'd found, and she was not willing to undersell what she had to offer. It was all or nothing. It had to be. She was more important to herself than this. She deserved an all-encompassing kind of love, if that was what she wanted. And it was.

If she wanted to be true to herself then this had to stop now, before it became unstoppable. Why was it that everything that was bad for her disguised itself as good and drew her like a moth to a flame?

Reuben's hand splayed on the bare skin at the small of her back as his other hand slipped to cup her neck, but as he closed in to capture her lips once more she pulled back, slipped off his lap, and stepped away.

"You need help, and I'm here to help you. So let's do this." Her braid had become loosened and she busied herself tidying it.

"I'm sorry," Reuben said, standing. He took two paces toward her but stopped when she held up a hand to ward him off.

"What we had was great while it lasted," she said, "but we are both adults and we should be able to work together and manage to not fall into bed."

"I'm sorry," he repeated. "I just lose my head a little around you."

"Well, don't."

She knew how crazy that response was, but she meant it. Shortly Gyla and Spencer would be married, so being around one another without tearing each other's clothes off was something they were both going to have to get use to. There was no time like the present to get started on that.

What better way to get used to the idea then in a small apartment in close quarters with one another? It would be the ultimate test, and even though they were attracted to one another, they were also adults. It was like any other temptation: you know it's there, but you learn to resist it until eventually the resistance becomes easier and the temptation subsides or goes away altogether.

"We're adults, Reuben, and on top of that we're family. All the special occasions that families share together? We'll be sharing them from now on. If we can't learn to control ourselves now we never will, and family get-togethers will just be awkward for both of us."

She ran her hand over the picture of two smiling little girls on the hutch. "And what about Ember and Terra? I love them like family already, and I want to be able to love them freely without feeling like I may at any second hurt them. They deserve for us to get along. The more people they have loving them, the better, right?"

Reuben ran his fingers through his still-damp hair and leaned back on the cupboard. A deep groan rolled from his chest in protest. "I just wish I'd never gotten a taste of you, is all."

"I don't regret our time together, but it was a bad choice considering the circumstances. We can't change what we've already done, but we can make better choices from here on."

"I get that, and I know you're right, and besides," he pushed from the cupboard to step past her, "you deserve a hell of a lot more than what I can offer you."

She watched him walk down the hall, his black t-shirt stretched taut across his broad shoulders. His long strides never faltered as he went into the bedroom and disappeared from sight.

She leaned on the buffet and was startled when it moved on its castors. Stemware clinked in the glass hangers and wine bottles jarred in their cubbies.

She needed a second before she followed him. His bedroom seemed like the worst place to be right now, considering what she was trying to avoid.

"It's okay if you changed your mind."

He stood in the doorway, a box dangling from his fingers. Overhead the rain pelted the roof, and from where she stood she could see out onto the patio. The bistro set glistened and the patio doors were speckled with drops of rain despite the awning overhead. The awning stretched and flapped in the uplift, but held steadfast. Its valance riffled in waves, water dripping in long rivulets from it's saw tooth edges.

The sky lit up as a streak of lightening zipped across the clouds, and a low rumble sounded overhead.

The next flash of lightening lit up the room. "I promise you I will be a complete gentleman if you stay. I would never force myself on any woman, no matter how attracted to them I am."

"I know that," Penny said. "And I haven't changed my mind."

She walked towards him just as a clap of thunder rumbled overhead, rattling the patio door. Her walk turned into a small leap and she shrieked a little in surprise.

From the doorway Reuben chuckled.

"Of course this is funny to you," she said, reaching out to jab him in the chest. "Now come on before I change my mind, or before the power goes out, whichever comes first."

She snatched the box from his hand and walked past him into the bedroom. "For starters, your boxes aren't going to go far if you just throw the clothes in any which way. You'll fit more if you take the time to fold them."

She upturned the contents of the box onto the bed. The seafoam cardigan slipped to the floor unnoticed, and she lifted the salmon blazer from the pile and started to slip an arm into it. "Is this okay?"

"Sure."

She peeked at the tag before slipping the blazer on. "Oh, Burberry. Your Eve went for the finer things in life didn't she?"

"Aren't I a case in point?" he said.

"You wish." She pulled the blazer around her. "As pretty as it is, I look sort of ridiculous in it." The sleeves went nearly to her fingertips, and the hem of the blazer past her rear end.

"She was tall."

"I remember wishing on 11:11 every chance I got that I could be tall." She took the blazer off and neatly folded it. "I guess the eleven-eleven fairy never saw fit to grant me my wish."

She placed the folded blazer inside the box. "How do you want to do this? I can just grab things willy nilly or you can hand them to me. I'm not sure how you feel about me looking through her things."

Walking past her he went to the closet and pulled the doors open wider. She saw him breathe in deeply before he reached in to trace a hand down a white blouse. "What did you do first?"

She knew what he was referring to, but when she didn't answer right away he elaborated. "With David's things. Did you deal with his clothes or his personal items first?"

He reached for a pair of sunglasses on a shelf. "Because, honestly, I thought getting rid of her clothes would be easier than sorting through her things, but now I have no idea."

He slipped the sunglasses onto his face, and lifted a toque to his nose. He inhaled the scent from the knitted hat, then sighed deeply. "I guess all of it is hard, isn't it?"

"It is," she said, her voice small. This felt like intrusion. She didn't belong here, pawing through the life of the woman who's husband she'd fallen in love with, but at the same time she couldn't think of another place she'd rather be. She wanted to be here for him. "Everyone is different, and the way you associate to one thing is going to be completely different than how I would."

She could tell that her words weren't helping. "With David, I found his desk items really hard, because for me that's where his passion was. I found all sorts of personal thoughts and words of wisdom in his desk. I found poems he'd started for me, but never finished."

She laughed at the memory. "David was especially bad at procrastinating. More than anything he had a problem finishing things." She stammered then, her throat becoming thick and husky at the memory. "I found unfinished poems, unfinished short stories, and letters, and unfinished lists."

At that her voice warbled and a tear pushed from her eyelids, despite her best efforts to keep it at bay. It just took the one to start a whole stream, and soon she was blubbering like a fool. "I'm sorry," she apologized, and warded him off when he reached for her.

"Just wait," he said, tossing the sunglasses onto the bed. "I have the perfect thing."

He reached for a box beneath the closet and started to rifle through the contents. She watched him lift something from the box and affix it to his face.

"You ready for this?" he asked, standing.

"I'm ready," she said, a hint of uncertainty in her voice.

"Are you sure? Because you sound unsure."

"I'm sure."

"How sure?"

"God, Reuben don't leave me in suspense," she laughed, reaching forward to swipe him on the shoulder.

"That's more like it," he said. "I think you're ready now."

When Reuben turned he wore a pair of bubble glasses with a large nose attached. A fuzzy moustache sprang out in every direction beneath the nostrils, and fuzzy eyebrows and sideburns completed the look, haphazardly sticking out from all directions.

And it did the trick. As soon as she saw him she doubled over into side-splitting laughter. Seeing Reuben's smile beneath the moustache made her laugh all the more.

It also made her heart ache. The more time she spent with him, the more she loved him. But it needed to be this way. She needed to learn how to laugh and cry with him without craving for more.

"So she has fancy high-end blazers, brocade shoes, *and* wonky glasses. She was a mix of everything wasn't she?" She said as her laughter abated.

"There's a story behind these," he said, pulling the glasses from his face and closing them.

"There's *always* a story."

"But you're right, she was a perfect mix of everything. She went from classy to redneck at the drop of a pin. But there's a funny story behind these. We were at a carnival; they used to do those, remember? Mostly around Canada Day. We were there and they had one of those games where you had to shoot these small palm-size targets and the target got smaller the bigger the prize was. At the time we weren't pregnant, at least not definitely pregnant, but I thought maybe we were because she wasn't feeling well and she was cranky as hell. I didn't tell her what I thought, though."

He clasped the glasses in his fist. "So to try to bypass her crabby mood I was being extra sweet and considerate and trying to do everything right, but when we got to this game with the targets I was about ready to snap."

He opened the glasses again and studied them, and she knew by the wan smile on his face that in retelling the story he was right back there at the carnival. With Eve. "It was either the last game at the carnival or the first depending on where you entered. For us it was the last game. She'd already threatened to vomit from the Ferris wheel and a bad hot dog she'd eaten, so she was more than ready to head home."

He reached into the closet and pulled out a shoe box. He flipped off the cover and continued, "That game was the highlight of the carnival for me, and there was a line-up of people on both sides waiting for their turn at a prize."

The pictures in the box were in order according to year, and the years were marked with divider guides. He flipped to the year 2015.

"I fell in behind the guy in the shortest line possible, and Eve went ballistic. She started pulling on my arm and telling me that no way was she waiting so I could try to win a stuffed panther. But I wanted to do this. I hadn't tried my hand at this game since I was a teenager and I was almost certain I was a better shot now. I wanted to prove it, but she was determined to leave. With or without me. So she got her attitude on and told me if I didn't want to leave, I could stay, but she was leaving and taking the car; I could find my own way home. I tried to be cutesy. I pouted and begged, and even told her how beautiful she looked with her angry face on."

He slowed as he neared the pictures towards the middle of the 2014 stack. "I was eyeing the prizes along the back wall, and I saw these glasses. I didn't want them, but the prize I did want was right beside them, and of course the two targets were close to one another and the stupid glasses target was twice as big. I had my sights on a cute blue elephant with a pink plastic face."

He pulled out a picture and looked at it for a second before he continued. "She was a hard nut to crack, so I went in with big guns. I pulled her close to me and pointed at the elephant. 'See that?' I said, and then I reached to cup my hand over her tummy. 'I want to win that for baby Eve.' And it worked. She melted. The whole while I was lining up my sights to get the elephant I now had her pumped, she was jabbering beside me. She was telling me how it made perfect sense now, and she was adding up days on her fingers and telling how she was five days late, and how she hadn't once thought it could possibly be a baby. And the happier she got at the idea, the more I began to sweat."

He held the photo out for Penny to see. She looked down at the beautiful woman in the picture. She was glowing. Her stomach was as flat as a washboard, but the aura around her and the twinkle in her eyes, despite the crazy glasses she wore, was a telltale sign of her excitement and the life inside her.

Penny glanced up from the picture to see that Reuben had flipped to 2016. "I wasn't at all sure I was going to be able to hit that target now. You get three shots for six dollars. I leaned over the shooting-line and because I was kind of cheating there was more power behind the shot. I missed the target but I walloped the back diorama with so much force it fell loose at the corners. Eve was squealing beside me. My second shot bounced off the elephant target and right when I was about to take my final shot a kid bumped into me and my aim veered to the right. Damn kid cost me an elephant."

He lifted the glasses and affixed them to his face again. "This was my final prize. And of course, after all that," he pulled a couple of pictures from the box, "they became a must in annual family pictures."

In the pictures, each of the twins had their turn with the glasses on. They were barely old enough to sit, and the glasses looked sort of ridiculous, but Penny knew that was the point. It certainly got the desired effect and Penny laughed at the craziness of it.

In one picture, the twin in the fiery red and orange dress, Ember she assumed, was sound asleep, oblivious to the ridiculous mask that covered her whole head, perched perfectly on the tip of her tiny nose. They'd laid her down on her stomach and propped her face up onto her hands in a traditional baby pose.

"If you look close enough you can see a small piece of tape on her nose to hold the glasses on. They kept falling down her face."

Terra, in a brown and green dress in her picture, she was more alert, her eyes cross-eyed as she tried to focus on the monstrosity her parents had taped to her face. Her rounded cheeks looked puffier than they normally would have had she not pursed her lips and pulled her chin out in a bid to escape the offending mask.

Despite the ridiculous glasses, the pictures were priceless. "Do you have any of you with the glasses on as well?" she asked, lining the three pictures up on the bed.

"Why of course." He plucked two more pictures from the pile and laid them on the bed next to the others.

There was one of him, and one of Eve. In Eve's picture she had mimicked Terra with her eyes crossed and her chin jutted out. Penny bust out laughing when she looked at Reuben's. He'd taken Ember's pose, his feet stretched out behind him and his gorgeous face perched on his hands, head lulled to the side, and the glasses perched on the tip of his nose.

"These are priceless," she said. "You need to frame them."

"That was the plan," he said, collecting the pictures and placing them back in their allotted spot. "But then she got sick, and well..." He replaced the cover on the photo box and rose to return it to the closet. "She ran out of time."

He returned the photo box and the glasses. "I have no excuse, really. I just keep putting it off, but maybe someday."

Penny pushed from the bed to join him at the closet. Although she knew the dangers involved in touching him, she reached for his hand that still rested on the box he'd placed the mask in, and laced her fingers with his. When he turned to face her she placed her other hand on the side of his handsome face.

"You do have an excuse. You have three very real excuses that no one will ever contest. You're raising two beautiful little girls while grieving for their mother and the woman you still love, and on top of that you're trying to balance a career and a home. It's okay to not be perfect, Reuben."

"I'm hoping to have more time after the move," he said, slipping his fingers out of hers and reaching to move her hand from his face, but he held hers for a second longer than necessary. She felt the gentle brush of his thumb across her knuckles and light squeeze on her fingers before he released her.

A flash of lightening lit up the room, and the lights flickered off and on. The alarm clock instantly started blinking on the night stand. "If we don't hurry we'll be working in the dark," he said moving away from her.

"You don't have candles? Or a lantern?" Penny lifted the box they'd been filling to the bed. "Plus if we hurry we might be able to fill a box, and maybe clear away the clothes that are hanging."

She stopped short as his words sank in. "You're moving? Where are you moving?" A clap of thunder punctuated her words, and the whole room lit up as two flashes of lightening lit up the walls in rapid succession.

"I don't know yet. I haven't managed to find a place," he said. "I did accept a job transfer to Cornwallis."

"Cornwallis is thirty minutes from Ridgeville, Reuben."

"Yes, Penny, I'm aware of that."

He lifted an armload of clothes from the closet and dropped them to the bed beside the box with their hangers all tangled. "Thirty minutes from my mother, and five minutes from where I was brought up."

Forgetting the sensitivity she was trying to give him in regard to Eve's things, she pulled a sweater from one of the hangers and angrily folded it. "I can't have you right under my feet all the time."

"Right under your feet?" he said sharply. "It's not my fault my mother and your father decided to fall in love. And do you expect me to punish myself and my children because of your bad decisions?"

She dropped the folded sweater and looked at him, shock written in her eyes. "My bad decision?"

"Well yes," he said, stuffing a cardigan in on top of the sweater. "*You* propositioned *me*, remember? Not the other way around."

"*You* manhandled me!"

"I don't recall any complaints. In fact, all I can remember is you practically begging for it. In fact I might even still have traces of the scratches you left on my back. If you want to start splitting hairs, I can match you strand for strand," he said, moving closer to her.

"You kissed me under the trees, remember? I tried to get away and you wouldn't let me."

"Oh please," he said. "As soon as I kissed you, you wanted to tear my clothes off. You even *told* me you were the one who seduced me, not the other way around. Remember? It was that day in your basement when you propositioned me."

"Oh God, Reuben, don't you know a joke when you hear one?"

"Were you joking when you told me you loved me?" he asked. Then, realizing the route he'd taken, he stopped short, remorse filling his eyes.

She dropped an armload of clothes into the box, closed the flaps, and then flopped down on the edge of the bed. She was suddenly freezing and without even thinking she pulled the cardigan up from the floor and thrust her arms into the arm holes.

"Unfortunately, I wasn't," she said solemnly, shrugging into the cardigan. "And that's why I can't have you under my feet."

She inhaled, allowing the air to fill her lungs slowly, and then with a long exhale she popped up from the bed. "What was I thinking?"

She walked from the bedroom, him close on her heels. In the foyer she slipped her purse onto her shoulder and turned to slip her feet into her sandals.

"Penny, where are you going?"

"Being here is like swimming in a pool of crocodiles and thinking I won't get eaten." She pulled her second sandal on and turned to look at Reuben. "It's crazy thinking. It's impossible."

She flipped open her purse and began rummaging through the contents. "Where'd I put my damn phone?"

With a swift movement she upturned her purse and spilled its contents onto the small table in the foyer. Keys, coins, and a comb went flying onto the rug. She quickly swept them up and returned them to her purse, protesting when he bent to help her. "My phone. Did you see my phone?"

Taking several steps deeper into the apartment, he made a quick sweep of the counter and the table. "I don't see it."

She pushed past him and made her own sweep, before slipping into his room. She tousled the blankets in her search, and swept a hand over the pile of clothing on top of the bed.

"I don't need it anyway," she said, pushing past him again to return to the door.

As she neared him, he reached out to touch her, but she was too quick and stepped out of his reach, pulled open the door and took off down the hall.

Reuben watched from his window as Penny emerged from the apartment building three floors down. The sidewalk shimmered under the street lamp, the pavement sleek with rain.

Eve's bad-news cardigan fanned out behind her as she ran across the street to her car. She fiddled with the keys and then slipped inside just before another clap of thunder sounded and lightening tore across the sky.

He leaned into the window and watched her out of sight.

He liked the idea of her phone being somewhere near him. It gave her a reason to return to him, or for him to go to her should he find it.

And there was something else, too. When she'd upturned her purse, something had bounced off the edge of the table and toppled to his feet. He held it up as another flash of lightening lit up the room, the light glinting off the key in his hand.

He had the key to the shack.

20

A stack of boxes sat by the front door the next morning. It had not been an easy task but Reuben had sorted through all of Eve's clothing.

He'd kept the brocade swing shoes to put away for Terra, and a pink lambskin Chanel purse for Ember. It would be a few years before either of his daughters would get the items, so he'd have to Google search the proper way to store them to keep the moisture out, and ensure they stayed in as good condition as they were in now for the next twelve years or so.

The power had gone out around midnight, but was back on in the early morning hours. The rain had eased, and although everything outside was still damp and dreary, Halifax harbour glistened under the orange sunrise. With the promise of a beautiful day on the horizon, Reuben made plans to head back to Ridgeville to tie up loose ends with his part of the oasis and collect his girls.

He shoved the key to the shack and Penny's cellphone into his pocket, although he still had no idea what he would do with either.

After Penny had left last night he'd taped off the couple of boxes they'd managed to fill. Although he knew he should probably continue clearing things out, the idea of doing it without Penny was not an appealing thought, so he'd crawled into bed instead. The thought of sleeping without her was hard to wrap his mind around, but eventually he'd willed his mind to quiet and had fallen asleep.

It was in the wee hours of the night, amidst the power outage, that the faint sound of a phone ringing stirred him awake.

It had taken him several seconds to realize it wasn't his own phone, and he threw back the covers to fumble his way through the dark toward the sound. He found it in one of the sealed boxes, wedged between the stilettos and the Burberry blazer.

By the time he reached it, the call had ended, and he needed a pass code to get to the phone's main screen.

He'd risen early and finished sorting the clothes in an effort to get started on the road early, and even though he'd been finished for some time now he couldn't get himself to leave the city.

She was still here. He could sense it. What if she returned for her phone and he were gone? Should he wait? Shouldn't he stick around to make sure she got her phone back so she wouldn't travel home without it? If she had car troubles or anything at all were to happen he needed to know she had a phone to call for help.

Where was she staying? He hadn't asked, and she hadn't volunteered. He couldn't very well ring up every hotel and bed and breakfast in the area. Well, he could, but it wouldn't be prudent. And in all honesty he didn't have the time. How many accommodations spots did Halifax have anyway?

So he did the only thing he knew to do. He swallowed a huge lump of pride and called Kyle.

"She's at the Marriott Harbour front," Kyle said reluctantly.

Reuben's stomach twisted. It hurt more than he cared to admit that she'd told Kyle where she was going but not him. But then her whole reason for leaving Ridgeville in the first place had been to get away from him. He wondered how she'd felt when she realized she was less than a ten minute walk away.

"She doesn't deserve this," Kyle was saying.

"Deserve what? I'm returning her phone. There's nothing nefarious about it."

"We both know that's not true."

"You don't know shit," Reuben said. "I would never intentionally hurt her."

"Well you did," Kyle said. "And she doesn't deserve this. Just leave her the hell alone. You don't deserve her."

"I already know how you feel about me Kyle. You've already passed judgment on me without knowing who I am. That's okay with me. I'm a big boy, I can handle it. But don't take it out on me because she's not in-terested in you."

"You're right, I don't know you, but my vision is 20/20, and from where I'm standing it looks like you saw a vulnerable woman and took advantage of her broken heart."

Reuben squeezed his cellphone in a death grip. "Have you appointed yourself her guardian?"

"She's my friend, and good friends don't so\it around and watch while others hurt them."

Kyle sounded too calm, too sure of himself, too confident in what he was saying.

"Yes I hurt her," Reuben said, compelled to confess his wrong-doings. "Was it intentional? Not even close. I don't pretend to be perfect, but I'm not some pompous asshole who sets out to destroy every beautiful wo-man I sleep with."

"Then leave her alone, man," Kyle said solemnly. "Don't take the phone to her room. Leave it at the front desk and have them give it to her. She said she needs space, right?"

"...She did."

"Then give her space."

"Yeah," Reuben said, resigned. "I guess you're right."

As much as he hated to admit it, Kyle was right. He needed to give Penny the space she asked for.

He approved of anyone who had Penny's best interest at heart, but he was unsure about Kyle. At the first chance he got he'd been all over her. So although he talked a good game, Reuben wasn't sure what he was really up to. "But Kyle?"

"Yeah?"

"You leave her alone, too. If I hear so much as a whisper that you've put your grubby paws on her, I'll break them."

"And what if she asks me to put my paws on her?"

Reuben hated the smug tone in Kyle's voice. What had Penny said? Something about Kyle being a complete gentleman and asking if he could kiss her? "Trust me, she won't."

"And what makes you so sure?"

"Because she loves me." He tried to sound confident. If Kyle had asked to kiss Penny, and he had in fact kissed her, then that meant she had consented. What if he asked for more? Would she consent to that too? "I'm serious Kyle," he said in a husky voice, "you so much as look at her in that way and I will break every bone in your fucking body."

Kyle laughed. "Just so you know, Rue, once you've eaten the cake, that's it, it's gone. Kaput. Finished. Time to move on."

"Don't test me, Kyle."

"You don't want her, but no one else can have her either? Is that seriously the kind of dipshit man you are?"

He wanted her. He wanted her so badly it hurt. He wanted her right now. He knew he'd want her tomorrow, too. He wanted her for all the tomorrows the world had to offer.

But what he wanted and what she needed were two different things. He just knew, somehow, that Kyle wasn't it for her. She needed someone better.

"She'll fall in love with someone else again someday, it won't be me, and it sure as hell won't be you," he promised.

"You don't know her at all do you?" Kyle said.

"I know her a hell of a lot better than you ever will."

"Just because you've rolled in the hay with her doesn't mean you know her. From what I'm hearing it doesn't sound like you know her at all."

Of course he didn't completely know her. Every second with her was like a new revelation. "Oh, and I suppose you're an expert?"

"I've sat with her. I've had long conversations with her. She's poured her heart and soul out to me. She's nothing like you seem to think she is."

"How so?"

"She doesn't just fall in and out of love on a whim," Kyle said. "I wish she did. I really do, because I truly believe I'd be a hell of a lot better for her than you. That doesn't matter now, though, does it? Because, for reasons I don't understand, she's fallen in love with you, and when Penny falls in love its forever."

He knew that too. He'd already discovered that. It was written all over her face. When she talked about David he could see the love radiating from her, he could feel it. And when she looked at him, it was with that same love.

But her love for him had a bitter undertone; he couldn't deny feeling that too. She loved him and hated herself for it. All he had to do was tell her the truth and that bitterness would disappear. If he could give her a lifetime, he'd wrap her in all the love she deserved. If she could see inside him, could feel what he felt at just the mere sight of her, all the bitterness and hurt would disappear.

But there was one problem. Although she could compartmentalize one love from the other, he couldn't. Although he'd safely tucked Eve away in the box in his brain he had reserved for the most precious love of his past he wasn't quite ready to close the lid on her yet.

"I don't think you know how lucky you are to have someone like Penny love you," Kyle was saying. "She's not just going to stop because you tell her to. She's going to love you forever. Even if she does find someone to fall in love with again someday, you are going to be another hard obstacle she's going to have to knock down. It'll take her longer to trust, and longer to open her heart again, but she will. But every time she gives love a thought, you're going to float to her memory. You are going to be the new David she has to learn to let go of." Kyle paused, and on the other end of the phone Reuben ran his fingers through his damp black hair. "It's going to be harder in a lot of ways to let you go than it has been for David, though."

"And why do you think that?" Reuben asked his voice thick with emotion.

"Because you're still here, and you're not going anywhere anytime soon."

"Fuck." He ran a hand through his hair again, pressing his fingers into his scalp. He was developing a headache, and all this talk about hurting Penny wasn't helping matters any. "Listen, I gotta go. I don't suppose you know how long she's planning to stay in the city?"

"Just the weekend, but Warren did say he suggested she stay longer. Whether she does or not is another story."

"I'm heading back to Ridgeville now to get my girls. I hope I can get out of there before she returns, like she asked me to do in the first place."

"Are you sure that's what you want?"

"Whose side are you on anyway? The way you were talking a moment ago I thought you'd be raring to help me pack."

"I'm on Penny's side. Always. I'm just not sure you're making the right move."

"Neither am I." Reuben admitted. "Neither am I."

He pulled the phone from his ear and ended the call.

21

Penny's morning was eventful. She had the opportunity to meet with the owner of *Spa and Sip*, and drop off some new and fresh products from her distillery. Everything about *Spa and Sip*'s environment felt perfect to her. It was the epitome of what she wanted people to get from her products: complete tranquility and relaxation. Seeing *Land of Lavendula* displayed and advertised made her a little giddy, but she managed to remain courteous and professional as she talked about her business and what they could expect from her in the future.

There was no denying that her business was finally stretching its wings, and she felt confident that *Spa and Sip* was the extra push needed to send it a flight. With any luck at all *Land of Lavendula* would be soaring before too long, and her only concern now was if she would be able to keep up with the demand.

Well, she would damn sure try. For now five acres would do, but if all went well she might need to set her sights on more land for expansion. Her dad's land was already tied up in his oasis project. Maybe next year, if all went as planned, she'd ask the Larkin sisters about selling their land beyond the brook.

Nothing was definite yet, and she had lots of time to think about it, but maybe putting the bug in Claire's ear now would be a start at getting her ducks in a row. That way Claire would have a whole year to maul it over and run it by Saulie, and Penny would have some time to drum up a second plan should this one fall through.

There was nothing wrong with securing your future was there? And it was okay to dream a little, right?

Now, as she neared the shack, her foot let up on the gas pedal and she engaged the blinker. As she eased the car into the narrow driveway the trees flittered in the breeze. The uncut grass around the cabin riffled in soft waves; a shallow ocean of green in her headlights.

The shack, a forbidding shadow of grey and black against the setting sun, stood desolate and lonely. As the lights washed over the rustic exterior, slowly spotlighting the place she'd come to know as the love shack, she noticed that someone had repaired the deck and secured the loosened clapboards, and that the stump that once hid the key was back in its usual corner, a discarded soldier refusing to fall by the wayside.

Parked in the driveway of the Larkin's shack, her arms wrapped around the steering wheel, Penny looked out over the small lake. The dark water shimmered beneath the orange sky, only the occasional ripple marring its glassy veneer. Clumped to one side were withering water lilies, long past their prime and decaying on the water's surface. Leaves from the maple trees caught in their pads and wilted petals; joined in death.

The summer had been a good one, all things considered. Her heart had been awakened again. She had learned to let go. Not once, but twice. She'd made a new friend, and he'd taught her the art of drinking. Her business had grown. Her family was growing.

And even while she was sad for what was lost, she was happy, too. Not a one-sided happiness, but an all-encompassing one. Because while she had loved another, and did love another, she loved herself, too, and it had been far too long since she'd done so. It had been a long time since she'd put herself first.

Having loved and lost David had made her cling to those around her. It made her lose herself in others, and in lavender fields, and things. But loving Reuben had awakened something new within her.

When she was alone with him, he awoke a hunger within her that she had forgotten existed. She'd not only forgotten what it was like to give to another, but she'd forgotten what it was like to get, and Reuben had given her herself again. He'd made her want again, he'd showed her her self-worth, and because of that she would never settle for less.

When she loved again, it would be with someone who loved her back equally. Who gave to get, and took to give. Who loved her beyond her imperfections, and smoothed away any rough edges with the soft caress of his words. Together they would fashion a life that could survive with just one, but flourished with two. A life where two became one, and one was better with two.

It was true that Reuben would be her step-brother, and she would learn to live with that. Later. Preferably, much later. For now he would remain only Number Seven.

Yes, all things considered, she was okay. And she would be okay. She started the ignition and backed from the driveway, a new determination and a new direction in her sights.

~

Even as the distance grew wider between Reuben and the cottage, the smell of lavender followed him, thanks to the plants wedged between the car seats. They would only ever be window plants in the city, which seemed like an abomination to him. After waking up to the sea of purple every morning for the last few weeks, he longed to have his own purple sea. The plants needed a full ground to stretch their roots in, and get larger and stronger. With any luck at all he would find the perfect home in the country and transplant them come spring.

Lavender would always remind him of Penny, but avoiding her would be hard to do anyway. He was going to have to get used to small bits and spurts of her leaking into his life now, and for the time being lavender was a perfect way to get use to the idea. It might be exactly what he and the children needed.

Maybe with time the smell would take on new meaning. Either way, the girls wouldn't leave the plants behind, so no matter how many memories the smell evoked he would just have to make new ones to associate with it.

It wasn't as though she held the trademark on the scent; he could assign it new meaning if he chose too. He'd add the plants to the girls' daily routines and, before he knew it, the plants would integrate themselves seamlessly into his life.

Earlier that day he'd driven to the hardware store and bought the supplies needed to fix the damage to the love shack. He felt it was his duty to spruce the place up; to give back in some way or another.

As he drove the nails into the clapboards he felt like it was respectful in some way. Sure, the shack had been a place for him and Penny to escape to, but it had been more than just a love shack. It had been a sanctuary, a place to let their hair down, and let go for awhile; a place of redemption.

As a finishing touch, he'd returned the stump to the deck; and because it felt right he placed the key back beneath it. It felt comforting to know it was there. It felt like there was hope, and right now even the illusion of hope was enough. For now.

He peered at his girls in the mirror. Terra stifled a yawn and tucked her chin into the blanket she held. Ember straightened Lacey's hair beneath the floppy sunhat the doll wore, and hummed softly. It was rounding on their bedtime, and he knew before they reached Lequille both girls would be sleeping.

"Is Nanna gonna live here forever?" Ember asked, pulling Lacey's hat down over the doll's perpetually open eyes.

"Yes," Reuben said. "But that doesn't mean we won't ever see her again."

"When will we see her again?" Terra asked, lifting her head from the blanket.

"We'll see her all the time. Just because she's not going to live with us any more doesn't mean she'll never come visit us, and we'll definitely visit her. Would you like that?"

"Uh huh," Terra said, her voice muffled as she yawned and tucked the blanket back up under her chin.

"Why does she want to marry Penny's daddy anyway?" Ember asked.

How do you explain love to four-year-olds? How do you explain that things change once love is added to the mix?

"Are they gonna kiss?" Terra asked from the folds of her blanket. She'd tucked her thumb into her mouth, something he hadn't seen her do in months. It was a security measure, he knew, and it made him sad to see her revert to her old habits.

Reuben said. "When two people meet one another, and realize how well they get along, sometimes they fall in love and never want to be away from one another. So the easy way to fix that is by getting married. Getting married is like a pledge to one another that you love them and want to spend the rest of your lives together."

"Did we get married, daddy?"

"No, silly," Terra said. "Getting married is for people who kiss and dance."

"I kiss Daddy, and he dances with us sometimes. Remember when he twirled you when you were singing the Bambi song?"

Reuben laughed. It was going to be hard, explaining love and forever when all he wanted to do was forget about it. "No, Ember we aren't married. The bond between a daddy and his daughter starts even before he sees her. It's a love that is so ingrained that it's not clear where it begins, and so it goes on forever and ever. Like a circle. You know what a circle is, don't you?"

Ember and Terra each drew a sloppy circle in the air.

"That's right." Reuben eased to a stop at the side of the road. He leaned forward and blew on the windshield. In the condensation he drew a circle. "See how a circle just keeps going around and around and around?'

"Uh huh." Both girls were leaned forward, watching in fascination.

"Well, that's how my love for you is. It has no beginning or end, because I didn't choose to love you. I just do. Now watch this.' He leaned forward and blew on the glass again. "See this?" he said, drawing an infinity symbol in the condensation. "That's an infinity loop."

"ninfininny loop," Ember said.

"That's right," Reuben said. "It reminds me of falling in love. It starts right here." He pointed to the intersection where the two loops converge. "You meet someone, and fall in love, like I did with mommy, and the infinity loop starts."

He traced the loop over and over, stopping at the intersection again. "If you're lucky, the loop goes on and on, but sometimes the loop can break."

"Did yours and mommy's loop break?"

"Well, sort of," he said, trying not to sound too solemn. "I still love your mommy very much, but when she died our loop did kind of break."

"Did you like the loop, daddy?"

He stared off at approaching headlights. "I did like the loop. Very much. And in a lot of ways I think a perfect life is having a circle, *and* a loop, but sometimes life doesn't work that way."

"So Nanna's gonna have a loop now?" Terra asked.

"Yes Nanna and Spencer will have their own loop, but she'll always have circles for us, and remember what I said about circles?"

"They go on and on forever," Ember piped up.

"That's right. Her love for us will go on forever, even if she doesn't live with us anymore. When you have a loop it takes a little more work to care for. So you have to live together, and take care of it together. Loving someone you've chosen to love is a lot like buying a flower. You have to take care of it so it will grow and be beautiful and strong."

The approaching car slowed as it neared, and Reuben's eyes locked on Penny's. "So once they're married, Nanna's going to live here with Spencer. That way they can take care of their loop together."

He turned on his blinker as Penny passed, and pulled back out unto the road again. He didn't accelerate until her taillights were out of sight, and only then did he allow himself to move forward.

But the move tore at his heart with each complete turn of the tires. It felt as though a lasso was around his heart, being pulled taut until it snapped and he was left reeling. He felt depleted. Gypped somehow. His loop wilted.

"We'll take care of our circles together," Ember said from the back seat.

"Yeah," Terra echoed.

"Yes," Reuben agreed. "That's what we'll do. We'll take care of our circles together."

Rhoda C. Hill

22

The gold fringe of Penny's gown brushed her ankles and rustled the leaves at her feet. The sun filtered through the trees, and the golden leaves embroidered in the skirt of her gown shimmered and sparkled as they caught on the scattered beams. The natural carpet crunched beneath her feet as she walked. Golden sandals dangled from her finger tips.

She was alone, for now. Soon the sun would set, the solar lights would illuminate the forest, and guests would make their way up the pathway towards the pagoda.

She'd see him. Soon.

Reuben hadn't been at rehearsal the night before, but she knew he was here now. She'd seen his jeep parked in front of the big house. She'd had nearly two months to get over him, and she had. So, even though seeing his jeep had caused a skip in her heart it had only been out of habit.

She was so over him. So much so that she'd accepted an invitation to dinner last week with Lowell, a man she'd met at her *Land of lavendula* booth during an end of summer fair. She'd accepted just to prove to herself that she was over him, and during the evening she'd only thought of him once.

If they hadn't stopped for ice cream, her night would have been Reuben-free. Would ice cream ever be the same again? Would she not taste the coldness on her lips and instantly think of him?

As soon as Lowell mentioned ice cream the memory of Reuben had stirred in her, but she'd fought to keep it at bay. She'd been succeeding too, but without any prior indication Lowell had reached to kiss her. It was just a light kiss, just a soft brush on her lips, but the kiss and the ice cream mingled together brought Reuben flooding to her mind at full speed.

She'd pulled back before Lowell could deepen the kiss and make the date more than it actually was, and they'd finished their ice cream in silence. Ended the evening with apologies.

She had moved on. Sure, memories bucked at her from time to time, but she had let go. She was fine now. So why the hell was her heart all aflutter? Why did she keep glancing over her shoulder in hopes of seeing him?

She tossed her sandals onto the steps of the pagoda and walked inside. It was three tiered, with the first level completely enclosed, but two large doors opened up level one, pulling it into the elements and the elements into the pagoda.

As she opened the big doors leaves danced inside and flitted about on the rustic floor boards. In the centre of level one was a spiral staircase leading up to the next two levels. The whole design had a bucolic feel to it: the entangled branches fashioned into a candled chandelier hanging from the ceiling, the black ash baskets in the corners, the primitive boards framing the windows, right down to the woven rug on the floor.

The leaves from the open door fetched up on the rug, clawed at its edges, and danced about on the rug's surface.

Gyla had suggested using The pagoda's when they had had to abandon the original spot to protect rare lady's-slipper orchids growing in the area. The ground was favourable for the orchids, and moving them was not an option since the fungi found around them couldn't be found in most soils. If they were uprooted they'd likely die within hours.

The next two levels were decks, opened out into the forest with rustic railings lining their edges. As she ascended the steps Penny watched as the tree tops, the brook, the big house, and the sky came more and more into view with each step. She wondered how the old location could have improved upon this view. It was perfect. Each step-up was more spectacular than the one before.

In a very short time Gyla would officially become her step-mother. She smiled at the thought. She couldn't have chosen a better person for her dad had she hand-picked her herself.

Gyla's only drawback was her son. After today any hopes of avoiding him could be thrown to the wolves. After today he would be family; her step-brother.

"I don't want to be your brother any more than you want me to be."

He'd had his fingers inside her when he'd said that, his other hand on her breast, his mouth on her skin, and she'd given herself to him in a wild frenzy of passion. She had practically begged him to upend her whole world and confuse the shit out of things. She'd clung to him like he was the only living male on earth, and she was desperate for love.

Then the whole thing had backfired on her. He'd been left no worse for wear and she'd skulked away with her tail tucked between her legs, resigned and hurting.

"Baby girl?"

Spencer's voice echoed up through the pagoda before she heard his footfall on the stairs. She pushed a tear, she was only just then aware had even fallen, from her cheek. The guilt at not being blissfully happy on her fathers wedding day consumed her. She felt numb. She felt non-existent. She felt disbursed and scattered, lost and lonely.

And here she was, feeling like all that, and what had she done to combat it? She'd rolled it up all together, and dressed it in a pretty gown. It would have to work for now. She'd sort through the chaos later. She'd fix her scrambled self at the end of the day, but for now, for her father's sake, she would pretend.

She plastered a smile on her face to complete the ensemble, and turned to greet him.

He looked dapper. More handsome than she'd ever seen him look before.

"You clean up nicely, Daddy," she said, reaching to straighten a lock of his hair. His brown tweed blazer had flecks of cider, sandstone, and honey. The buttons, pocket square and flaps were a spicy brown. He wore a light grey cravat rather than the traditional tie. Grey cotton pants and tawny shoes completed the look.

And on his face was the truest smile she'd ever seen. It went straight to his eyes, and burst from him in the most infectious outpouring of happiness.

"Look at you," he said, cupping her face in his hands. "You truly are your mother's daughter."

The compliment upended the vial of tears she'd been trying to keep upright, and she crumbled in front of the groom.

"I'm sorry," she said, dabbing at her eyes with the back of her hands.

"Don't be," he said, folding her into his arms. "Here." He pulled the pocket square from his blazer and handed it to her.

She pressed the square of cotton into the corners of her eyes, trying not to disturb the makeup she'd applied earlier. She didn't wear makeup well, but she'd added a small dusting to soften her pale complexion and help complement the taupe gown she wore.

"Could Gyla ask for a more beautiful maid of honour? I think not." Spencer ran a finger down the tousled waves of her hair and smiled. "How did I get so lucky? A gorgeous bride with a heart of gold, a son with such a brilliant head on his shoulders who still thinks I'm the cat's meow, and the most precious daughter any man could ask for, who has lived through hell and is no worse for wear, and is still my rock."

"Oh, daddy." She said wrapped her arms around him. "You *are* the cats meow. Warren and I are the lucky ones. And you are absolutely right, Gyla *is* amazing." She pulled back and looked at him. "I couldn't be happier for you. I absolutely love her. Warren loves her. It's a win-win."

"Love always finds a way, Penny-Laine. Remember that."

"I'm not even going to tell you how much I hate that name, it's your wedding day and I don't want to spoil it." She stretched up to kiss his cheek.

He laughed, and held her out at arm's length. "There's something missing," he said, eyeing her from head to toe.

"There is?" She reached to check for the pearls on her earlobes. They were still there. She felt along her braided crown, patted at the tousled waves of her hair, and stepped back to search about her feet. "Oh I know what it is. I left my sandals on the steps."

"Oh, I found it," he said.

He'd removed a gold necklace from his pocket and it dangled between them. She reached out to hold the heart extending from the chain against the palm of her hand. Both of their birthstones, topaz and amethyst, dangled together in the heart's centre.

"I wanted to get you something."

"You didn't have to." She turned for him to clasp the necklace around her neck.

"It felt right," he said, and she turned back around. "You mean so much to me. Not only are you my daughter, but you've been my friend, my confidante, my go-to person. My love for you far exceeds any explanation I could ever come up with. You are a treasure I wouldn't trade for anything, and I hope you always remember that."

Footsteps sounded on the stairs behind them, and they both turned. Reuben stood before her, a bronze god in a grey suit and a taupe shirt with a spicy tie. He wore the same tawny shoes as Spencer, and the same-colour pocket square. His hair loose and soft hung down his back.

"Sorry," he said and stepped back. "I didn't mean to intrude; I just thought maybe I ought to touch base with the maid of honour before we walk down the aisle together."

Penny's stomach did flip-flops, and even though she longed to be alone with him, another part of her wanted to beg her father not to leave.

"And so you should. I was just leaving," Spencer said. He gave Penny a parting hug. "I approve," he whispered in her ear before moving aside and heading down the steps.

~

"You look beautiful." Reuben moved closer to Penny, making sure to keep a good distance between them for comfort's sake. She was already making it hard to breathe, and he reached up to tug at the tie around his neck.

"Thank you," she said. He heard the tremble in her voice and saw the shake of her fingers before she tucked them within the crook of her elbows, her arms crossed protectively over her chest. "You look nice, too. I don't like it."

That caught him off guard, and he chuckled. "You don't like it?"

"It's just not you."

"It's still me. Just in nicer clothes."

"Yeah. I don't like it."

If their relationship were more relaxed he'd ask her if she'd like to remove them later, but that wasn't where they were at. He'd halted the forward steps they'd made together. Now the only way onward was to step back and start over.

"Me either," he said truthfully. His arms ached for her, his lips twitched to kiss her, and his heart was both squeezing in his chest and fluttering against his rib cage. "How have you been?"

"Fine." She reached to smooth the skirt of her gown. "Doing great, actually. You?"

""I've missed you," he said, and, as he had anticipated, she recoiled. He spoke quickly, to try to save her from crashing inward. "No please, listen to me."

And then he reached for her. After two months of never seeing her, he finally had his hands on her, and she felt like home.

Her lips quivered and she tried to speak. A tear pushed from her eye and hovered at the edge of her eyelashes. He quickly reached to catch it on his fingertips. His eyes locked with hers as he raised the moist finger to his lips and kissed the tear away.

"Two months ago I left you. Parked alongside the road watching your taillights fade out of sight was one of the hardest things I've ever had to do, but I did it because I wasn't ready. I told my girls a loop needed two to grow, and the whole time I explained why Mom and Spencer needed to be together I was in denial. A loop needs two people to help it grow; two people to tend to it and polish it and keep it flowing perfectly. Two people who love one another and are willing to work at it together. Two people who are present and willing."

"A loop?"

"A loop," he said, taking her hand in his. "Let me show you." He led her down the stairs to level one of the pagoda and walked over to the window. Breathing on the pane of glass he placed his finger in the middle of the condensation. "This is where I realized I loved you." Slowly his finger drew out from the centre and he quickly drew the infinity loop, retracing it over and over again. "No matter what life throws at me, you, and I know you dislike this word, but us," he said, still retracing the infinity loop as he spoke. "It always comes back to the same thing."

His finger stopped in the centre again, at the intersection where the two loops converged. "Right here. Back to three simple words." He turned to her, not daring to touch her. Fearing it was too late for them. Fearing that she'd let go forever.

"What three words?" she asked, her voice a hitch.

"I love you," he whispered.

She shook her head, and tears spilled from the corner of her eyes. "Don't do this. Not now. Not today when everyone is supposed to be happy."

"Don't do what? Don't tell you that the last two months have been hell for me? Don't tell you that my life without you is just a small flicker compared to the blaring fire it could be if you were next to me? Don't tell you that you're all I think about? That I've been like a lovesick teenager stalking you on Facebook and wondering what you are doing?"

He cupped her face within his hands and leaned in to her. He didn't kiss her. He wouldn't do that again until she was ready. "I've been half a person without you." He traced her lips with his fingers. "I love you. I already know I want you with me tomorrow and the next day and all the tomorrows the world has to offer us, but I won't do that to you without first showing you I mean it."

"And Eve?"

"Oh Eve." He smiled fondly. "She was such a pretty part of my life, and in two ways she'll always be a part of my life, and I'll always love her, I'm not denying that. But our loop has lain down. It's still there, it always will be, but it's had its time. It's gone out. And now it's a sweet memory I will cherish forever. It's run its course. It's our turn now."

"Are you sure?" she whispered. "Because I can't stand it if you're lying to me."

"I want us to start over." He reached into the pocket of his coat. "I want to date you properly. I want to take you out into the world and show them that you are mine. And then when you are ready I want to marry you."

He flipped out the box. An infinity loop dangled from a delicate gold chain. One end of the chain passed through one loop and ended in a gold heart. "But for now, this is my promise to you. My promise that I love you now and forever, and someday when the time is right I want you to be my wife."

"I want that too," she whispered. "More than anything."

She didn't turn for him to put the necklace on; instead she leaned forward and lifted her hair from around her neck.

He leaned into her to clasp the necklace. It dropped against her throat, hovering just above the necklace her father had given her.

"Kiss me?" she asked as she dropped her hair back around her shoulders.

"Gladly."

His voice was deep and husky, but his kiss gentle and sweet.

As he folded her against him and deepened the kiss he heard the squeals of delight as two little dark haired girls came bounding up the steps of the pagoda. He didn't release Penny,. Instead he whispered in her ear, "You have no idea what you just got yourself into."

She pulled from him and bent just in time to gather the girls into her arms, rising with a child on each hip, their frilly gowns shooting out at all angles.

Terra's tiny finger reached forward, and she made a circle around the infinity symbol still visible on the window.

"Ninfinninny loop," Ember said, touching the chain on Penny's neck.

"I know exactly what I'm getting myself into," Penny said, and she leaned in to kiss Reuben again. As their lips touched Ember and Terra leaned in and planted a kiss on each of her cheeks, their arms encircling Reuben's neck to draw all four of them into a circle.

As the sun sat on the horizon and the solar lights activated all around them, they walked from the pagoda to join the rest of the wedding party. A promise on the horizon, a better tomorrow in sight. The first joining of the Lafford and McCall family, but by no means the last.

THE END

Acknowledgements

Just before I sat down to write this acknowledgement, I was having chicken soup and tea. I am never very good at these things, so I tried to write it in my mind in between blows to cool off my soup. "I could thank this person and this person and this person," I was thinking, and before I knew it I realized that I had a whole plethora of people I could attribute my writing to. Suddenly I realized that as a single person I kind of fall short, but with the help of a ton of others who played in different facets of my life I was able to grow and stand on my own two feet.

First I want to thank my Mom and Dad, who never allowed a television into our home. As a child I regretted that, but now I believe that living without it is what turned me to books and ultimately turned my creative wheels spinning and got my fingers itching. Thanks for buying me that monstrous brown typewriter and letting me waste piles of loose leaf.

Thanks to God for giving me this talent in the first place, and helping my fingers to fly over the keyboard. Despite what others believe, I think you are the driving force behind it all.

Thanks to my best friend Suann (Soupie), who first stepped out into the world of writing with me and was my very first critique partner. I still take all your writing advice to heart and cannot wait until the world gets to read your amazing masterpieces. Your talent runs deep.

I also want to thank my aunt and one of my best friends, Marlene, who is always a sounding board for me. She lets me vent and bounce ideas off her and for that I will forever be grateful.

I thank my daughter Evelina for always being willing to watch her younger brother so I can have a few more minutes to write, and for encouraging me to put myself out there, and not sell myself short.

I thank my son Arless Hill for constantly correcting my poor English and for ALWAYS being the voice of reason. I love that you are only a message away when I have an English question, and your love for the language is palpable.

I could go on for pages, if I took the time to write all the reasons I am thankful for my husband, Clifford. He has never lost faith in me, even when I've lost faith in myself. He's been the one to push me when I'm procrastinating. I cannot count the number of times he's told me to not worry about the house and instead write, and if he's come home to a house in shambles he's not once complained about it. All the car rides he's taken our younger, autistic son Elijah on so that I can have writing time in quiet are too numerous to count. I cannot express my appreciation for you enough.

I want to thank my grade five English teacher. Mr. Veinot, for always pointing out my writing in my journals and having me read aloud to the class when he felt they were especially good. I will forever be grateful for you for pulling me to the desk to talk privately about my potential and telling me I could make it so much better if I used my five senses to do so. The vote of confidence is one of few treasured memories from my school days, and still resonates with me in 2020. The world needs more teachers like you.

I would be remiss if I did not mention my friend Larry Smith. We have never met in reality but our 20+ years of friendship has been one of my favourite things about my life. Always supportive and one of the best critique partners I've ever had. Many years ago he told me my dialogue was very weak and I worked my butt off to get it up to par. I hope I've succeeded. I am blessed to get such words of advice from such an amazing writer.

I want to thank Lari Smythe, Michelle Helliwell, and Stella MacLean for being the first readers of *Loving Number Seven*. I am very appreciative of your time and your beautiful words.

I want to thank the owner of Moose house Publications, Brenda Thompson, for taking a chance on me. I hope your investment and time proves to be worthwhile.

A massive thanks to my editor, Andrew Wetmore, for the magic you worked that made my jumbled words coherent to others. Also thanks for taking my small tantrums with such grace and talking me through them.

And thanks as well to all of you who take a chance on *Loving Number Seven*. I have poured my all into it and I hope that shows. I truly hope you enjoy it at least a quarter as much as I have enjoyed writing it.

Thanks

Rhoda C. Hill
October 22, 2020

About the author

Rhoda C. Hill writes a broad array of fiction that spans several genres. Her writing has appeared in *The First Line*, and she was a finalist in Harlequin's Killer Voice contest in 2014. Two of her short stories appear in *Moose House Stories, Volume 1*. She is hard at work on the next books in the *Love Shack* series.

Rhoda thrives on the love of her family, rainstorms, books, and writing. She lives in Doucetteville, Nova Scotia with her husband, three children, and five furbabies. Rhoda can be reached on Facebook (rhodaswritingpage) and Twitter (@Creaeh).

Chapter 1 of 'Tough All Over'

Tough All Over is book two in *The Love Shack* series. We hope to have it in bookstores sometime in 2021. For now, here's an early look at chapter one.

"Has my bouquet arrived yet?"

The look of excitement in her mother's eyes got to Claire every time. She'd be lying if she said the question didn't aggravate her, too, because it did. The first few times her mother asked in the run of a day were bearable, but hearing it over and over became increasingly tedious.

Claire positioned the cushion on the wicker chair in the corner of her mother's room, and breathed deeply to help mollify her agitation before turning to reassure her mother. "Not yet, but as soon as it does I'll let you know."

Claire's parent's, Bill and Pidge Larkin, were prime examples of true love. Right up until his death six years ago, Bill never forgot a birthday or an anniversary. He carefully thought out his bouquet for Mother's Day, that the local florist assembled, and Bill never handed over so much as a cent until every flower and bud met his approval.

He chose whimsical over romantic, so a rose rarely made the cut. King Proteas, buttercups, panda anemones, and silver dollar eucalyptus were some of his favourites, and every year Pidge had the anticipation of wondering which would appear.

Pidge forgot the names of her children on most days, and she often forgot how to perform simple tasks, but Bill's bouquets were always fresh in her memory. In her mind Mother's Day was every day, even when she forgot she even had children.

Claire knew there was no right or wrong way to answer her mother. Every doctor gave a different opinion. "Always correct her when she's wrong," said one doctor; "Just play along." said another. It was the doctor who told her to choose her battles that Claire decided to listen to. And whether it was Mother's Day today or not seemed less of a problem at the moment. So, today, she chose to play along.

"I think spearwort will dominate the array this year."

A dreamy smile crossed over Pidge's face. "It just feels like a spearwort kind of year, doesn't it?"

"It sure does," Claire chirped. She pulled up the corner of the mattress on her mother's bed and peered beneath. No photos.

Spearworts were the flower of the day. Yesterday it had been dahlias. The day before, larkspur. Eventually all the flowers made a complete circle back around. It always confused Claire that although Pidge only had two daughters she still managed to forget their names, or that they even existed sometimes, yet she still remembered the names of hundreds of flowers. She tried not to take it personally, but it wasn't always an easy thing to do. Some days it hurt more than others. Right now? She just didn't care.

Today she chose to focus on finding all the photos her mother had confiscated from throughout the house. That was the battle she chose today. If that were wrong of her, then so be it. At the moment it seemed more prudent than what her mother remembered and what she didn't; more important than a simple dream of a flower bouquet. So she let her mother pretend while she upturned cushions and rummaged through trash cans trying to unearth snapshots of years gone by.

Pivoting in the middle of the room, Claire wondered what she'd forgotten. She'd checked all the beds, the chairs and sofas, the closets, dresser drawers, the trashcans, jewellery boxes, and laundry baskets. She'd even sifted through the ashes in the fireplace, and came up with no evidence that anything had recently been burned. She'd covered the whole 3,340 square feet of living space in the house. What had she missed?

"I *do* love butter, Bill, but you already know that," Pidge said from the corner of the room. She had plucked a book from between the bookends and was riffling through its pages. The other books fell to the side. Slowly the bookend, now taking the brunt of the weight, slipped and fell to the carpeted floor with a quiet thud. "But if it's spearwort you want than who am I to argue?"

She giggled, lost in her world of pretend. "After all I'm just the gracious wife who puts up with you."

As she walked from the room, she bent her head to rub her nose between the pages of the book.

Claire loved that her mom was mobile. It made taking care of her that much easier, but it also posed a risk. She'd added coded locks to all the doors, and safeguards on all the windows to control how far they could be opened. So far her mother had not tried to wander, but it gave Claire peace of mind to know that she couldn't.

She wanted to ask her mother where she'd put the pictures this time, but she knew if she did that Pidge would send her on a wild goose chase. The first time the pictures had gone missing from the stairwell, Pidge had given her some cock and bull story about how she'd secured them to the blades of a ceiling fan so they could go on an inexpensive trip to see the moon. Claire had fallen for it and pulled a ladder from the shed so she could check the blades of all the fans in the house. All she found was dust and cobwebs; no pictures. Instead she'd found them tucked behind the flour bin and the rice canister in the pantry.

Another time, when pictures of Saulie, Thomas, and Archie had gone missing from the mantel, Pidge had told Claire that she'd 'put them to bed' because 'they'd been standing with that poor baby for far too long'. That time she'd found the pictures in a basket of tart apples a neighbour had given her for pies.

So no, she wouldn't ask her mother where the pictures were. There wasn't any point. She'd find them eventually; she always did.

Claire crossed to the shelf in front of the window and bent to retrieve the bookend that had fallen. It was wedged between the chair and the wall, and the rag quilt which usually hung free over the back of the chair looked more bulky than it ought to. She dropped to her knees for a closer look.

When she reached to move the quilt aside the mass beneath was so obvious she nearly laughed out loud. She knew exactly what she'd find before she even lifted the quilt.

Sure enough, a neat pile of frames sat behind the chair, but when she lifted them she realized all the pictures had been removed. This was a first. Finding bulky frames was one thing. Finding straight up photos was another. That could take days. That would mean upturning every register in the house and peering beneath any loose wainscotting.

"Not today, Satan," she mumbled under her breath as she rose from the floor with the frames and the bookend. Today she'd let it go. At least she had the frames. Later she'd figure out which pictures were missing and have them reproduced. It wasn't a big deal, and she wouldn't stress over it, especially not today. Today was respite day.

She glanced at her watch. Any minute now a continuing care assistant would show up and give her some much-needed time off. It was the cedar tree outside her bedroom window this morning that helped her decide what she would do with her free time. The changing leaves and partially bare trees were perfectly picturesque at this time of year.

She sat the frames down in a basket and crossed to her bedroom. She'd moved into her sister Saulie's room when she'd returned home to be closer to her mother. Although she'd been home for some time, she had not completely unpacked. She wasn't sure why. She'd already signed contracts with the village as the new general practitioner in the medical centre, so she wasn't going anywhere soon. However each time she lifted a bag to her bed and opened it, she found something more pressing she needed to be doing, and set the bag aside for later.

The doctor in her had all kinds of theories as to why that was, but the individual person she was always debunked them. As soon as she got full swing into her work life, she'd get the urge to completely settle. For now she liked the feeling of living right on the edge of leaving.

She lifted her camera backpack and secured the tripod to the front. She was hoping to beat the rain, but just in case she made sure she'd tucked her rain protector in the side pocket and attached a small umbrella to the strap system. Slipping the bag unto her shoulders she went downstairs and waited.

~

For Beau Green, hiking was akin to freedom. Exploring in a vehicle just wasn't the same. It was boxed in, cold, and uninspiring. He wasn't so crass as to not understand the importance of a vehicle, that would be hypocritical of him seeing as he owned an old Dodge Ram Laramie and a BMW sedan. He just didn't like how impersonal it was.

In a vehicle you didn't get to experience nature, and the only smells from the outside were what the vents and windows afforded you. The tires rolled over the rough edges of the road and jostled everyone and everything inside the car, and everything outside just zipped by unnoticed. Nothing slowed down and yelled, 'hey, check me out,' because you couldn't look around, could you? Not really. You had to obey road sign and be on alert for other drivers who didn't give a damn you were there. There was no time for sight seeing when you were the one behind the wheel.

Nature demanded respect. If you weren't attuned with it, you couldn't completely enjoy it. Hiking, you got to know the trails. You could feel all the bumps and holes with your feet, feel the wind on your face, and smell nature right up in your face. Nothing zipped by, because everything was right there at your fingertips, waiting to be explored at whatever pace you chose.

In a vehicle as long as you stayed on the road, drove safe, were mindful of other vehicles, and had plenty of gas nothing else really mattered, but on foot you had to let your body and nature adjust together in order to get the full experience. It was great. He never felt more alive.

Of course it had its disadvantages, but in his opinion the pros far outweighed the cons. And if you were clever enough, you could make allowance for the cons by crafty ideas and well thought out plans. All of which Beau was an expert at.

It had been years since he'd explored the woods he was in now, and although he thought he would forget all the well-worn paths and spots from his youth, it all came flooding back as though he'd never left.

Mayo, his Border collie, had ran on ahead, but she kept returning every few minutes to ensure her master was okay. For the first time in a long time, he *was* okay. He'd finally given into the voice telling him to come home, and now here he was and everything felt perfect.

He could hear the brook before he saw it; it was just a few feet in front of him. The trees lining its edges had grown to three times their size, deciduous trees that burst with a fiery array of yellows and reds, with the odd splattering of magenta and purple.

Someone or something had recently been over the ground near the brook, crushing tall grass and thickets to the ground and breaking tree branches away. Usually if someone wanted to fish they did so in the clearing near the road, so he doubted it was for this reason. Probably another hiker.

From the angle he was approaching the brook he knew exactly where he would come out. It was *their* spot. It was the only flat ground near the water, and was perfect for a picnic. Even though he had no right to, he'd cleared away the only tree growing in that spot so they could better spread a blanket and stretch their legs.

He'd taken the small tree by the roots and replanted it at her request a few feet away. As he approached he could see the top of a tree over the sloping ground and just knew it was the same tree.

The whole spot was probably grown over by now. Pushing aside a branch, he stepped into view—and instantly slunk back again.

Someone was there. Someone had trampled the vegetation to a flat surface, and in its centre sat a tripod and a bag.

Beau scanned the area for the person owning the stuff. The day was winding down. Greyness overtook the sky as the sun slid behind the clouds. Thick puffy clouds that he knew would soon give way to orange and reds as the sun slid out of sight. In all honesty it looked like rain was on the horizon. The sky was darkening too fast for the time of day.

The photographer had set the tripod up in a perfect spot. From where it was the kaleidoscope of autumn colours would be a perfect foreground for the setting sun. If they timed the shot just right all the colours of the trees and the sky would converge together and reflect off the brook in the most alluring way.

He could almost see the shot already. It would definitely be frame-worthy. And if a deer were to cross the path at the same time, it would be even better. But perfect shots like that didn't just happen without some pre-planning and some well thought out tactics.

The photographer in him had been quiet for a long time, but now he itched to stand here and watch. It seemed creepy somehow, but he just couldn't pull himself away. This was wrong; creeping on someone without their knowledge was not his way. Hadn't he just told Nancy off for doing this very thing? No he would not be that person.

He looked down at the bed of needles and fallen pine cones at his feet, but right when he was about to turn away he saw someone step into view, and he froze on the spot.

It was her. Even with twenty years between them he knew her. She'd cut her waist-length hair and her awkward girlish figure was gone. The straight lines of her hips had softened into curves, and he could see the swell of her breasts beneath her waist-length plaid jacket. She had definitely filled out from the gawky teenager he once knew.

Her head was lowered, the bill of her hunter's-orange cap shading her face from view as she attached a lens to her camera. She turned to affix the camera to the tripod, but the camera slipped and in her scramble to catch it the cap fell from her head. "Damn," she cursed.

That was all Mayo needed. He zipped off towards Claire at full speed.

She raised her head, her bangs a shaggy fringe across her forehead, a look of panic in her dark blue eyes.

He didn't want to make his presence known, but he had no choice. "Mayo," he called, stepping behind the trees to shield himself from sight. "Mayo, come."

Within seconds he spotted the blue merle coat of his Border collie bounding over some brambles towards him. He turned and ran, Mayo on his heels.

A series of clicks and beeping sounded from behind them as Claire gathered proof of their escape.

Sign up for our newsletter at moosehousepress.com to be the first to know when *Tough All Over* is available!